CLEAN EXIT

AN AJAX CLEAN FORENSIC THRILLER

J. KENT HOLLOWAY

CHARADE
MEDIA

Clean Exit (An Ajax Clean Forensic Thriller)

ISBN: 979-8-9876847-5-7

Charade Media, LLC

www.charadebooks.com

CHAPTER 1
AJAX CLEAN

MegaCon Orlando
Gilbert-Seely Hotel and Convention Center
Saturday morning, February 3

t was after midnight and the nerds were still partying like it was the first time they'd left their parents' basement in a parsec. Though the MegaCon Comic Book Convention had officially closed its doors for the night two hours before, there were easily three dozen Han Solos, Wonder Women, Supermen, Daleks, Dalek-human hybrids, and at least four different varieties of the Doctor from Doctor Who loitering in the hotel lobby lounge area when I walked through the automatic sliding doors. And I'm pretty sure there was at least one Flash wearing a trench coat that might have been about to take his name quite literally to a nearby Supergirl.

Of course, I'm not one who should talk. I live in my dead grandma's basement when I'm not on the job, and currently was wearing an equally colorful comic book costume I'd made from scratch. Granted, I wasn't there to get my pimply-faced jollies by hooking up with the hottest Xena lookalike like most of the guys were. I was here to work. Plain and simple. It didn't matter that I, myself, was in nerd heaven as I walked through the lobby and took in the incredibly creative costumes these kids had lovingly crafted.

The Iron Man with blue-hued repulsor beams flashed me a thumbs up as he caught me taking it all in. I smiled a silent thank you—not entirely certain my grin quite revealed any of my pearly whites—as I lugged the huge suitcase behind me and made my way toward the southeast cluster of elevators. Casually, I let my suitcase roll to a stop, adjusted the two Japanese swords strapped to my back, and pressed the elevator button as I whistled the theme to the A-Team. A few moments later, the doors opened and a group of scantily clad female cosplayers stepped out, winking at me as they did.

Hmmm. Maybe I need to reconsider the whole job thing and hang out down here for a while.

But that just wasn't me. I took what I did very seriously, and I was paid exceptionally well because of it. Taking one last glance back at the professional cosplayers, I sighed and stepped into the elevator before pressing the button for the fourteenth floor. The doors closed, and I was rocketed up through the building in what felt like a jet-powered elevator. In seconds, there was a ding, and the doors opened onto a spacious open air hallway with a view all the way down into the lobby below. Resisting my impulse to look down, I walked along the hallway until I came to the third potted plant on my left, stuck my hand into the thick green fronds, and grabbed hold of what I'd expected to find.

I glanced around, making sure no one was watching, and withdrew a hotel room keycard. *So far, so good*, I thought, continuing my stroll down the corridor until I came to room 1423. I inserted the card into the lock slot, and froze when the red LED blazed to life. The card didn't work. I withdrew the card, and turned it over. 1423 was scrawled in black Sharpie on the back. I hadn't attempted to enter the wrong room.

All right, Clean. Give it another shot.

I placed the card in the lock again, holding my breath, and almost let out a victorious shout when the green light flashed and the tumbler clicked inside the door frame. Letting out a breath, I pulled down on the handle, and let myself into the room.

The moment I turned the lights on, I wished the keycard hadn't worked after all. The room was a mess. Lamps and tables turned over. A mirror shattered and hanging catawampus on the wall. Broken beer bottles lay strewn across the carpeted floor. But I knew this had nothing to do with partying conventioners. It was infinitely more sinister than that. It had to be in order for me to be called in.

Judging from the mess, things hadn't gone exactly according to plan either. Someone had put up quite a fight. Either that or…

No. No, there's no way they would have hired him. Fontaine knows I won't work with Ellis.

Nervously, I turned to face the closed bathroom door, turned the knob, but it came off in my hand. The door swung open of its own accord, no longer being constrained by the latch. It had obviously been kicked in.

I looked inside. The blood covered almost every surface of the tiled and porcelain room. High velocity blood spatter coated the walls, mirror, and toilet. The body lay face down on the floor. His face pressed against a dark pool of his own blood. He was a big man too. Too big for such a small space in which to work and I quietly cursed the hitter who'd pulled this job off—I still refused to believe it had been Ellis. But whoever had been the contractor had definitely not been subtle, making my job all the more difficult.

When it came down to it, however, it didn't matter. I was a cleaner, after all. It was my job to remove all traces that either Muldoon or Ellis had even been there at all. It was more difficult work than one might think. Locard's Exchange Principle—the forensic law that states that an individual cannot enter a scene without leaving traces of themselves behind—was a bitch. It was a cleaner's job to minimize as much forensic evidence left at a scene as possible. It was the work of a *great* cleaner, however, to negate the principal entirely. I have a reputation for being a great cleaner. The best, in fact, which meant that no matter how incompetent the hitman was, I was about to make him look like a freaking artist.

I sighed, then moved back into the hotel room, and removed my swords, bandolier, and gun holsters. Once I'd set them safely aside, I knelt down at my suitcase, and unzipped it. Inside, I pulled out the white Tyvek disposable suit, and slipped it on over my costume, following it up with two pairs of thick latex gloves, and a filter mask.

"Okay. No sense moping about this. Time to get to work."

I started with tidying up the main living space of the room. Picking up the broken pieces of glass, clothing, and other detritus scattered everywhere. I wasn't too concerned with the mirror. My job, in this case, wasn't to erase the entire existence of the victim. It was simply to destroy any possibility that anything criminal had occurred here. Later, when hotel staff came into the room to clean, they'd find a mess, the guest's clothes and property gone, and their guest skipping out on the bill. That is, of course, what I hoped was all they'd find anyway. And I have a pretty good track record that said I'd be able to pull it off.

Thirty minutes later, I stood by the front door and surveyed my handiwork. To the uninitiated, it looked as if our man had just had one too many drinks and trashed the place before packing up and leaving. That was the easy part. Now it was time for the in depth work.

I reached into the suitcase and withdrew a folded sheet of ten by ten foot clear plastic. With a flick of my wrists, I laid the sheeting on the floor flush with the exterior of the bathroom door. Ripping several liberal strips of duct tape from a roll, I fastened the edges around the wall, being sure to tape some of the plastic over the lip of the doorway. I then placed another sheet on top of the first, before securing more plastic along the walls and ceiling until I had a roomy plastic tent in the foyer of the hotel room.

Satisfied the sheeting was properly sealed, I stepped into the bathroom and crouched down at the body for a closer look.

Victim's name was Carl Muldoon. Divorced with three kids. Ex had full custody. From the paunch bulging at the buttons of his shirt, and the creased wrinkles quite evident in the man's earlobes, I figured Muldoon's murder was a bit overkill. Give him another six months with a diet of double cheeseburgers, fries, and Jack Daniels, and the guy probably would have dropped dead from a massive coronary. But he had handled the books for Jimmy Fontaine. Not the greatest career decision in its own right, mind you. But when he decided to turn State's evidence after he'd been nicked in a rather ambitious Ponzi scheme, a slow cardiac death just wasn't in the cards for him. Now he had two holes to the back of the neck. And from what I could tell of his flattened face pressed against the tile of the floor, was probably beat near to death by the hitter who'd killed him, which explained the chaos in the rest of the room.

My guess is, the hitter entered the room and a fight broke out. Mr. Muldoon, realizing he couldn't win, ran to the bathroom to escape—it's easy to ask why he didn't just run out his room's door to freedom, but when a person is in that situation, they're not always thinking straight. I've seen it a hundred times before. Anyway, not letting a flimsy hotel bathroom door stop him from completing his task, the assassin forced the door open, shoved Muldoon to the ground, and pop! Pop! Dead accountant. Time to have Fontaine call in the cleaner.

Although I complain a lot about the mess, I really didn't mind. After this job, I was going to take a very long vacation. Something I'd owed myself for a while now. The money I'd make from this gig would tide me over quite well for several months at least.

After examining the back of Muldoon's head, paying particular attention to the two round holes in the back of his skull and at the base of his neck, I rolled him over and began undressing him. Ordinarily, I'd leave the clothes on and dispose of the body with them intact, but I was in the middle of a busy hotel now. That meant I had to be creative, which also meant that I was going to have to throw convention out the window for now. No pun intended.

Once he was stripped down to the suit he'd been born with, I grabbed hold of his ankles and dragged him from the bathroom onto the plastic sheeting. It wasn't easy. Not only was the guy ridiculously overweight, he was already slipping into rigor mortis, making his limbs too stiff to maneuver easily through the doorway.

The next portion of the job was not for the squeamish or children under the age of twenty-six. I grabbed a butcher's cleaver from the suitcase, scooted up to Muldoon's right shoulder, and brought the blade down between the humerus and scapula.

I wasn't trying to sever the arm right now. Cutting through human bone and ligaments isn't as easy as they make it look in the movies. What I was attempting to do was essentially score a slot within the skin and muscle tissue to make it easier to use the specially modified skill saw I'd brought with me for that particular portion of the job. For now, I did the same thing at each of body's major joints. The elbows, the hips, and knees. Once a good sized slot had been scored into each joint, I withdrew the battery-powered fully-charged saw and set to work biting through the bone and tendons until one by one, Muldoon's limbs detached from the torso.

What might surprise most people is that there was very little blood displaced by the activity. One of the reasons was in the modifications I'd made to the skill saw. First, I'd removed the guide, allowing for deeper cuts. Then, I'd fashioned a special handheld vacuum hose to it that was designed to pull most debris —both body fluids and bone dust particles—into a special container.

For this job, however, it hardly mattered. Most of it was already congealing on the floor of the bathroom. Because his heart was no longer beating, and therefore, no longer pumping blood through his veins, only the little that remained inside his body sprayed in mist-like clouds as the saw blade cut through the limbs. When it was over, my Tyvek suit and the plastic lined walls and floor was coated in fine pinprick dots of crimson. But there was no pooling, and more important, none of it had seemed to seep out into the carpet.

I vowed to keep it that way as I began carefully making my way around the edge of the plastic sheeting, and dislodging it from the walls, floor, and ceiling until—still standing on the first sheet of plastic I'd laid down—I wrapped Muldoon's body up tight and duct taped the plastic into a compressed package.

I stood to my full height, stretching my back, as I let out a tired sigh.

KNOCK! KNOCK! KNOCK!

I stiffened at the sound of knocking at the door.

"Mr. Muldoon, this is hotel management."

CHAPTER 2
AJAX CLEAN

hardly breathed as I crouched down and pulled out my Ruger LC9 semi-automatic pistol from its front pocket. I wasn't a murderer by any stretch of the imagination, though I had killed before...when it had been necessary. I hoped tonight wouldn't prove necessary, but the gun's weight in my hand was a reassuring feeling.

Another triple tap at the door. "Mr. Muldoon? Are you there?"

I glanced over at the clock on the nightstand beside the bed. It was three forty-five in the morning. What on earth was management doing here? The battery-powered saw shouldn't have been loud enough to wake any neighbors. Especially with the festive cacophony of comic book geeks reveling up and down the hallways all night.

"Mr. Muldoon, I'm sorry. But if you don't answer the door right now, I'm going to be forced to enter."

I crept up to the door, and placed my back against it before pulling back the slide of my Ruger with a soft click. A looked down at the wrapped up, dismembered corpse just two feet away and sighed.

This job was becoming more troublesome than it was worth.

I had to think fast.

"Do you have any idea what time it is?" I growled at the door, giving my voice the raspy garble that comes from being awakened from deep sleep. I hoped the manager had never met Muldoon or heard him speak before. With the crowd the hotel had staying with them for the weekend though, I doubted he would have remembered even if he had.

The manager cleared his throat. "I'm sorry to disturb you, sir." He paused. I watched him from the door's peephole. He was a wiry little rat of a man, with a round, bulbous nose of a chronic drinker. He was also fidgeting nervously, switching the pressure from one foot to the next as he tried to think of how to explain his reason for disturbing his guest. "It's just that we received a noise disturbance complaint earlier this evening. They said it sounded as if a fight had broken out in here. Unfortunately, with the convention in full swing, this is the first chance I've had to check on you. We were concerned for your well-being."

My racing heart began to slow as I released the breath I'd been holding. Then, I grinned as a devious idea popped in my head.

I paused. Counted to ten. Then let the poor manager have it. "What? Someone thought I was in trouble and you waited this long to check on me?" I yelled. "I could have been dying, for crying out loud!"

"Well, it's just that…"

"This is unbelievable!" I told myself I needed to tone the dramatics down just a notch, but this was just too much fun an opportunity to pass up. Plus, it would provide the perfect cover for why Mr. Muldoon would disappear in the morning without a trace. "Absolutely reprehensible. Yes, I had a bit of an accident in here. Slipped and feel in the shower. Knocked some things over. But I'm fine, no thanks to you."

This would also give a great explanation for any blood I might miss when I finally got around to cleaning the bathroom.

"Mr. Muldoon, if I could just speak with you face to face, I'm sure…"

"I don't think so. I'm going back to bed now and I'm leaving first thing in the morning."

"But sir..."

"And you'll sure be hearing from my attorney, I can tell you that."

"I'm very sorry, sir. It's just that..."

"Go away. I'm going back to bed now."

I watched the manager fidget a few seconds longer. He then raised his fist to knock again, then lowered it before turning and disappearing down the hall.

A wave of relief washed over me and the thumping in my chest continued to settle into a more stable rhythm. If my gloves weren't covered in blood, I would have wiped away the sweat streaming down my brow. As it was, I decided the best course of action was to finish the job as quickly as I could and get the hell out of that crazy hotel.

That meant it was time to play the part of hotel housekeeping and get the bathroom cleaned up. Pulling several bottles of industrial strength cleaning solution, towels, a squeegee, and a retractable mop from the suitcase, I stepped into the bathroom prepared to get to work.

That's when I saw it. The handful of shiny copper pennies stacked ten high encircled with a ring of ash from what looked to be from a cigar on the side of the bathtub. A freaking adimus. An offering to the spirits of Palo Mayombe. Or Santeria. Or whatever voodoo religion that psycho practices.

"Ellis," I growled softly, as I snatched the pennies up and tossed them in a biohazard bag.

CHAPTER 3
LUNA MAO CHING

Office of the Medical Examiner, District 11
Miami, Florida
Saturday morning, February 3

Today wasn't going my way at all. It was bad enough that it was a Saturday—my day off—and I had already performed two autopsies. And I was about to start a new one. A possible homicide of an unidentified decomposing female. It was my birthday too, and no one in my life seemed to know or care. I suppose it is my own fault for that. I am rather fond of keeping to myself most of the time. Since coming to Miami two years ago to start my pathology fellowship with the Medical Examiner's Office, I had not put much of an effort to make a lot of friends.

Of course, that could be the result of spending much of life in China and on the run from some very bad people. This, however, was not my fault. It was my father's. And though I don't blame him for the unstable childhood he provided for me after my mother died, I do wish things had been different. It is a difficult thing to learn to form attachments when one has been forced to hide most of her life—not to mention the necessity of being able to leave everything you know and love behind at a moment's notice when danger rears up without warning.

I let out a self-indulgent sigh as I raised the scalpel to perform my final autopsy of the day.

"You okay, Dr. Luna?" Gerald Jimenez, the forensic technician assisting me, asked.

Gerald, who always addressed me by my first name, was the closest thing I could consider to be a friend at the office. Though he didn't know it, he and I had a great deal in common. He and his family had fled Cuba when he was only eight years old and had spent much of his own childhood hiding from the U.S. Immigration Department. That is, until his family managed to garner the attention of a Florida senator who granted them asylum here. He was kind. Very intelligent. And he always had a knack for making me feel safe and at home in this strange country I'd only just begun to understand.

"I'm fine," I said, forcing a smile. "Simply tired, I think."

He flashed a brilliant smile in return. "Well, we're almost finished." He had just finished taking photos of the body and sat the camera down on a nearby workstation before picking up a scalpel. "Just one more and we can get out of here."

He slipped his scalpel into the deceased's right shoulder, and drew it down at an angle to the center of his chest.

"Hold up," I said, pointing to a single maggot inching its way down the autopsy table toward the drain. "Let's collect that. Looks like it's ingested some of the victim's blood. It might be better preserved if we need to get DNA for identification."

He nodded, scooped up the larvae with a pair of tweezers and placed it carefully into a glass tube. As he labeled the specimen, I took my own scalpel and completed the Y-incision across the victim's chest, and sliced through the abdomen, and past the navel. Then, in unison, Gerald and I began flaying the skin back on our respective sides of the chest until the rib cage was revealed.

Gerald, like everyone else in the office, was unaware that it was my birthday. I hadn't bothered to share this information with any of them. So I was not certain just why I was feeling so down about no one making today special for me.

I did have a brother. But he went away when my father went into hiding, and I'd never actually met him. Two years ago, when I received my fellowship here, my brother and I had begun emailing and finally started getting to know one another. But we were hardly what one might call close. I wasn't even certain he knew today was my birthday either. I hadn't expected him to make a big deal of it, but it would have been nice.

"Luna!" Gerald shook a set of tree loppers in front of me to get my attention. "You're a million miles away, *chica*."

"Sorry." I accepted the loppers with an apologetic nod, and placed the two blades against the lower portion of left side of the rib cage. With six or seven crunches, I cut through the bone and cartilage and began cutting the tissue away from the chest plate. "A lot on my mind too, I guess."

"Want to talk about it?"

I shook my head. "Thanks you, no. I appreciate the offer though."

He shrugged and plunged a needle into the victim's heart, drawing a portion of congealed dark goo that had once been blood to be used for toxicological testing. I, in turn, began the process of carefully removing each organ from the dead woman's torso and continued with my reflections.

There was only one person in this country who really knew me, but he was more of a casual acquaintance than anything. He was a freelance journalist, Remy Williamson, doing a story on a mythic criminal I'd published a paper about in my first year as a Pathology Fellow. Remy had come to me to learn more about this criminal and the techniques he was known to employ. He was cute, but the ring on his finger immediately made him off limits to me, so we had become very good friends instead. He always came to visit me when he was in town, and I'd grown to cherish those visits more than I would have ever thought possible.

I smiled when I thought of the reporter. As I said, there was nothing romantic between us, but there was just something about Remy that made me feel safe. And genuinely cared for. It was a nice feeling. But unfortunately, he seemed to have forgotten my birthday, as well.

Oh, Luna, you are behaving like a child with all this melancholy. You are blessed beyond belief, whether anyone knows it's your special day or not. I frowned. *If only father was here. He always knew how to cheer me up.*

I continued pondering these thoughts, finishing the autopsy in silence, removing my protective gear, and heading to my office with a polite "Thank you" to Gerald, who remained behind to clean up the autopsy room. I was finished for the day, and unless histology revealed something very different from what I suspected, it was safe to say that our unidentified homicide victim had died from manual strangulation. The crushed hyoid bone and bruising on the inside lining on both sides of the neck revealed as much. Now, all was left was to dictate my autopsy report and I could go home and enjoy a nice glass of wine, sit back on my couch, and immerse myself in a good mystery novel.

A perfect night.

For the first time that day, I allowed myself a genuine smile of amusement. Most people would marvel over the fact that I had become so complacent in my career that a mere work of mystery fiction would enthrall me so. But truth is honestly very rarely stranger or more entertaining than fiction. In fact, my profession can be rather mundane. The same homicide over and over again. The same drug overdoses. The same ridiculously obstinate doctors who do not understand the laws that govern them.

But a good locked room mystery or a thriller involving the perfect crime? Now that was something anyone could find great joy in.

I stepped into my office, and came to an abrupt halt. A bouquet of China lilies sat ornately on my desk, bringing my smile to a radiant glow. Someone had indeed remembered and had sent my favorite kind of flower to me. I looked around to see if any of the skeleton crew from the office was lurking about, ready to surprise me, but there was no sign of anyone. Curious, I walked around my desk, pulled the flower arrangement closer to me, and pulled a small envelope from the floral pick.

"So, who are you from?" I said allowed as I opened the envelope and withdrew the card with its note written in impersonal typed print.

"TO MS. LUNA MAO CHING. I HOPE YOU ENJOY YOUR BIRTHDAY THIS YEAR. YOU NEVER KNOW IF YOU'LL HAVE ANOTHER ONE."

I blinked as I reread the first part again. Was that a threat of some kind? After reading it a third time, I continued with the note.

"PLEASE SAY HELLO TO YOUR FATHER FOR ME, AND THAT I LOOK FORWARD TO YOUR UPCOMING FAMILY REUNION. SINCERELY, AN OLD FRIEND OF THE FAMILY."

I sat the card on the table, slumped into my chair, and stared up at the ceiling. This was about my father. Somehow, someone from his past had tracked me down to America and they weren't aware that…well, they weren't aware of what happened five years ago that had cut my stay at medical school in Beijing short and had brought me here to Miami.

This is most definitely a threat, I thought as I stood up, tossed the bouquet into the garbage, and gathered my things. I needed to figure this out. I needed to discuss this with someone and try to make sense of it. But who could I turn to? My brother, of course, knew about our father. Knew of the trouble that followed us through most of Asia. Because of that, he'd always felt it best to keep our distance from one another—for safety reasons—and only allowed communication through email. I couldn't be certain when he'd get any message I might send, and at that moment, I didn't feel safe to return home without discussing the strange message with someone.

The only other person I could think of was Lindsay Hogan. I would not exactly call her a friend, but I knew I could trust her. She was my sparring partner at the dojo where I continued my training in Shequan Kung Fu and knew how to take care of herself. I would be safe with her around, and she would at least offer an ear as a sounding board for my current dilemma.

My course set, I scooped up my keys and my backpack filled with case files, and left the office determined to get to the bottom of the threatening message. I could not, however, help but feel as though unseen eyes were watching me as I got into my car and pulled out of the office's parking lot.

CHAPTER 4
AJAX CLEAN

The dismembered body inside the oversized suitcase groaned as I yanked it from the back of the rented Escalade, and let it hit the ground with a thud. I kid you not. Guy was as dead as Macaulay Culkin's acting career and he actually groaned.

Not many people are aware of this particularly disturbing triviality when dealing with corpses. They like to make noises, and it invariably creeps the heck out me every time they do. Dead dude...not breathing...not moving...you shift their body weight just right, and they'll practically sing an undead cantata right where they lay. It's the freakiest thing you could ever hear.

Of course, on those rare occasions that this kind of thing happens, I'm fully aware that it's not the beginning of the zombie apocalypse. It is, after all, easy enough to explain scientifically. When a person dies, their body retains much of the air the lungs had pulled in just before their ticker gives out. Additionally, the body begins breaking down, and is converted into gasses that build up along their abdominal wall. Then, when you give their body just the perfectly random little nudge, all that gas tends to try to escape out of the most convenient orifice it can find. Most of the time, it slips through the victim's gastrointestinal tract, but every once in a blue moon, it whips up through the esophagus, into the throat, and over the vocal cords. Crazy vibrations ensue, and *voila*! Instant creepy zombie groan.

Knowing this, of course, didn't lessen the groan's effect on my nerves as I heaved, and dragged the luggage down my driveway. The tiny wheels dug deep into the gravel as I pulled, threatening to topple the suitcase—and the dead Mr. Muldoon inside—from one side to the other, and I struggled to keep it upright as I maneuvered around the corner of the quaint little ranch-style house I'd inherited from my grandma, and over to the storm cellar door.

"Why can't they ever be thin?" I grumbled, bringing the case to a stop and steadying it as it wobbled slightly to the left. I then crouched down to spin the combination of the padlock that held the doors secure. "Millions of people in the world, a hundred and fifty pounds or less, but every stinkin' time some trigger-happy goon decides to whack someone, they're at least a hundred pounds heavier." I glanced down at the suitcase. "Why is that?"

The lock popped open with a well-oiled click, and I swung open the double doors to the cellar, pulled the luggage up over the doorway's ledge, and shoved with all my might. I'll admit to a rather unprofessional satisfaction each time I imagined Muldoon's head smacking hard against the oak steps leading down into the cellar. "That's for not eating a salad every once in a while," I said as the suitcase crashed against the concrete floor after the last step.

Still at the top of the stairs, I pulled the cellar doors closed behind me, and barred it from the inside. Satisfied I'd have no unexpected company, I began trotting down the steps until I heard the *brat-a-tat* of video game gunfire coming from the television on the other end of the cellar.

Yancy.

I took the last three steps in a single leap, and landed in a clumsy crouch. The costume I was still wearing was tight, unwieldy, and made almost entirely of leather and latex. It was also packed with so much foam muscle, it was two sizes too large for me. But that was kind of the idea.

"So you decided to go with Deadpool, eh?" Yancy shouted from the couch, his back to me. Though I couldn't see the video game controller in his hand, I could tell he was thoroughly engrossed in the latest Rainbow Six game when he shifted his shoulders left to right to keep his character from getting pelted with terrorist lead on my 78-inch flat panel television hanging on the opposite wall. "Lousy costume. You didn't even wear his mask."

"I opted for the cancer-faced Deadpool look. That's what all the latex on my face is for." I rolled my eyes, then stepped over the suitcase at the foot of the stairs and trudged to the bathroom to strip from the prosthetics and makeup. "Besides, I wasn't trying to win any prizes, buddy. Just needed the disguise."

"So, I take it everything went well?"

The adhesive remover ran past my eyebrows, into my eyes. "Ah, crap! That stuff stings!"

"Use cotton balls. It'll absorb most of the fluid and let you apply it more carefully."

"The hell do you think I'm using now? A funnel?"

"Just tryin' to help."

Just tryin' to help. It could have been Yancy Fortner's motto. Yancy was kind of like my butler. Only, he never did any actual work. Though I'd brought him on to be the caretaker of my grand-mother's house, all he ever really found time for was eating nachos, playing video games, and hacking into some of the most well-protected computer systems in the world. Other than that, he had no real interests. He also didn't mind what I did for a living, which was a major plus.

I finally worked off the latex makeup to reveal my angular Asian features. Dark, almond-shaped eyes. Straight, black hair, which I promptly spiked with gel. And the dark complexion-mixed tan of a near-lifelong Floridian. After soaping my face down and rinsing it off, I left the bathroom and walked over to the small bedroom set on the northeast corner of the cellar. I opened the top drawer to my dresser when Yancy let out an angry shout.

"No, no, no!" He jumped from the couch and tossed the game controller across the room. "You jerk! Vogon12 just cheated. My own teammate snuck up behind me and popped me in the head."

"Isn't Vogon12 Cathy Jennings? The thirteen year junior high girl from Vero Beach?"

Yancy turned to glare at me. It was a rather scary look actually. Despite his crew cut and thick glasses making him look like the classic image of Drew Carey in his fatter heyday, his formidable six foot eight inch frame of puffy, steroid-induced muscles made him a force to be shunned whenever agitated.

"Shut up." His eyes brightened a little. "Oh, don't bother with any of those." He nodded to my t-shirt drawer. "You got a package in the mail yesterday."

I looked over at the end table next to the sofa to see a sealed plastic envelope and grinned. "It finally came?"

Yancy just shrugged, walking over to the refrigerator next to the television and snagging one of my Corona Extras. "Oh, and you got an email too, but I didn't read it." He turned and grinned at me.

"Gee, thanks." It was the biggest issue with being roomies with a world class hacker. He liked breaking into my accounts and going through my sundry emails. I pulled on a pair of faded jeans, walked over to the table where the parcel was sitting, and opened it like a kid on Christmas morning. "It came! Finally got it!"

I pulled the shirt out, unfolded it, and took in all the glory. There was a picture of an old Korean man—Chiun, the Master of Sinanju from my favorite book series, The Destroyer. Underneath his squinting mug, bold Asian-style letters read, "KOREANS ARE SIMPLY BETTER." Excited, I slipped it on, spun around, and spread out my arms.

"What do you think?"

"Meh. You know I'm not a big fan."

"That's because you are white and stupid," I said in my best imitation of the racist master assassin. "Not wise at all, like us Koreans."

"Yeah, yeah. Don't you have a body to get rid or something?" Yancy plopped back down on the couch after retrieving the controller, and continued his game. "If it starts decomposing and leaking all over the floor, don't expect me to clean that mess up."

"I stopped expecting anything of the sort years ago."

Of course, he was right, and I knew it. This was my last job before I could finally take the vacation I'd denied myself for the past two and a half years. When it was finally over, I'd be well on my way to live life to the absolute fullest—by doing a perfect impersonation of my slacker live-in butler. Games, beer, and nothing else. When my reluctant sense of responsibility finally kicked in, I upended the suitcase, and began hauling it toward my private workshop in the back of the cellar.

Calling it a cellar was a bit of a misnomer actually. More accurately, I suppose, it was originally intended to be a bomb shelter, a throwback from the Cuban Missile Crisis. The home's builder, Jerome Jax, had constructed it back in the 60's when he'd married his high school sweetheart, Bernice. It had been quite a feat of architectural engineering on the old man's part—building an underground bomb shelter in the soft, porous soil on a central Florida citrus farm. But then, Jerome hadn't been your typical farmer either. Having served with the Corps of Engineers during the Korean War, he'd learned a thing or two about constructing bunkers in the most inhospitable of environments. Of course, his connections with certain high tier members of the New York mob had provided the finances necessary to make it happen.

So when Jerome had married the woman that I eventually came to think of as 'grandma', he put his knowledge and resources to good use in order to protect the woman he loved from the Communist 'Pinkos' that threatened the world. Though he and I never saw eye to eye about anything, I've got to give him credit of that. He lived for Bernice. He eventually died for her too, but that's another story.

The shelter, reinforced with four feet of steel and concrete, was buried nearly twelve feet below the house's foundation, and boasted a very spacious two thousand square feet of living space big enough to sustain a family of four comfortably for several months if properly stocked.

When I inherited the place after Bernice passed six years ago, I immediately saw the cellar's potential as a combination laboratory, work station, entertainment hub, and hideout for when I just needed to lay low for a while. It's why I'd converted it into a rather comfortable apartment and kept the place secret from everyone save a handful of people.

Stopping at the locked door of my workshop, I popped open the padlock with a flick of the combination, opened it, and flicked on the light. When I stepped inside, I stopped to perform my ritual check of the room to ensure no pesky intruders had paid it a visit while I was away on business. Despite his apathetic laziness, I trusted Yancy implicitly. However, as much as I wish things were different, he didn't always hang out in the cellar and didn't have a particularly good eye for details like signs of forced entry.

The dust on the floor inside the doorway lay undisturbed save the impressions of my own footprints from my last visit inside. There were several drag marks as well, which could easily be accounted for by my last job.

"Have they been stocked recently?" I asked over my shoulder.

"Oh yeah. Ted came by here Thursday night. Brought a fresh supply of those nasty things and dumped them down the vent outside just like you asked."

Good. At least, I'd have more than enough for the next phase, I thought while continuing my assessment of the lab. So far, I saw nothing untoward, but I hadn't survived this long by being impatient. Standing perfectly still, my gaze swept the room from left to right, past the enormous Remo Williams movie poster, its corners peeling slightly where the tape's adhesives had begun to yellow and erode. But it was exactly how I'd left it, so I knew without question that the state-of-the-art Drekter 3250 wall safe hidden behind the poster was still secure. The bookshelves to my right—filled with old paperback novels ranging from such literary greats as Robert E. Howard and Lovecraft to modern thrillers by authors like Robinson, Preston and Child, and Butcher. The largest, and most prized collection lining the shelves, however, was all fifty-one volumes of The Destroyer series, featuring the world's greatest assassin Remo Williams, and his wiseass teacher, Chiun, the Master of Sinanju.

Realizing my mind had wandered from its task by mentally inventorying my collection, I focused again on my security ritual. After a few seconds, I knew that the books had not been rifled through, and were as undisturbed as everything else in the room. I allowed myself a satisfied sigh.

My bat cave appeared to be very much secure.

After one more careful scan of the room, just to be safe, I took a deep breath, and savored the sweet aroma of the honeysuckle Febreeze air freshener plugged into a nearby outlet. I looked across the room to the work table and old, inoperable freezer chest, then at the suitcase next to my leg.

"Okay. I hope you enjoy your new accommodations," I said to the dead man inside the suitcase. "No expense has been spared."

Yes. I occasionally do talk to my guests. Don't judge me.

Grabbing the suitcase's handle once more, I wheeled it across the room. Once in position, I carefully maneuvered it onto a rectangular metal platform cut into the floor immediately in front of the freezer, and pressed the green button mounted in a panel on the wall. With a hiss and a whir, the platform rose on hydraulic legs until just above my waist.

"Now, let's have a look at you, shall we?"

CHAPTER 5
AJAX CLEAN

U nzipping the suitcase with one swift motion, I flipped its cover to the side to reveal the various pieces of Muldoon, still wrapped in the sturdy plastic sheeting inside. It'd been hell squeezing him inside, even after removing his limbs. But it was far easier than if I'd forgotten to bring the saw considering how much rigor he'd developed when I finally got to him. But why focus on the negative? Getting him out now should be a piece of cake in comparison.

I slipped on a pair of latex gloves before grabbing a box cutter from a rolling cart nearby, and slicing through the polyester material of the case on all four corners until I had a flat surface on which to work. First, I pulled out his discarded clothing, and tossed them on the floor by my feet. I then began gave him a quick onceover.

My curiosity had been getting the better of me ever since finding that voodoo-whatchamacallit offering left at the scene. The only hitter I knew who practiced that mumbo-jumbo was Ellis, but I knew Jimmy Fontaine was smarter than that. He knew how I felt about that Haitian madman and would never knowingly pair the two of us up.

Would he? I thought about it a minute and shook my head. "Not if he ever wants to hire me again, he wouldn't." Any good mobster knew that the only thing more important than having a good hitman was having an even better clean up artist.

Still, I needed to be sure. The overall violence displayed at that scene, along with the offering was just too big a coincidence to ignore.

Curious, I gripped Muldoon by what was left of his right shoulder and tried flipping him over on his stomach. This is where I regretted the dismemberment. By now, rigor would have been full, making it much easier to maneuver a corpse. The wonderful thing about rigor is that it makes manhandling dead weight so much easier—like having an instant lever to work with. "Let the rigor work for you," Lou Nikopoulos, my old mentor, had always said. And it was one piece of advice that had been employed wisely throughout the years I'd been doing this job. Unfortunately, with no arms or legs to work with, turning the body over was like trying to hold onto a greased pig—with no arms or legs.

After several embarrassing tries, I finally managed to flip him onto his stomach. I leaned to my right, took hold of a swiveling magnified lamp mounted to the wall, and pulled it directly above the corpse's head. Flicking the florescent light mounted inside the lens to life, I looked through the magnifier and glanced down at the bullet wounds at the base of the man's neck and head. Just as I'd thought at the scene. Two shots. From the stippling patterns, it looked like at least the shot to the neck had been fired from an intermediate range. Possibly three to four feet away. The second wound, however, was seared around the edges. A cylindrical pattern—with a very distinctive marking cut into its center—had been imprinted against the skin. A muzzle impression. Contact gunshot wound.

The killer's first shot, fired from a few feet away, had apparently not been enough. Since no blood had been found inside the hotel room except in the bathroom, I figured the killer had busted in the door knocking Muldoon to the ground and shooting him in the neck instantly, but not killing him outright. Struggling to survive, the marked accountant had probably tried to scramble away on his hands and knees—at least for a few precious moments, before the assassin had casually walked up to him, placed the barrel of his weapon against the back of the man's head, and pulled the trigger.

I instantly recognized the muzzle from the strange marking in the impression, as well as the skillful, yet brutal, handiwork of the kill itself.

For a second time today, my gut had been right. Stupid Fontaine had indeed contracted Ellis.

You've got to be kidding me. What the hell are you thinking, Jimmy?

I should have been pissed. The entire criminal underworld knew my feelings about the psychotic hitman. Knew I adamantly refused to work with him. Granted, Jimmy wasn't exactly the kind of guy to fret about my feelings when there was work to be done. I, of course, knew better than to call him on it too. In the end, I guess he *had* considered my feelings on it though. After all, he had kept the two of us separate. We hadn't technically *worked* together. Ellis had done his job. Now it was time for me to conclude mine. I'd already spent half the night cleaning up the murder scene and, by sheer dumb luck, I'll admit, setting up a great cover story for why the guy had disappeared from the luxury hotel.

Now it was time for the final step in my job. Arguably, the most important. To ensure the victim, or any trace evidence the body might contain, was never found. Needless to say, it was often the messiest and smelliest task of my profession.

Opening a metal cabinet immediately to my right, I slipped on a plastic surgical apron, a fresh pair of latex gloves, and a face-shield. I then grabbed hold of the handcart I'd taken the box cutter from, and pulled it over to the raised platform before picking up a scalpel. With a practiced swipe of the wrist, I brought the scalpel blade down across the dead man's neck, and within minutes, two blood-soaked slugs sat harmlessly on a folded paper towel resting on the handcart. For several long seconds, I watched as the crimson liquid on the bullets was absorbed into the towels. Then, I dabbed the excess blood away with another towel, picked up a magnifying glass, and peered closer at the projectiles.

It didn't take long to solidify my suspicions. Though each bullet were squashed beyond recognition, the same strange glyph that had adorned the muzzle imprint could plainly be seen—though slightly mangled from crushed metal—cut into each piece of lead. Ellis's personal mark. I forced myself to calm down as my blood began to boil over yet another piece of evidence linking that Haitian goon to the hit. It wasn't my job to question my clients' judgment—no matter how boneheaded it might be.

I decided I needed to just let it go for the moment. I needed to focus on the grisly work that lay before me without being distracted.

I walked around the hydraulic platform to the freezer chest, and was just about to lift the lid when my cell phone in my pants pocket chirped. I looked at my gloved hands, still covered in blood and viscera, and growled. "It never freakin' fails. Phone never rings until I'm elbow deep in body fluids." But the phone was insistent as it rang again, urging me to remove my gloves and answer it. Reluctantly, I obeyed, and on the fifth ring, I dug into my pocket, and pulled it out.

"You got Mr. Clean," I said after pressing the *TALK* button. Yeah, a bit of a juvenile way to answer the phone, but it's fun.

"I've got another one for you."

I recognized the voice without having to look at the incoming phone number. Ed Massey. I called him Mass for short, and he hated it, which only egged me on. If I worked in the world of publishing or motion pictures, Massey would have been my agent. In the world of organized crime, I guess you could think of him as pretty much the same thing. After all, were any of those worlds truly all that different? Point is, Massey was the go-to headhunter for your average underworld boss. A fixer. He connected clients with contractors for a wide variety of specialized tasks.

"Not interested," I said, slipping on a new pair of gloves. "Once I'm finished here, I'm on vacation, and you know it. We've talked about it like a million times."

"Hiding out in your basement playing PlayStation isn't exactly a vacation."

"You say 'toe-may-toe', I say 'blowing a brain-eating zombie's head off is quite relaxing'."

"Ajax, this one's a big deal. You're really gonna want to hear…"

"Sorry, Mass, got to finish up. Call me in three months. We'll see how I feel about work then. Ciao."

I pressed the *END* button, and sat the phone down on the hand cart with a sigh. I knew Massey would be ticked at me for that, but we'd been pals a long time. I'd also made him bookoo *dinero* over the years. He'd get over it. Besides, now wasn't the time to worry about fragile egos and strained friendships. It was time to get back to work.

The phone rang again, but I ignored it, and instead, lifted the lid to the freezer chest with a scowl. Now most people use a freezer to preserve perishable items. But where's the fun in that? Since the silly thing broke down in 1989, it had been collecting dust in the bomb cellar…until I figured out a great way to use it for the business. 'Great', however, doesn't mean pleasant. Of everything I do in this job, the contents of the chest were my least favorite. After all, who in their right minds would enjoy a giant container filled with beetles and insect larvae? But that's exactly what I kept in there, thanks to my supplier, Ted, from Crescent City.

Thousands of the ugly critters writhed and squirmed inside the confines of that 4x6 freezer, fed into it via a six inch hole in the wall behind it with an accordion dryer tube leading up to the surface on the southeast side of the house. To paraphrase the old song, the bugs crawled in, the bugs crawled out—all at will—but I tried to keep a healthy portion of decaying meat inside to maintain a steady supply of insects at all times. Fortunately, with the current food supply buried under fifty pounds of writhing insects, there were no flies inside to escape into my workspace.

There are a number of ways to effectively get rid of human remains. Chemicals—like acid or quicklime—are extremely efficient, but they're highly regulated, and too easily tracked. I'm the proud owner of a defunct crematorium in southeastern Tennessee, but cremation equipment is not only expensive, it's bulky and impractical. If I have a job near Knoxville, great. Otherwise, it's pretty much useless. Gator baiting is just plain dangerous, not to mention unreliable. The list goes on and on like that. In reality, there was probably only one way better for disposing of a body, but there was no way I was going to take up pig farming. So, in the end, my method of choice was insects. They could pick a body clean of its flesh in a matter of weeks during the summer time. Maybe months if the victim was big like Muldoon. But ultimately, the only thing left after they were done would be the bones. But I had a guy in the medical supply business who'd happily take those off my hands with no questions asked, and would make a little extra money in the process.

The only downside to it really was…well, I'm just really not a big fan of bugs. Let's leave it at that.

Pulling my eyes away from the disgusting insect colony, I wrinkled my nose and stifled a gag. Then I looked down at the dead man, and quoted my favorite Firefly line, "I aim to misbehave."

I was just about to pull the dead man's torso from the raised platform into the freezer when my phone rang for a third time. "Oh, for cryin' out loud!" I shouted, giving the body one quick jerk, and slid him quickly into the insect-infested container before tossing the limbs in behind him and slamming the lid shut again. I then slipped out of my gloves, scooped up the phone to my ear, and growled, "What?" But no one responded. Instead, there were three loud bangs against the outside metal doors of the cellar. I jumped at the sudden rhythmic cacophony. "Mass? Is that you?" I asked into the phone, while reaching for the 9 mm pistol tucked in the back of my jeans.

There were another three bangs.

"Um, Anton," I heard Yancy say from the living room area. "I think you've got a visitor."

"No, really?" I walked back into the main living quarters of the cellar. "Ever think about checking to see who it is? What am I paying you for?"

The big lug rolled his eyes at me, and returned to his game unfazed by my quip.

Carefully, I moved toward the steps. "Mass? Dude. You didn't use the 'knock'."

There was a pause, then a rhythmic beat echoed against the metal doors. The rhythm to Gilligan's Island.

"Is that better?" Massey said from outside. "Come on, Ajax. You know it's me. Let me in."

"But I'm on vaca…"

"Don't give me that vacation crap." The tone of his voice had changed since his first phone call. It sounded almost frantic now. "This is big. You're going to want to hear me out on this." He paused—I'm pretty sure it was for melodramatic effect—then, added, "If you do this, you'll get to see Luna again."

My throat burned at the mention of her name, as if someone had jammed a Magic 8 Ball down my gullet. Massey was right. I definitely wanted to hear him out now.

CHAPTER 6
AJAX CLEAN

Yancy, grumbling over having to pause his game, shuffled into the kitchen to pour a bowl of Lucky Charms to give us some space to talk. Massey sat down on the couch, and I handed him a beer before plopping down on the beanbag chair against the wall.

He was dressed as he always was...to the hilt. In a silk suit that could not have cost less than five grand, and a bright red tie that cost about as much as my laptop. Every crease was crisp, and perfect, even while seated on my old, raggedy couch. His salt and pepper hair was cut short, and his neatly trimmed mustache and goatee made him look more like a gigolo who'd aged very well over time, than a mob Fixer. But it was his bright, blue eyes with tiny flecks of gold sprinkled throughout that always seemed the most dichotomous about the man. They were deceptively kind. The beguiling eyes of a serpent in the very first garden paradise. One look into them would convince a man dying from thirst in the desert to give his last bit of water to Massey because it was the right thing to do.

Scary dangerous, those eyes.

"Okay. So what's this about Luna?" I asked, avoiding my agent's customary small talk.

He took a sip of the beer, and shifted in his seat uncomfortably, before loosening his tie, and leaning forward. "My client's planning a job in her neck of the woods. It's in Miami."

I scratched my head at this, and shrugged. "So?"

"It's scheduled for a night she'll be on call. It'll be her case when it comes in."

I jumped up from the beanbag, and made my way for the stairs, gesturing toward the doors. "It was really great seeing you, Mass, but like I said, I'm on vacation, and every second you're here, is another that I'm not enjoying myself."

"Wait. I'm not finished."

There was a crash in the kitchen and Yancy shouted a string of curses as he crouched down to scoop up the shattered cereal bowl spread across the tile floor. Embarrassed, he looked over at us and mouthed, "Sorry" with a shrug of his shoulders. After a moment, we turned to look at each other again.

"Then get on with it. No more beating around the bush."

Massey exhaled, then downed the rest of his beer. "My client has contracted the Peyton brothers for the job."

I pinched at the bridge of my nose at the news, and shook my head. "You've got to be kidding me. Who's your client?"

"Can't tell you that."

"If you want my help, you're going to have to. I mean, what's going on with these people? First, Fontaine hires Ellis for the Muldoon hit."

He looked up sheepishly at me. "Yeah, sorry about that."

So Massey had known about Ellis too, without bothering to tell me. I gave him an irritated glare, but decided to let it pass at the moment. I really was ready to get started on my vaca. "I thought hiring the Haitian was crazy enough, but the Peytons? When did the patients start running the asylum?" I walked back over the couch, and sat down beside him. "Seriously. If I'm going to have to pull a job over on Luna, I'm going to need to know everything. And I mean everything, Mass."

"I thought you'd revel in matching your wits against hers

again. You two do have that weird...thing...between you, after all."

The 'thing' he was referring to wasn't exactly what Massey suspected, but I couldn't tell him that. Couldn't tell anyone. For all intents and purposes, Luna Mao Ching was simply an incredibly skilled pathology fellow at the Dade County Medical Examiner's Office. They had been incredibly fortunate when they'd accepted her request for a pathology fellowship a few years before. She was constantly being courted by every medicolegal and law enforcement agency in the United States, including the FBI, but she was content in Miami. She had originally chosen to live there because it was her father's—a bitter old man who didn't deserve the girl's devotion— favorite American city. Of course, a desire to remain close to her father wasn't the only reason she batted away every job offer that came her way. She was also obsessed with me. Or rather, the idea of me. Somewhere along the line, she'd caught wind of my existence. During some research, she had detected a vacuum of evidence at a scene I'd manipulated—a kind of signature I had inadvertently left at every murder I'd cleaned. In my entire career, she had been the only person of authority who'd ever come close to knowing I even existed. Even worse, by interviewing several colleagues of mine in the state prison, she had discovered my *nom du guerre*, Ajax Clean.

Girl was bad for business. But that's not why she mattered most to me, though no one could ever find out the truth.

"The *thing* we have between us is that she's the only one smart and tenacious enough to get me sent to the clink," I said. "No thanks. Your client is an idiot for hiring the Peyton brothers. Let him clean up his own mess."

"It pays a hundred and twenty-five grand."

That stopped me in my tracks. "10-9?" Cop lingo for 'repeat that'.

"You heard me the first time."

"One twenty-five. Over four times my usual fee. Just for a simple cleanup job?"

Massey's nose scrunched up in an ugly bunch. I knew the look well. It was his 'you're really not going to like this' face. But with ten percent on the table for him, he wasn't about to give up now.

"There's a little more to it than cleaning, yeah." He reached into his suit jacket, and pulled out his phone. Swiped through the apps, and pulled up a photo of a balding middle-aged man of Hispanic descent with gleaming white teeth.

"This is the victim? He looks like a freakin' dentist or something."

"That's exactly what he is."

"A dentist? Really? What in the world could a dentist have done to someone to deserve a hundred and twenty-five grand paycheck?"

Massey shrugged. "Have no idea. I just know he's the target. Dr. Dominic Hernandez. A naturalized citizen from Cuba. And the paycheck is precisely because my client isn't as stupid as you think. He trusts the Peyton's for the job itself, but not for the planning. They want finesse. They're not interested in the 'shock and awe' of the Peyton's trademark. They want you to plan it. The brothers will execute it, and then you clean up afterwards. They don't want this to look like a hit. They want it to look like anything other than a murder, and I convinced them that you're the man to make that happen." He handed me his phone, and then he pulled out a pack of cigarettes.

"Don't even think about smoking in here," I said, studying the photo on the phone's screen. "Anything, but murder?"

He nodded.

"Even suicide?"

"Perfectly fine. I asked that one myself. Apparently whoever's doing this isn't worried about life insurance, so the wife's probably out."

I shook my head. "Nah, that's a fallacy. If the guy had his insurance long enough, most insurance companies still cover for suicides too. At least in Florida anyway."

"You'd know better than I do on that."

I cocked my head to one side and growled. "Why the heck would you tell them I could plan their hit? You know I don't work on the front end of something like this. Wet work isn't my thing."

He slipped a Salem between his lips, but had sense enough not to light it. "Look. Here's the thing. This job can't register on anyone's radar. It simply can't be suspected of being a homicide, and with Luna being on-call the night it's supposed to go down, they want someone who can best plan it out without raising her suspicions. Personally, I believe you're the only one who can slip this past her." I watched as his hands trembled ever so slightly. The guy was jonesin' for a smoke in the worst way. "Let me put it this way to you, Ajax. Was I wrong? Couldn't you pull it off if you put your mind to it?"

Oh, now the creep is appealing to my ego. Massey knew me all too well.

I stood up from the couch, walked back into my workshop, and lifted the freezer's lid as I pondered his question. Muldoon's body was already showing signs of major tissue degradation. The insects were working much faster than I'd expected, but it would still be a few weeks before his bones were picked clean.

I closed the lid, and turned to look at my old friend. "I'm not a hitter. Grandma would have had a conniption at the very idea. Look at how she felt about Jerome when she found out he was still hitting years after he was supposed to retire."

Massey laughed. "Don't kid yourself. Bernice was just as much in the family business as he was. Besides, she is dead. I don't think she'll mind. But I'm not asking you to actually do the hit. Just want you to plan it. That's all. And the good news is, you're in charge of those bozos for a change. The Peytons will carry it out —to the letter. And if you do it smart, there would hardly be any cleanup work to do afterwards, right?"

I moved over to the living room area again, and looked down at him. "Who is this guy, Mass? Why such a high paycheck for a simple dentist? You know what Lou always said about jobs that pay too much, right?"

"Yeah, yeah. 'If a job pays more than the victim's actually worth, start counting the pennies in your own life's piggy bank before you accept.'" Massey stood, tapped some keys on his phone, and looked up at me. "Look, I just Dropboxed you all the information I have. Think about it. Get back to me tomorrow. I honestly don't think you'll regret it."

With that, he stood from the couch, pulled on his sunglasses, and moved for the stairs.

"Wait," I said. "I'm serious. I want to know who's paying the bills on this one. I won't even consider it unless I do. And that's no bluff and you know it."

He turned to look at me, pulling his sunglasses down on his nose to look me over the rims. His legs shifted nervously where he stood as he pondered my ultimatum, then he sighed. "Fine, but you didn't hear it from me." He slipped his cigarette lighter from his pockets. "Murphy's the one setting it up. Not sure who the paying customer is though. Just know Murphy's the one who contacted me." He pushed the glasses back up onto the bridge of his nose. "So think about it, will you?"

Without another word, he bounded up the stairs and slipped through the cellar door, leaving me with my thoughts.

Murphy? Holy crap. Wade 'The Raid' Murphy. I was already screwed and I hadn't even given my answer yet. *No wonder the payday's so big.*

Despite the danger I was getting myself into, however, it didn't take me long at all to decide what I was going to do. After all, a hundred and twenty-five thousand dollars could buy an awful lot of vacations.

CHAPTER 7
AJAX CLEAN

The Delano Hotel
Miami Beach, Florida
Monday, February 5

E verything about me is a lie. Even my name, Anton Gabriel Jax, is an outright farce. Don't even get me started about the name the criminal underworld knows me by. I mean, Ajax Clean? Come on! If I had to be honest, I chose it purely for the play on words, and for the kick in the pants I get whenever some tough Guido is forced to use the prefix 'mister' in front of it. Point is, I've been using aliases since I first stowed away on a merchant ship from my South Korean homeland when I was twelve years old and came to America.

Names are only part of my duplicitous arsenal too. My personalities are as varied, and manic as an asylum full of schizophrenics. There is no aspect of my public persona that is completely accurate…if I can help it, that is. Depending on the individual, certain colleagues know me as a dour, straight-laced professional who feels more comfortable in a suit and tie, than a pair of jeans and sneakers. Others might know me as having a major Peter Pan complex—a perpetual geek with a propensity for Captain Caveman t-shirts and all night games of D&D or Risk. No one knows the real me, not even myself. Though, I suspect the truth is, I'm all those things, and none of them.

But masks are just part of the business. Bank robbers, burglars, and serial rapists wear ski masks. Terrorists wear hajibs. Ajax Clean wears personalities.

And fake mustaches.

I reflected on all this in my luxurious art deco suite at the Delano in Miami Beach as I dabbed the theatrical glue just above my upper lip, and prepared to slap on the thick walrus mustache that would make Chumley from Tennessee Tuxedo proud. Disguises were essential for survival in my line of work. No matter how good one might think he is as a cleaner, there was always a risk of being spotted near a crime scene. Always a chance of being noticed slipping away through the shadows. And in my experience, the shadier you look, the more people take note, and even worse, remember the details.

A guy in a fedora and a trench coat, or more appropriate in today's culture, a hoodie, will always draw someone's attention. Whine about it all you want, everyone profiles in one way or another. Sure, you should have the right to cover your head in a shroud of darkness if you want, but don't be surprised if others exercise their right to take notice. After all, nothing good ever wears a hood. Case in point: the Zodiac Killer, the Unabomber, the Grim Reaper, and my personal favorite, Emperor Palpatine. People are naturally going to be distrustful of a suspicious looking dude in a hood.

Now take that same suspicious character, and put him in a clown suit and makeup. He'd certainly creep people out, but he'd look so ridiculous that the average passerby would only recall seeing a clown meandering down the street—possibly looking for his itsy-bitsy jalopy. The average witness would have no clue as to your hair or eye color. No idea how tall, short, fat, or skinny you were. All they'd see is the ridiculous get up and ginormous red shoes you were wearing. It's the next best thing to being invisible.

Of course, I had no plans to dress up as a clown. I'd already tried that on a gig I had a few years back, and to this day, I still can't stomach the sight of cotton candy. But the disguise I was putting together now was just as brilliant…an ensemble that just screamed 'Sunday stroll' boring.

Mustache now in place, I pulled on the salt and pepper wig, and adjusted it to sit properly on my head. Once secured by bobby pins, I grabbed the ends of the wig, bunched them together, and formed a long, greasy pony tail. I then slipped on the tweed jacket, complete with elbow patches, and stared amazed at the middle-aged English professor looking back at me in the mirror.

Was the disguise a cliché? Absolutely. That was the whole point. Any would-be witnesses would allow their subconscious to use those stereotypes to form the inevitable erroneous conclusion I was hoping for. They wouldn't see my slightly almond shaped eyes or yellow-tan complexion. They wouldn't notice my slight build, or fine, straight black hair. They wouldn't see a thirty-six year old Korean man wearing a fake mustache. They'd only see the caricature I'd presented to them as a whole. They'd only notice a mild-mannered, hippy-throwback professor of the liberal arts.

My phone rang as I continued to appreciate my disguise. I glanced down at the caller ID, and smiled. "Luna!" I said into the phone after answering it. "Thanks for calling me back so quickly."

There was a cheerful laugh on the other end. "Remy, how could I not? It's been a very strange couple of days. Your message was—how do you say it—a fresh air breath?"

I laughed. "Breath of fresh air, actually."

"Yes. That is what I meant. So how have you been?"

Luna didn't know my real name either. She was my friend. Possibly my very best friend. But she had no idea who I was. What I really was. She'd met me about a year and a half ago. I'd met her twenty-five years before that. But when I'd caught wind of the paper she'd published in the Journal of Forensic Pathology —a paper that actually named Ajax Clean—I just had to introduce myself. Call it hubris if you like, but I had to learn more about the person I knew beyond doubt was even more brilliant than myself. So I became Remy Williamson, a homage to my favorite literary character. Remy was a fellow Korean immigrant, adopted by a loving couple in Clearwater when he was just a boy. I'd introduced myself by explaining that I was an investigative journalist who was looking to write an expose on this mysterious Mr. Clean himself. We'd become fast friends from the moment we met.

"Been good. Just wanted you to know I'm in town," I said, straightening the glued on mustache, before slipping my Ruger into its shoulder holster, and buttoning the sports coat. I didn't expect trouble, but whenever dealing with the Peyton brothers, it's always best to be prepared. "I have business plans the rest of the day, but was hoping we could grab some drinks or something before I leave."

"I'd love to, but I'm on call for the next three nights. No booze. Unless you'll still be around Thursday."

I moved over to my motel bed, and rifled through my duffle bag; cataloguing its contents for one final check. Everything seemed in place.

"Leaving tomorrow night actually. Was an unexpected trip. Two days only. How about coffee later tonight? Rudolfo's still open?"

"Best beans north of Colombia," she laughed. "Sure. Sounds great. How about we meet at eight?"

I glanced down at my watch and made some mental calculations. It was just before noon. Hernandez's office closed at five. From what I'd learned, he usually left at four-thirty to go to the gym. He'd stay there about an hour, then go to his favorite watering hole before heading home. The Brothers were going to intercept him when he was leaving the gym, and meet me at the office around seven-thirty. Should be plenty of time to do the job and head across town to Rudolfo's. His body wouldn't be found until the office opened tomorrow morning, so it'd give Luna and me plenty of time to catch up.

Still, to factor in any unforeseen circumstances...

"How about we make it around nine? Not sure how late I'll be."

She paused. "Nine's fine with me, though if you keep me out too long, I'm liable to turn into a pumpkin. Early day tomorrow, you know."

"Completely understand. I'll have you home well before the witching hour." I needed to get moving. The clock was ticking. "Look, one of my meetings is about to start. Wish me luck?"

"Always! See you soon."

She hung up and I tucked my phone into my jacket pocket before pulling out a tablet from my suitcase, and firing up Skype. A few finger swipes and the all-too-familiar ring tone of an out-going call sounded from the tiny speakers.

A minute later, I was greeted by the bespectacled face of Yancy Fortner. His mouth on one side was bulging and he had a spoon in one hand as he crunched down on the cereal he'd been eating before receiving my call.

"Hey, I just remembered," he said between crunches. "Did you ever read that email I told you about yesterday? It was from Luna."

I shrugged. "Not yet. But I just talked to her. She seemed fine to me. I'll check it later. It's time to work now."

He nodded. "No prob. Just wanted to remind you. Everything good to go?"

"Depends. You get the information I needed?"

"You know it. Weird thing about his office though. I did get the specs to his security, but there's a dead zone."

"Dead zone?"

"Yeah. A space, near the center of the office, that's completely off any blueprints I've been able to find and no security feed video to access either."

After a second to ponder this information, I smiled. "Don't worry about it," I said. "I know exactly what it is. For now, just concentrate on hacking the security system around six tonight, okay?"

"Got you covered there."

"Good. Now what did you find out about the dentist?"

He shoved his cereal bowl aside and began tapping on the keyboard of his computer. "Whoa, dude. The better question is 'what didn't I find?' This guy is in some serious trouble, man. I'm emailing you the details now."

"Any idea who's behind the contract with Murphy?"

Yancy shook his head. "Not a clue. But I caught wind of something kind of weird when I hacked into the Peytons' email like you asked."

I stared at my tablet's screen and shrugged when he didn't come out and tell me what he'd found. "And?"

"Oh, yeah. I'm not sure what it is."

"What's that supposed to mean?"

"The email is encrypted. And I mean, it's a serious piece of work too. I'm having trouble hacking it and you know what that means."

I nodded into the camera. It meant that whoever sent the email was a heavy player. Since the Peytons were penny ante hitters compared to the likes of Ellis and a few others I've worked with over the years, the fact that someone was contacting them with the capabilities of encrypting an email Yancy couldn't crack was something I should definitely be concerned about.

"Forget the email. What about tracking down the IP address from the emailer?"

"Tried. The account's untraceable."

I chewed on that for a minute. Suddenly, the hairs on the back of my neck stood on end. "Okay, crack the email. Do whatever it takes. Just do it, and let me know ASAP."

"Will do."

"And Yance. You know that 'untraceable' account?"

"Yeah."

"I want you to un-untraceable it. Got me?"

"Sure thing."

The second I disconnected, my hotel phone rang, making me

jump. Only one person knew where I was staying, and if he was calling, it couldn't be good.

I nervously picked up the receiver. "Mass?"

"Anton, I'm in trouble!" He sounded out of breath. Panicked.

"Mass, what's going on?"

"I can't explain now, but something is terribly wrong!" I could hear him moving around on the other end of the line. The sound of clothes hangers whipping across a closet bar echoed in the background. He was packing...and seemed to be in a major hurry. "I'm at my place in Coral Gables. About to head your way. Be careful until I talk to you again." He let out a sharp hiss, then lowered his voice to a mere whisper. "You can't trust any..."

Suddenly, the phone went dead. I tried calling him back, but the phone went straight to voicemail. I hoped he'd probably hit a dead zone or something, losing his signal. But those neck hairs were now stretching way past their follicles now. Whatever was going on, I didn't like it one bit. Unfortunately, I had a job to do and I had never failed a client in my life. I wasn't about to start now.

I switched on my laptop and reviewed the files Yancy had sent me, periodically trying to reconnect with Massey. An hour and a half later, a solid plan, as well as at least three contingencies, had been conceived and relayed to the Peyton brothers.

Satisfied that the planning stages were now complete, I scooped up my keys, strode out the door of my suite, and headed toward my car as I dialed my old friend Massey one more time.

CHAPTER 8
AJAX CLEAN

H&G Dental Associates
Miami, Florida
Monday evening, February 5

I met the Peyton brothers in the parking lot of H&G Dental Associates off Claremont Avenue a few minutes before seven-thirty. The brothers stood outside the back of their 1978 Chevy 'shag' van; their arms folded over their thick chests as they glared at my car driving up. John and James—I never could tell which was which, although I'm fairly certain, like me, they weren't using their real names anyway—fiddled with the suppressors on their pistols as I climbed out from the driver's seat, and walked back to my trunk. I retrieved my duffle, and gave the parking lot a quick once over.

Dr. Hernandez's Lexus sat in his assigned space, just as I'd instructed. Good. It wouldn't do to have his body found dead at his work place if his vehicle wasn't there as well. A small detail, but one that could have easily derailed our plans. Satisfied that everything was going well so far, I sidled up next to the hit squad twins.

"Gentlemen." It was like calling a hyena a kitty cat. "You have him, I assume."

The brother with a mane of long, greasy brown hair nodded silently. He wore black BDU trousers, and an equally black T-shirt. The brother with the shaved melon of a head—wearing a matching set of clothing—simply slipped his sidearm into his shoulder rig as he sucked on some gristle caught between his front teeth.

"And there were no complications drugging him, I take it."

"I know you don't trust us," said long hair. "But we really do know what we're doing."

"John..."

His eyes narrowed at me.

"I mean, James." His expression relaxed. "It's not that I don't trust you. It's just that your little fiasco in Chicago last year proved to me one simple thing."

"And that is?"

"That you two are stupid." I smiled at them. "I mean it from the bottom of my heart. You guys are the Laurel and Hardy of the International Assassin's Union."

John the Skinhead, took a step forward. His hand gripped the handle of his pistol to the point his knuckles whitened.

"Easy there, Stanley," I said, holding up my hands submissively. "I meant that as a compliment. Laurel and Hardy were hilarious."

James placed a firm hand against his brother's chest, silently holding him back. Brotherly love. It really does save lives.

"You're the one who is hilarious, funny man," James said. "Now want to get this show on the road or what?"

"I think that would probably be for the best." I gestured to the van's rear doors. "Seriously. You haven't left any marks or anything on him, right?"

James shook his head as he opened the doors. "As pristine as a baby's bottom."

I looked inside the back of the van to see a man wearing a black hood over his head, duct taped tightly, lying on a wooden pallet. I stepped forward, examined his bindings, and shook my head disapprovingly. "Laurel and Hardy," I mumbled, then looked over James. "Duct tape? Really?"

"What?"

"You used a heavy adhesive. It sticks to clothing. The plan is to make this look like a suicide. Hard to sell a suicide when our victim has traces of poly-ethylene resin on his threads."

"You said not to use ropes. Anything fibrous that could leave marks. What else were we supposed to use?"

But I was already walking back to my rental car. My thumb pressed down on the key fob, and the trunk lid popped up once more. I was nervous as it was. I hadn't been able to get a hold of Massey and Yancy had yet to break the encryption on the Brothers' email. Something wasn't right and I felt like I was going into this whole thing utterly blind. I peeked around the open car trunk to watch my collaborators. They stood there, impatiently, glaring at me with contemptuous disdain painted across their brows. They probably trusted me about as much as I did them, which said loads about the camaraderie this business nurtures among its contractors. Putting my doubts aside for the moment, I reached into the trunk, grabbed a parcel of clothing I'd laid aside for just such an emergency, then strode casually back to the Moron twins.

"You guys actually did me a favor," I said, holding up the lacey brassiere, fringed crotchless panties, and fishnet stockings.

"Now who's the idiot?" the shaved one, John, said with a sneer. "You don't think the cops are going to get suspicious with the dude dressed in women's clothing?"

"Actually, no. They won't."

I didn't offer an explanation. Truth is, autoerotic deaths are more common than you might imagine. Someone with really messed up sexual urges decides it'd be a swell idea if they got all decked out in their favorite Frederick's of Hollywood ensemble, cut off airflow in a variety of creative ways, and then get busy pleasuring themselves. Most of the time, they have an escape route planned—a means to allow oxygen to return to their system

—but all too often, something messes up, and they're found the next day by their mom or wife wearing Aunt Gertrude's granny panties and a leather mask with a zipper where his mouth is.

It's the weirdest thing, and no matter how long a detective has been working the mean streets, there's just something about this kind of death that screams 'perversion' somewhere in the back of his mind. Though the detective knows he has to do his job, and investigate the death, he's not entirely certain he wants to look the corpse over any more than he has to for fear that he might look into those dead eyes and see his own staring back at him. So, if we don't want a lot of scrutiny on a case, and suicide is no longer an option, then autoerotic death is the perfect way to go.

I handed the lingerie over to James just as they finished placing Hernandez into a cheap, drugstore wheelchair. I watched as they struggled to get his feet onto the stirrups, and could only shake my head in dismay. The dentist was dressed in a pair of plain aqua-colored scrubs, and a pair of black Crocs. A black, silk pillow case was pulled over his face, obscuring his features.

I glanced down at my watch. It had been dark for the last couple of hours, so it was no surprise that it was now 7:45 in the evening. Knowing Luna's penchant for always arriving early for any engagement, she would probably arrive at Rudolfo's in forty-five minutes.

Plenty of time.

"Hold up a sec," I told them, bringing my phone to my ear, and dialing a number.

"What's up, boss?" Yancy said when he answered my call.

"Security set?"

"Roger that."

"And the other thing?" I glanced over the Peytons. There was no way they could know I was talking about their email, but paranoia isn't exactly rational to begin with.

"Still nothing. I can tell you this though. This encryption is state of the art. Like NSA quality tech here. It's…"

"I get it. Just keep at it. And make sure to keep on the security grid 'til you hear from me."

"Sure thing."

The phone went dead and I slipped it back in my pocket. "Okay. Let's go," I said to my accomplices, taking hold of the back of the chair, and wheeling the victim toward the dentist office's front doors. I glanced up at the security camera below the entrance awning, and hoped Yancy had remembered this part of the security system. Turning off the alarms was simple enough, but the plan called for him to remotely loop the feed as well. Should be a simple enough job, but my 'butler' tended to get distracted very easily. I made a mental note to check the monitors before I called it a night, just to be safe.

John moved up ahead of me, making a beeline for the security key panel. With a few swift motions, his fingers danced over the keys, and we were rewarded with the sound of the door being unlocked. John opened the door, holding it so I could push the dentist into his office.

I looked at John, then at the keypad. "You had the code?"

He grinned. "Yep."

"How?"

"Our client," James said, moving around and holding the door open for me. "Now go ahead and get everything set up. John and I will get the gas canister you requested from the van, and bring it inside."

There were those rising neck hairs again. It was starting to become a habit. I couldn't understand how or why they had the key code, and I, as the planner, didn't. Why had the client trusted them with it? Why hadn't I been told it was even an option? Heck, I'd been having Yancy work his butt off all night getting the security system hooked up for us.

Then, there was the canister comment. Though I was certain the dentist's office would have the majority of the equipment we needed to pull my plan off, I've always been one to leave nothing to chance. I'd asked the brothers to bring a fresh canister of nitrous oxide with them, in case we had to tap off the tanks that were secured inside. And while most canisters would be easy enough to maneuver with a dolly, I knew it would take both of them to lower it from the back of their van. Still, my Spidey sense was ringing to beat the band, but I couldn't quite place why.

"Hurry," I said, eyeing my companions up and down. I could read no deceit on their faces. No telltale nervous ticks that telegraphed any subterfuge on their parts. "I'll be in Exam Room 6."

I began wheeling our captive through the posh reception room boasting oversized beige leather chairs, and a flat panel TV mounted on the wall. The place was spacious, and open air with no doors separating the waiting room from the rest of the office. I wheeled the dentist past the curved reception desk, and took a hard left to navigate down a long hallway peppered from left to right with examination rooms.

I'd chosen Exam Room 6 for two reasons. First, it was directly across from Hernandez's private office. After all, it would only make sense for a weary dentist to go to the most convenient space available to him after a long day's work in order to unwind. It would be much stranger for him to choose any other room for a suicide, as my original plan had been. The autoerotic thing worked just as well for his weird nocturnal forays into drugs and porn.

I reflected on my plan as I wheeled him inside the exam room. It was a well-known fact that the dental profession had a dirty little secret they wanted to keep from the rest of society—an addiction often thought to be so harmless it was hardly worth mentioning. But the cold hard fact of the matter is, dentists tend to love the one drug they have so readily available. Nitrous oxide. Few people realize just how widespread the problem is, but law enforcement understood that the lax regulations with the substance affectionately known as 'laughing gas' was creating a major epidemic.

The drug has even been used quite a few times as a dentist's personal choice for committing suicide. That was why my original plan had been to make Dr. Hernandez's death appear to be suicidal in nature. Yancy's research had revealed that he was in some dire straits in regards to money owed to certain unseemly people. Gambling debts mostly. And his beautiful wife had taken his two kids, and moved in with a boyfriend who was nearly half her age. Plenty of reasons to want to do yourself in.

But after digging a little deeper, I was glad for my foresight to pack the lingerie. Seems that the good doctor, having tendencies outside the female persuasion, wasn't all that sad to see his wife leave. Furthermore, he had, on more than one occasion, expressed concerns that his children, might in fact, not be 'his children'. Besides, just the brief glance at all the trophies and photographs of celebrity patients smiling their porcelain whites next to their favorite dentist told me Hernandez might actually love himself too much to ever take his own life.

That's where the autoerotic asphyxia would work perfectly. Autoerotic deaths were never considered intentional. They were accidental deaths taking place during bizarre rituals of self-gratification. Something that a narcissist like Hernandez might easily do. In his case, I was combing two vices in one. It's why I needed the Peytons to keep him alive to set everything up. The plan was to make it look like the dentist was enjoying a bit of the nitrous oxide, while placing a plastic bag over his head and sexually gratifying himself. As he inhaled the nitrous, he'd become more disoriented. Without oxygen to counter the laughing gas, he'd soon succumb to anoxia, pass out, and eventually die. Clean and simple.

I brought the wheelchair up next to the dentist chair, and glanced down at my watch again.

7:57 PM.

What is taking them so long?

The second reason I'd chosen Exam Room 6 was that it was the farthest away from the front doors. Should an enterprising employee decide to return to the office hours to do some paper-work, it would be much easier to avoid detection. Of course, the downside was that it made it more difficult for me to check on what my compatriots were doing at that precise moment.

I slipped my duffle bag from over my shoulder, and sat it down on the floor next to the dentist's chair. Unzipping it, I rifled through the contents and withdrew a bootleg DVD. I then walked over to a nearby cabinet, opened it, and slipped the DVD into the office's entertainment center. The equipment quickly hummed to life, and a small television screen mounted into the ceiling flickered on. Seconds later, the gay porn I'd inserted into the DVD player began playing just above the dentist chair.

I looked at my watch again. 8:00 PM. *They should be back by now.*

Then it struck me. The reason I'd felt so uneasy when the Peyton brothers had told me to go on ahead. My mind replayed the moment they'd opened the van's door, and I'd looked in to see Hernandez trussed up. There'd been nothing else in the back. There'd been no nitrous containers. Just an old wooden pallet, and nothing else.

My stomach lurched at the realization.

"Hang tight," I told the duct taped dentist, jogged out of the room, and down the hall. When I reached the large picture window of the waiting room, I knew my suspicions were true. The Peytons' van was gone.

My phone vibrated in my pants pocket. I slipped it out, and answered it with a swipe of my finger.

"Yancy!"

"Dude! You need to get out of there. Now!"

"I was just…"

"No, seriously. I just hacked that email. There's a second contract and you're the target."

"Let me guess. It's a set up job."

"Exactly. How'd you know?"

I looked out past the parking lot and could already see the blue and red lights of two marked police cruisers speeding over the Interstate bridge and heading straight for the off-ramp that would lead them directly to Dr. Hernandez's front doors.

"Oh, just a hunch."

CHAPTER 9
AJAX CLEAN

'd been set up. My instincts screamed for me to run. Every nerve in my body was pulling me toward the exit. But there were times to listen to your instincts, and there were times to tell them to shut the hell up. Something told me this was the latter situation. Something in the back of my mind was clawing its way to the surface. Something I'd missed.

And just as the absence of the nitrous canisters had slapped me in the face like Grandma Bernice when I'd 'sass talk' her, so too did the image of the Peytons struggling to get Hernandez's legs into the wheelchair. It had seemed like such a small thing at the time. Hardly worth a second glance. But that tiny, insignificant detail had told me everything I needed to know.

The man in the wheelchair was already dead; his limbs already freezing up with rigor mortis. If he'd still been alive—as my plan had called for—then it would have been easier to get myself out of this particular jam. Leaving a corpse, however, without eradicating the evidence would most likely lead the police directly to me. After all, why go to all this trouble to place me at the scene of a murder, then call the cops, and *not* place key pieces of trace evidence on the body that would finger me as the suspect?

I took another look out the window. The cruisers had pulled

off the Interstate, and were already merging onto Claremont Avenue. I only had minutes.

After quickly dead bolting the front doors, I ran back to Exam Room 6, grabbed the pillow case hiding the target's face, and pulled it off in one smooth motion. The sight that greeted me brought me to my knees with a stifled whimper. The man was dead, just as I'd suspected. His head had been wrapped tight in Saran Wrap that staved the flow of blood from the dozens of knife wounds all over his face and the one surgically precise incision drawn across the jugular. But it wasn't Dominic Hernandez staring back at me with those lifeless eyes. Through the semi-opaque plastic wrap I could just make out the perfectly manicured salt and pepper hair and goatee of my old friend, Ed Massey.

My limbs shook at the sight. I'd known the fixer most of my life. He'd been friends with Jerome Jax since before Grandma had adopted me. He'd looked after me. Helped me through some pretty difficult times. While we didn't always see eye to eye on things, I counted him among the few in my life I saw as 'family'. And he was now dead. Brutally murdered.

His last phone call to me replayed in the back of my mind. *"Anton, listen. I'm in Miami. I've just learned something you need to..."* The phone had gone dead. I'd assumed he'd simply lost service. Now I knew better. More than likely, I'd actually been privy to his murder at that precise moment or sometime soon after.

Reflexively, I took a deep breath. My mind was threatening to go numb, but too much was at stake. I had indeed been set up. That much, I knew. But I knew something else, as well. I knew that somewhere on my friend's corpse, there was evidence linking him directly to me. I knew also that that was something I couldn't allow.

My phone started vibrating inside my pocket. Numbly, I pulled it out, and glanced down at the caller ID. It was Luna. I didn't have the heart to answer. I was going to have to stand her up because I was currently stuck at a murder scene that would eventually end up being her own case. Worse still, she'd met Massey before. Though she had no idea what he did for a living, she knew he and I were friends. It wouldn't take long for her to put certain pieces together. This was going to crush her. I ignored the call, and slipped the phone back into my pocket, before visually sweeping the room for a way out of the trap that had been so expertly sprung on me.

Expertly. One word that does not describe John and James Peyton. Someone else had to have orchestrated this. I didn't have time to dwell on it at that moment. I pushed the thought to the back of my mind, and returned to my current predicament.

I estimated I only had a few minutes before the cops would arrive on scene. Another minute or so for them to check the door and find it locked. Then, a sweep of the exterior of the building. They'd walk around the back, which was surrounded by a small parcel of woods, and look into each window in a search for anything suspicious. If anything caught their eye, they'd force open the door and barge in on me. About ten minutes altogether. Fifteen tops.

My options were limited, so I acted instinctively—letting my years of forensic cleanup do most of the initial work. The first thing I did was shut down the entertainment center, as well as the lights to the exam room. No need attracting the officers with a light and sound show. With the lights now off, I withdrew my alternate light source from my duffle bag, flipped it on, and watched as the pale blue light flickered to life. Taking a pair of amber colored glasses, I slipped them on, and waved the ALS wand up and down over the body of my dead friend. It took only seconds to discover several strands of fine, black hair—consistent with my own. A handful of fingerprints, no doubt belonging to me, erupted on the bare skin of Massey's wrists and throat. The amount of evidence was overkill, but whoever was setting me up knew I'd do what I could to eliminate as much of it as possible before I got pinched for the murder.

Thankfully, there was still something called reasonable doubt in this country, and the more doubt I could create in the minds of any future jury would be better for me. The question was, how could I do that with the dwindling time I had left?

Digging through my duffle, my fingers grazed against a brown glass bottle. It was corked with no label, but I knew exactly what it was. Acid. Hydrofluoric acid to be precise, and had the concentration necessary to eat through skin, tissue, and bones in minutes flat. I picked up the bottle and walked over to Massey. Unfortunately, there was nowhere near enough of it to properly dispose of an entire body. Not even enough to reliably destroy any trace evidence on the body. Besides, before this night was done, I might need it for something else. Best not waste my precious resources unless it was a sure thing.

The sound of something banging near the waiting room caught my attention. Someone was pulling at the door, testing to see if it was locked. The cops had finally arrived, and that meant I was out of time. According to protocol, they would begin their patrol around the building any second, and...

An explosion of glass shattering echoed down the hallway. They were forcing entry into the office without their customary search, which meant that they weren't here responding to some general alarm. They'd been verbally tipped off that something criminal was going down in here tonight. They weren't going to waste any more time than was necessary if they believed a life was being threatened, which meant that my luck had truly run out.

"Well, crap," I muttered, giving the exam room one more once over and hoping for inspiration.

"You take the north wing," I heard someone say from down the hall. "I'll take the south."

Just swell. I suppose I'm in the south wing.

I heard the soft rustle of booted feet scurrying over the plush carpet of the office, and I reached around and took hold of the Ruger LC9 tucked away behind my belt. I'd done a lot of bad things in my time—even killed a few people—but I was in no way a 'murderer'. Those I'd killed in the past had certainly deserved what they'd gotten. Or I'd been fighting for my very survival. But I'd never even entertained the notion of killing a cop before. Heck, I liked those guys. They had a tough, thankless job. At the end of the day, all they wanted to do was make a difference, and make it back home to their wives and children. They weren't my enemy.

I took hold of the gun's slide, and slowly pulled it back; arming the weapon.

"Anything?" I heard the one farthest away shout from the other side of the building.

"Clear so far!" Sounded like the other one was only a few doors down from me. If I was going to act, I needed to do it now.

I dove for a nearby cabinet next to the door, and pressed my back against it hoping the officer would see the body in the wheelchair, and pass me by entirely. I had no desire to kill the man, but if I couldn't run past him, and make for the door, I couldn't see any other alternative.

"Rick, come check this out!" said the cop on the other end of the office, and my heart skipped a beat.

"What is it?" Rick's voice was dangerously close. Perhaps only two or three feet away, and I tensed, waiting for the inevitable.

"Not sure. My flashlight battery's dying. I need yours for a sec."

To be honest, I was confused. The two cops were being too overt—too loud—to be clearing a building they suspected of being occupied by an assailant. It was almost as if they didn't expect to find anything at all. But if that was the case, why bust the window out to make entry? What had been so important?

Whatever the reason, when I heard Officer Rick start to make his way to his partner, I praised whatever god was looking over me for even the briefest of respites. Creeping to the edge of the door, I peered into the hallway, and watched the two cops converge. The other officer pointed into one of the other examination rooms, and Rick swept the beam of his light inside.

"There's nothing there," Rick said irritably.

"But I'm positive I heard something. Hold on—over there! Did you hear it that time?"

Officer Rick shot the flashlight in the direction his partner indicated, and paused. His head cocked slightly to one side as if straining to peer into the shadows. I wasn't sure what they were hearing, but I wasn't about to waste the opportunity. As the two cops searched for their phantom noises, an idea that would solve all of my problems simultaneously sparkled to life with the brilliance of a ninety watt bulb.

Pulling myself back into the room, I turned to the cabinet I'd been leaning against, and opened it. The DVD player met my gaze at eye level, but what I was looking for was on the next shelf down. A clear hose attached to a nose and mouth mask. The same mask I'd planned on using on Hernandez. I followed the length of the hose down to the lowest tier of the cabinet, and found two knobs. One was labeled simply O_2. The one connected to the face mask and hose read N_2O. Nitrous oxide. I smiled to myself as I pulled out my pocket knife, sliced through the hose, and let it fall to the floor. I then turned the nozzle to the right, allowing the gas to pour out into the room for a few minutes before digging into my trouser pockets for the Zippo lighter I always carried with me.

Standing up, I moved closer to the door, flicked the lighter to life, and dropped it near the hose of the NOS. Instinctively, I tensed, waiting for the fireball I imagined would come. Instead, the slow moving gas from the nitrous oxide blew out the lighter's flame in an anticlimactic huff.

That's when my high school chemistry class came back to me —or rather, my days of drag racing down Barley Road when I was a teen. In my panic, I'd forgotten that nitrous oxide was a relatively stable compound, and required intense heat—almost 525 degrees—to combust.

Great. Now what Einstein?

"...still have two more rooms to check down there." Rick's words oozed back into my conscious mind. The two officers had obviously cleared the north wing, and were making their way here.

I was screwed. There was no way around it. I withdrew my pistol again, pressed my back against the wall beside the door, and stifled a giggle. The excitement was apparently getting to me. The adrenaline pumping through my veins was starting to make my head swim. The room around me began to spin out of control.

Crap. The nitrous. I'd forgotten to shut the gas off. There wasn't much danger. Laughing gas is slightly denser than air, therefore, it was hovering near my feet. On top of that, it tended to diffuse rapidly in air, therefore, the concentration was much lower than if I inhaling it with a mask. Still, in my present situation, the slightest misstep could prove fatal, and being even a little inebriated could have disastrous consequences for me.

Clutching my weapon tighter, I spun around, crouched down to the nitrous knob, and turned it off. As I did so, my eyes drifted ever so slightly to the right, and I found myself smiling once more —this time of my own free will.

O_2.

I'd just found my solution.

CHAPTER 10
AJAX CLEAN

"2380 to HQ, we're still 10-7. Just a few more rooms to check out, and we'll be clear," Rick said into his radio. "So far, we haven't found anything."

"10-4, 2380. Standing by."

My uninvited guests were still a few doors down. If I was going to act, it had to be now. But first, I needed something. Latex gloves would work nicely. Just needed to figure out where they kept them in the examination room. They hadn't been in plain sight, so they must be kept in one of the storage cabinets.

I sidestepped to my right, to the next cabinet over, opened it, and found an assortment of dental instruments, picks, drills, and other medieval torture devices. But no gloves. I moved to the next cabinet, and nearly scream when I opened the door and a naked, and very dead Dr. Dominic Hernandez slid from his hiding place onto the floor.

You have got to be kidding me!

Two bodies now. Of course, I should have known. The dentist's car was in the parking lot. Mass was wearing a set of scrubs. Only made sense Hernandez would be around here somewhere. And naked.

Unfortunately, his sudden intrusion made just a little too much noise.

"Who's there?" shouted one of the officers.

"Police!" shouted Rick. "Come out of there. Now!"

I held my breath. My mind raced through all my dwindling options. It looked grim. I had to stall for more time. They already knew I was in here, so I could only think of one recourse.

"Stay where you are!" I shouted in my most country twang accent imaginable. I made sure to stay in the corner of the room farthest away from the door, well outside of anyone's line of sight. "I got Hernandez in here. Any false moves, and he's dead!"

Okay. So I watched way too much television as a kid. But they could critique my acting performance once I was long gone. All I cared about at that moment was that I was dealing with two 'by the book' cops, and not a couple of cowboys. If they were the latter, I was soon to be a dead man. If they were the former, they would, according to SOP, withdraw and call for backup—including a S.W.A.T. unit.

For several eternal seconds, there was nothing but silence from the hallway. I couldn't even hear the sound of their boots against the soft carpet. Then, one of them sighed before answering, "Alright, buddy. Everything's going to be fine."

Typical cop. A bit dense, but he meant well. He had no idea whether I had a hostage or not, but he wasn't going to take any chances.

"We're backing out now," said the other one. "But don't make this worse for yourself than it already is."

They were worse on the melodrama than me. I guess all of us had seen one too many cop buddy pictures, but I figured that would ultimately work to my advantage. After all, they had to play by the rules. I didn't.

"Before you go, toss one of them radios of yers into the room," I said. Accents. Just another kind of disguise.

There was a pause, then, "Um, why?"

"'Cause how will them negotiator people contact me later? There ain't no phones in this room, and we're not plannin' on budgin' from this spot any time soon."

Several seconds ticked by, then a small black object tumbled into the room from the hallway. I saw it come to rest, and immediately identified it as a handheld radio. It would come in handy for listening in on their conversations—at least, if I could keep up with their frequency changes.

I waited until the two officers had completely backed out of the office, then stole down the hallway. I came to the corner adjacent to the waiting room, and peered around. The cops were skulking back over to their vehicles, and I began scanning the radio's frequencies until I found their conversation.

"Dispatch, this is 2380. Suspect located. He appears to be signal zero with a gun. Possible hostage situation. Requesting backup, and SWAT."

"10-4, 2380. SWAT will be 10-51 to your 10-20 ASAP."

Just as I thought. Backup would be there in minutes. My gambit had bought me a little time, but not much. I dashed back to Exam Room 6, stepped over to the windows, and pulled the blinds closed before resuming my search for the gloves. I found them in a drawer next to the sink, grabbed the entire box, then moved over to Massey, and pulled him from his wheelchair to the dentist chair. Once in place, I carefully unwrapped the Saran Wrap from around his head, and stuffed the bloody plastic into his shirt pocket. If this worked, the plastic wrap would melt along with all the other evidence.

Satisfied Massey was in place, I glanced over at Hernandez's crumpled form on the floor near the cabinet, then immediately disregarded him. The cops could have him. The way I saw it, my old friend was the biggest danger to me. He was the one the Peytons had planted the evidence on. The dentist was only an incidental. Collateral damage. More than likely, they wouldn't have thought to plant any evidence on him. So, disposing of Massey was my number one priority—outside of escaping the office with my brains still in one piece, that is.

Opening the box of gloves, I grabbed a handful, and scattered them in Massey's lap. I then dropped several down his shirt, as well as the inside of his pants. To top everything off, I wadded a pair up, and stuffed them into his mouth, being sure to leave a portion of the gloves protruding past his lips. Once the body was adequately blanketed in latex fuel, I crouched down at the gas niche, uncoiled a fresh hose, and attached it to the O_2 nozzle. I turned the knob, heard the unmistakable hiss of gas pouring through the tubing, and pulled it over to Massey's corpse. I let the hose rest on his right shoulder, being sure to position the opening down his chest to provide the maximum flow of oxygen I could.

The walkie-talkie suddenly crackled to life. "2380, 4571." Another officer, possibly a detective or a supervisor was calling Officer Rick. "We'll be 10-97 to your location in five minutes. What's your status?" The cavalry was only five minutes out. It was time to put my money where my mouth is.

Thanks to Yancy, I'd been able to study the layout of office quite extensively while planning the hit. I knew things about it that even Hernandez wouldn't have known. And of course, there was also that 'dead zone' Yancy had referred to earlier that day.

Yeah. That'll come in handy, I think.

Grabbing a stool, I moved it directly under the exam room's sole fire sprinkler, and slammed it with the butt of my handgun with three hard whacks. The force bent the device at a weird, forty-five degree angle, completely disabling it. I then hopped down from the stool, pulled out my trusty Zippo lighter from my coat pocket, and flicked it to life. With the excess oxygen in the room, the lighter flared brighter than I'd anticipated, and nearly took my eyebrows off in the process.

Good. That'll work nicely.

With that, I tossed the lighter onto the pile of gloves in Massey's lap, and watched the flames slowly build. The gloves bubbled and spewed as the heat rose, and the fire jumped from one glove to the next, climbing up my friend's chest. The fire also took hold of the nylon fibers of the scrubs and began moving casually down his legs. It wouldn't do too much damage to the body—some charring of the epidermis and that would be about all—but if allowed to burn long it enough, it should definitely remove any of the evidence left on my old friend.

After a few seconds, I moved back over to the nozzle, and opened it up all the way. The flames surged with the new wave of oxygen, and the gloves and clothing quickly became engulfed. The pleather padding of the dentist chair hissed, and popped as it, too, began to melt under Massey's weight.

Satisfied that whatever evidence had been left on the body was now little more than ash, I grabbed the bottle of acid from my bag, and doused the wheelchair with every last drop. I didn't bother to watch it though. Instead, I skulked out into the hallway, and took another quick peek outside. The parking lot was now lined with red and blue lights. A perimeter of yellow police tape had been strung up around the building, and dozens of assault rifles were now aimed directly toward the building. Toward me.

I found myself smiling at the situation. I couldn't explain it, but I'd not felt so alive in a very long time. And let's face it, if I pulled off I what I was about to, I would be forever counted among the gods of the criminal underworld. Hey, a guy needs to take pride in his work, right?

For several long moments, I watched as the Miami-Dade police officers scurried around, back and forth, like antsy children chomping at the bit to get past the gates of Disney World. From my vantage point, I couldn't see a whole lot, but I could at least make out a few sets of worried, fearful eyes. Eyes that betrayed their own fears that they might not make it home tonight. Fears that they might take one misstep and blow the entire operation. Fears of failure and fears of success at too high a price.

Good people, cops. No matter what a number of my colleagues might say about them. Personally, I respected them a great deal. Then again, that might be because my own dad had been one for twenty-three years before his world fell apart.

The radio squawked again, jarring me from my thoughts. "This is Detective Sean Tice, Miami-Dade Police Department. Are you there?"

I slunk deeper into the shadows, making my way back to the burning exam room. The fire had grown much more than I'd anticipated, and I hoped beyond hope that the cops wouldn't notice until I was ready for them.

"I...I'm here." I hoped my voice sounded worried enough. Haggard. Lord knows I was scared enough to piss myself, but I'd been in so many tight spots before, I had to force myself to let that fear shine through.

"Good. Good," replied Tice in a calm, soothing voice. "What about Dr. Hernandez. Is he okay?"

I paused, looking down at the dead dentist. One gaping gunshot wound to his right eye. "Um, yeah. I reckon he's alright." *Sell the hick, Anton. Sell the hick.* "We're both just a bit scared is all."

"Perfectly understandable. It's a scary situation. For all of us."

I knew what Tice was doing. On the one hand, he was trying to gain my trust—showing sympathy for my situation—while assessing my own mental state. On the other hand, he was stalling. He was giving his men time to get themselves into position for a strategic strike. Which meant that very soon, someone would be approaching the window to the exam room, and would see the blaze between the blinds. Then my entire plan would be shot all to hell. I had to move this along.

"I...I...think the doc here was screwin' my wife," I said.

"I can understand why that might make you angry, um...can I get your name? Much easier to talk to you if we had a name."

I paused, counting to ten as if contemplating something, then answered with just a touch of vengeance coating my words. "Names John. John Peyton." There was that smile again. It just felt too good. Jerk and his brother tried to pin this crap on me. At least maybe this would put them under the looking glass when this was all over.

"Okay, John. I can see why you'd be upset. Anyone would be if they found out their wife was cheating on them, but this isn't the answer."

Quietly, I crept across the hall into Hernandez's office, and opened the closet door to the left of the door. The large iron safe sat in the recess, exactly as I knew it would be.

"I don't know, Officer Tice. I just don't think I wanna go on livin' knowin' what this piece of shit did to my wife." I depressed the walkie's button, then started spinning the tumbler, rifling through a series of numbers I'd known were important to the dentist. After the fourth try, I heard a click, and the safe popped open. I took a quick look on the bottom platform of the safe and started searching for what I'd hoped I'd find. After a few heart-pounding seconds and nudging a few odds and ends aside, I chuckled. *Just what I thought.*

"Surely there's some way we can talk about this," Tice said. "I'm sure we can work all this out without anyone having to get hurt."

Satisfied everything was ready, I moved back into the exam room, unscrewed the suppressor from my gun as I listened to Tice's pleas. I then squeezed the radio's talk button, but my act was now directed at the dead dentist for all the world to hear. "Don't you dare lie to me, you rotten son of a bitch! I know you did it. I know you was with her...just last night! I'll blow you to hell if ya deny it again!"

I let off the button.

"John! John! Take it easy. Come on, brother. Don't do anything rash."

"Too late," I said softly into the radio, before pulling the trigger. The gun barked in my hands; its projectile striking Hernandez in the neck. I then pressed the weapon flush with the right side of Massey's head, careful not to let the smoldering heat burn my hand, and fired again. Contact gunshot wound. It was essential to selling a possible suicide.

"Jesus!" Tice shouted into the radio. "John? John? You still there?" I paused again, using the time to fulfill the final act of my plan. I tossed the gun down on the floor where Massey's right arm hung before dashing back into Hernandez's office. I moved over to the safe, dropped to my knees, and pushed back on the hidden hatchway in the back of the safe before crawling through.

"We're coming in, John." Detective Tice sounded agitated over the radio. "Lay down your weapon and surrender immediately."

The office exploded with the sound of tactical boots rushing back and forth through the hallway. Shouts and cries of dismay echoed all around me. A whirlwind of motion as police, firefighters, department brass, wailing estranged spouses, and medical examiner personnel—I assumed Luna was among them—traipsed in and out of the office for the next twelve hours. I was there the whole time. Watching. Enthralled with the activity. But not a single person ever knew I was there.

CHAPTER 11
LUNA MAO CHING

H&G Dental Associates
Miami, Florida
Tuesday Morning, February 6

The clock on my dashboard read 01:23 as I pulled up to the parking lot of H&G Dental Associates. A uniformed police officer nodded at me, then lifted up the yellow crime scene tape, allowing my car to pass through and ease in behind the sheriff's office's crime scene van. Before climbing out of my car, however, I switched on the dome light, and gathered up everything I might need for my investigation at this homicide scene.

Though I'd consumed a considerable amount of coffee earlier, I was still a little groggy from being interrupted from my sleep. It had taken me a considerable effort to calm my mind enough to fall asleep after Remy had failed to show up for our get-together at Rudolfo's. I had waited there for nearly two hours—my irritation building with each passing minute—before deciding he wasn't coming. I had tried calling him, but after a few rings, I'd gotten his voice mail and decided not to leave him a message. Instead, I'd simply paid my bill, gone home, and had finally begun to drift off to sleep when I'd received a call from dispatch requesting my presence on scene at a possible murder-suicide. Such was the life of a fellow in forensic pathology.

Slipping the chain holding my badge around my neck, I was just about to grab my gear bag when my phone began to vibrate in my blazer pocket. I pulled it out and glanced down at the Caller ID.

UNKNOWN CALLER, the display read.

If it had been my personal phone, and a decent hour of the day, I wouldn't have even considered answering figuring it to be a telemarketer of some kind. But when you're the on-call M.E. for one of the busiest cities in the southeast and the call is coming on your work cell phone, one better answer it to ensure it wasn't another call out.

I was just about to press the TALK button, when three gentle taps came from my driver's side window. Startled, I look around to see the smiling face of Detective Sean Tice waving at me.

"Dr. Ching! Sorry to call you out this time of night," he said, his voice muffled from behind the glass.

Smiling back at him, I held up one finger to ask him to wait, then answered the still-ringing phone.

"Dr. Luna Ching," I said.

There was brief shifting of cloth on the other end of the line, then a haggard breath.

"Hello? You've reached the medical examiner on call."

More rustling on the other end, then the distinct sound of a hand taking a tighter grip on the phone and a throat cleared. "Ah, Luna Mao Ching. It's very nice to hear your voice again." The voice had an Asian accent. It sounded Korean, but spoke in flawless English. My mind raced to the strange bouquet of flowers I'd received the day before yesterday, and my pulse quickened.

"I'm sorry. Do I know you?"

The caller shifted once more. His breathing grew more labored, then a gentle hiss. *Is he taking oxygen?*

After a few seconds, he spoke again. "We've met. A very long time ago." He seemed to wheeze. "It doesn't surprise me you don't remember me though. You were such a young, pretty thing back then. So innocent. Only two years old, if I remember correctly."

My throat constricted as I listened. The panic of the last two days threatened to consume me unless I took control of the situation immediately.

"I'm sorry, sir. I'm afraid you have me mistaken for someone else." I looked over at Tice, who stared at me with a concerned expression on his face. I gave him a weak smile of assurance, and a nod to let him know I was almost finished with the phone call. "Listen, I need to go. I'm working at the moment and..."

"Ah, yes. That horrible incident at the dentist's office," he said, cutting me off. He was determined to maintain control of the conversation. Demonstrating his dominance over me. And that was his mistake. I'd had enough of domineering men in my life, and I no longer tolerated such behavior.

"Look, I don't know how you know about what's happening here, and frankly, I do not care. I have to go now, so..."

"Just one more thing, Luna Mao Ching." He said my name like it left a foul taste in his mouth to speak it. "Be *safe* in there, Mao Ching. Be *safe*." He placed special emphasis on the word 'safe' both times he said the word, then chuckled between a fit of rasping breaths. Then, the line went dead.

I took a deep breath, trying to regain control of my rapidly beating heart and pondering the meaning of the strange call. *Another threat? Or something else? What was he trying to tell me in regards to be safe?*

Tap. Tap. Tap.

"You okay in there, Dr. Ching?" Tice asked.

I sat there in silence a few moments more, staring straight ahead and not looking over at the detective. Sean Tice and I had worked on a number of cases together. He was a good man. A good detective. And he made no effort to hide the fact that he was interested in me in a romantic way. His concern for me right now was genuine, but I could not confide in him. No one could know about my past. My father's past. And whatever was happening to me right now was obviously linked to it.

After taking another deep breath, I opened the car door, grabbed my bag, and climbed out. "I'm sorry, Detective Tice," I said, shaking his hand. "Simply a question from a Hospice nurse in regards to a dying patient. Nothing to be concerned about."

He nodded at this. "I've told you a million times, Doc. Call me Sean." He gestured toward the dentist's office and I followed him inside while he briefed me on the case. "We have a weird one here, Doc. And I mean weir-erd."

He proceeded to tell me how 911 received a call from an anonymous source explaining that a crazed maniac had broken into the office of Dr. Hernandez, and was threatening to kill him. When the officers arrived on scene, they found the office secure and all the lights were off. However, having received permission from Hernandez's partner to force entry, they'd shattered the glass door, and began searching the premises.

"The officers thought it was a hoax," Tice said, walking me down a long hallway toward the examination room at the end. A crime scene technician stood at the exam room's door, snapping photographs. "But when they got close to exam room six, they heard a noise, and announced themselves. That's when our suspect made contact with them. Threatened to kill them if they didn't leave. Wisely, they backed out and called for backup."

"What happened next?"

He shrugged. "That's where it gets a little confusing. I'm the first detective to arrive on scene, so I establish communication with him."

"How?"

"Before he sent our road guys out, he demanded they leave a radio."

I blinked at the detective.

"What? You're giving me that weird look you always do when you have one of those brilliant thoughts of yours," Tice said.

"Well, it's just odd. Clever, actually. Too clever for a run-of-the-mill crazy person, don't you think?"

"What do you mean?"

"I mean, of all the things to ask for, he asked for a radio. He was anticipating your protocols. He knew you'd want to make contact with him. More importantly, he knew that while much of your strategy would be discussed over cell phones, a radio was the perfect way to keep a finger on what the police were up to."

His eyes narrowed, then he shook his head. "Still not really following you. How's this help us?"

"Because it suggests that this isn't some random psychotic. This is someone who seems to know how to play the game. Knows what they're doing."

"Damn. You're absolutely right, but it doesn't really matter much."

"Why's that?"

"Because it looks like our perp is dead. He killed the dentist, then lit himself on fire and put a slug in his own head."

"Really?"

"That's what it looks like. GSW to the right temple."

"And why do you suppose he set himself on fire?"

"Who knows? Like the caller said, he must have been crazy." He gestured toward the exam room. "Anyway, we're still processing the scene, but I wanted you to come out and take a look before Crime Scene got too involved."

"Thank you for that."

"Savile," Tice said to the Crime Scene Technician taking photographs. "Can Doc Ching go on in and have a look-see?"

The tech stepped back and nodded. "Sure. Just be careful where you step. I've got everything photographed, but haven't taken measurements just yet."

I stepped into the room and that's when my entire world changed.

CHAPTER 12
LUNA MAO CHING

White powdery foam lay like a coat of snow over the body lying on the dentist's chair and the surrounding floor where police worked to put out the smoldering fire with extinguishers. Another man, dressed only in a pair of briefs, lay on his back with his head resting on the bottom of a medical cabinet.

That must be the dentist.

Ignoring him, I moved up to the chair and slipped on a pair of gloves before pulling a towel out of my gear bag. Carefully, I dabbed the foam away from the man's darkened face and neck, then leaned in for a closer look.

"Caucasian male," I said to the detective who was standing silently behind me. "Roughly fifty years old, I'd say. In excellent physical condition." I paused, and turned to Tice. "Why is *he* the one wearing the scrubs? Why isn't the dentist? How do you know who's who?"

"D.A.V.I.D., the driver's license database, confirmed the man near the cabinet is Hernandez. We don't have a hit on our suspect yet. He claimed to be one John Peyton, but there are a few on file, and no matches. Rapid ID found no prints on file for him either." He shrugged. "Point is, the guy in his undies is the dentist. We have no idea why our suspect is wearing the scrubs, but like I said…this is a weird one."

I nodded and continued my examination. Taking my index finger, I rubbed at the dead man's soot-covered temple to get a better look at the gunshot wound. When I pulled away, there was a streak of unmarred flesh underneath the black substance, but the star-shaped wound was much more pronounced.

"Contact gunshot wound," I said. "Which is consistent with a suicide. Statistics show that most suicides by GSW are usually contact. People are afraid they might miss otherwise. It's also rare to be seen in homicides too."

"Why's that?" Tice asked.

"People put up a fight. They're not just going to sit still for someone to press a barrel of a gun against their head."

"How do you know it's a contact?"

I pointed to the injury. "See this pattern?"

The skin and tissue around the wound was ripped in at least five different directions, giving the impression of a star-shape. Black burn marks, not a result of the fire, could be clearly seen on the edges of the wound. The detective nodded.

"This is seen only in contact gunshot wounds," I said. "When the weapon is fired, the gasses push the projectile out of the barrel, and enter into the wound. The area around the wound begins to inflate with all those gasses building up until the elasticity of the skin gives and you get this familiar ripping pattern." I pointed in various spots around the face. "If the weapon had been a few inches away, we wouldn't have seen this, but we would have seen clear evidence of stippling, which we don't. So, it's got to be a contact gunshot wound."

"Makes sense." Tice moved up next to me to get a closer look. "So case closed, right? It's a suicide? This is our shooter."

I shook my head. "I don't know yet. We still need to perform an autopsy. And there's just too many things not adding up." I looked at the floor and glanced around. "Where's the gun?"

"Crime scene already took it. It was found right there by your foot, at Marker #7."

The yellow marker sat about seven inches away from my right foot, directly underneath where the victim's hand hung over the edge of his chair. My mind imagined the scenario. The shooter had just shot the dentist. He knows there's only seconds before the police SWAT units burst through the doors and take him down. So why go to the trouble of laying back in the chair?

It's not unusual. Many people like to get comfortable before ending their own life, I thought. *Yeah, but to take the time to grab a box full of gloves and work a hose of oxygen to help fuel a fire? Why set himself on fire? It makes no sense.*

"What kind of weapon was it?" I asked.

"A nine millimeter. A Ruger, I think."

I glanced back at the man's blackened face and the streak I'd left when clearing the head wound. Curious, I took my towel and began wiping away the grime around the rest of the face.

"Looks like the fire damage is only superficial," I said. "Just soot. Most of the fire damage was to his clothing, arms, and neck."

"Hey!" the crime scene tech shouted. "I told you to be careful. I haven't taken my measurements yet!"

"Stow it!" Tice said. "The lady's working."

I smiled at Savile while dabbing away more of the soot. "I promise. I'll be careful. This shouldn't affect your measurements at all."

I continued cleaning away his face and gasped when I pulled the towel away.

"I know this man," I said.

"What?"

"I said, I know him." I glanced back at the detective. "Or at least, I've met him before." My mind raced, trying to recall his name. It had only been the one time, but he'd been introduced to me by...

Oh, God. Remy!

I bit my lip, afraid of blurting something out I might regret later. Was my journalist friend involved in this? Was this why he wasn't able to make it to Rudolfo's?

"Luna," Tice said, placing a hand on my shoulder. "Are you okay?"

I nodded. "Yes. I can't remember where I met him," I lied. I didn't know why I did it, but something deep in the recesses of my subconscious compelled me to do so. "But I think his name is Edward. Or Ed." I strained to remember the last name. It had been nearly a year ago and he hadn't really made an impact on me other than his exquisitely tailored suit and charming smile. "Moore? Or Malley. I know it started with an 'M'."

"It's okay. It'll come to you. It's always a shock when it's someone you know."

But I didn't know him. Not really. He was merely an associate of someone I did know. Or at least, I thought I did. The coincidence, however, of Remy Williamson being in town and standing me up for our coffee date when his friend is involved in something like this was…well, Father never believed in coincidences, and neither did I.

I was about to turn away and begin my examination of Hernandez when something caught my eye. I stopped and leaned in toward Ed Massey's neck. Something didn't quite look right and I began dabbing away the soot along the throat with my towel. After a few swipes, I pulled away with a sigh.

"We have a problem."

"What? What do you see?"

I pointed at the approximate eight inch jagged deformity just under the man's chin. "That."

"Is that a…"

"A sharp-force injury, yes." I pulled a magnifying glass from my bag and pulled in for a closer look. "Incision from the top of the victim's mandible, across both carotids, and up to the left ear."

"His throat was cut," Tice said. I understood the unspoken question behind the statement.

"His throat was cut," I confirmed.

"So it's not a suicide then."

"No, it isn't." I shook my head in disbelief. *Oh, Remy. What are you involved in?*

I finished my examination of both bodies, then called for the body removal team to come to scene to transport both victims to the medical examiner's office. I glanced at my watch as I climbed back into my car. It was a quarter past four. I'd only be getting a couple of hours sleep, and that was only if I could quiet the whirling thoughts flowing through my mind.

Someone else had obviously been in that exam room when the police officers began their search. Whoever it was, had set Ed Massey's body on fire, but had left the dentist alone. Why? The only possible answer I could think of was to get rid of evidence. But why not do the same thing with Hernandez? Did he run out of time?

"No, I don't think so," I said out loud as I started my engine. He fired a shot, knowing it would bring law enforcement. He had their radio. He knew the police wouldn't storm the place until they had a better idea of what they were dealing with. He could have easily burned both bodies before shooting Massey. *So why just Ed Massey?*

My mind drifted back to the phone call I'd had when I pulled up to the crime scene. The mystery man who'd called me. Threatened me. *Be safe,* he'd said. *Why 'be safe'? And what does Remy's friend and the man from my past have to do with a dentist in Miami?* It was all so confusing, but I hoped a few hours of rest would help to clear my mind before the autopsies.

Putting my car in reverse, I backed out of the parking lot and headed home. As I entered the Interstate, I pulled out my cell phone and dialed Remy Williamson's cell phone number. But I already knew he wasn't going to answer.

CHAPTER 13
AJAX CLEAN

H&G Dental Associates
Miami, Florida
Tuesday Morning, February 6

M y legs tingled asleep as I huddled safe inside the closet-sized panic room hidden behind Hernandez's safe. The pins and needles in my leg only increased the discomfort I'd so far endured since going into hiding.

I'd first suspected the good dentist had a secret panic room installed when Yancy had mentioned the 'dead zone' earlier that day. Then, while scouring the building's blueprints during my preparations—searching for possible points of egress should the need arise—I'd spotted what he'd been talking about. It had been a peculiar little niche tucked away inside the target's walk-in closet of his personal office space. A small hatchway that led to a three-foot squared cubby hole, tucked behind a large solid steel combination safe. Gambling debts and associations with the mob can make people take the most extreme actions and a panic room in your workplace is one of the most extreme I'd seen. I only hoped that the cops weren't aware of its existence.

The room had been tricky to find though, even being aware of where it was supposed to be. I'd eventually found the entrance on the lower tier inside the safe; a hidden panel, haphazardly concealed by an assortment of prescription medications and dental apparatus. I'd gambled on the combination, but a man as self-involved as Hernandez seemed to be was fairly predictable. Only a handful of combinations were necessary. His date of birth. His wedding anniversary. The birthdates of his children. The identification number of his forty-foot yacht. In the end, the yacht had won out, making it even easier to see why his wife had left him. And maybe why someone would have wanted him dead.

Squeezing into the panic room had been pretty tight, but fortunately, I'm a skinny guy. And limber. I'd popped the safe open, and ducked inside the secret hatch just as the whirlwind of Kevlar and AR-15s stormed the building. A shiny red button in the interior of the panic room, had closed the safe's door with a soft click.

And so, there I huddled. My legs numb. My nose vexing me with an unscratchable itch. The building pressure against my bladder ached with every beat of my heart. For twelve solid hours in those miserably tight confines, I waited for the moment it would be safe to leave. Patience is definitely a virtue in my business. A cleaner needs loads of it to do his job well, and I'd known from the start, an investigation like this would take hours.

Standard operating procedure for a high profile multiple death scene would first include clearing the building. Once it was determined that all parties were accounted for and the scene was secure, all law enforcement personnel would back out, and calls would be placed to the Homicide unit, the M.E., and Miami-Dade's crime scene unit. It would take at least an hour for each of these units to respond from their downtown offices, and another seven or eight to properly process the scene—all of this being done before the bodies were even examined by Luna or the M.E. investigators under her direction.

So, yeah. I'd expected to be holed up for the long haul. It had given me enough time to reflect on everything that had happened that night. Initially, my mind raced, trying to fit the pieces of the puzzle together. I struggled to discern the identity and the motive of the one who'd set me up. In the end, I knew I'd have plenty of time for that later, so I reflected on something much more important to me at the moment—how well I'd handled a rather impossible situation. All in all, I'd been pretty pleased with myself. There'd been a few moments of self-doubt, such as when I'd chosen to hold onto the walkie-talkie, but logic had won out in the end.

First of all, I needed the radio to discreetly keep tabs on what was happening beyond the four walls of my hiding place. Sure, there was a chance that some savvy investigator would wonder why the radio wasn't near Massey's body, but chances were, they wouldn't think to question that until I was long gone.

Besides, my ruse was never intended to fool the cops indefinitely. Once they got the bodies onto the autopsy tables, it would only be a matter of time before they discovered that they were both long dead before the shots had been fired. And while on scene, the fire damage to Massey's body *might* have concealed the slit throat. But once the pathologist—Luna—had him on her table she'd realize that the charring and skin splitting from the heat didn't match up with that around his jawline. She would most definitely discover the fatal wound with relative ease, if she hadn't already.

No, the plan had only been intended to give the police something to sink their teeth into while I waited out the storm, and from the sound of things out there, that time was fast approaching.

I shifted the weight of my body on one butt cheek, allowing the other to regain some circulation as I strained to hear what was happening out in the office. From the sound of it, things were wrapping up. Foot traffic had settled down to only two or three people from what I could tell, but they were currently inside Hernandez's private office.

"You get everything you need?" It was the same voice as the one who'd been talking to me on the radio. Sean Tice.

"I believe so," said another. His voice was softer than the first.

What's more, I recognized it. Steve Savile. Crime scene guru with Miami-Dade Sheriff's Office. Former Florida Department of Law Enforcement wiz kid until he'd gotten a better offer with Miami. He'd consulted me once or twice on a case, though he had no idea what I really did for a living. Good guy. Brilliant too. "But this just might be one of the craziest scenes I've ever worked. I may need to come back later for more samples from the carpet, and wall."

Their voices grew softer as they moved out of the office, and into the hallway. "Shouldn't be a problem. I'm stationing two patrol officers outside until at least after the autopsies. Maybe for the next forty-eight hours."

I'd already counted on that piece of bad news. Once again, it's basic SOP to leave officers to guard active crime scenes. The news didn't undermine my plans in the least.

I waited a full thirty seconds before turning the police radio on, but kept the volume as low as possible. Ten minutes passed. Fifteen. As I waited, I could imagine the cops outside jabbering on about the weekend's upcoming game or where everyone was planning to grab lunch. Cops can be such yappers when they want to be. Finally, after nearly twenty minutes since the detective and Savile had left the building, I heard what I'd been waiting for.

"2617, HQ."

"Go ahead 2617."

"We're 10-98. I'll be 10-51 to the station. Going to leave 4324 and 4362 on scene until they're relieved next shift."

"10-4, 2617."

10-98. Assignment complete. *10-51.* The detective was heading back to his office. It was about bloody time.

I WAITED another two hours before sliding out from my hiding place, and performing a quick sweep of the building. No cops lingered about. No hidden G-men lurked in the shadows, ready to pounce. I was completely alone.

Creeping on all fours, I made my way to the glass entrance. Part of it, where the officers had forced entry into the office, had been hastily boarded up. But it wasn't exactly Fort Knox material either. It would be simple enough to remove when the time came.

I discreetly peeked outside the front window, being sure to remain well within the concealing veil of the venetian blinds. My rental car was now gone—obviously taken by the forensics crew for processing. I wasn't too concerned about that. It's exactly why I use rental cars for every job. Hundreds of previous occupants had used them for business trips, visits to grandma's house, or clandestine trysts with the secretaries. Hundreds of different DNA strands locked within an equal number of hair and fibers littered throughout the inside the automobile would render locating anything that could identify me hopeless. And of course, I didn't use my real name with the rental agency either, so the car really was no big deal.

I continued scanning the parking lot. Except for the two patrol cars sitting side by side—each driver's side window rolled down to allow the officers to chat away the boredom of their vigil—the lot directly in front of the dentist's office was empty. There were, however, a handful of cars parked here and there in other sections of the lot, revealing that the police had allowed the other doctor's and lawyer's offices within the complex to open for the day.

My reconnaissance complete, I made my way back to Hernandez's desk and plopped back into a ridiculously comfortable desk chair. I then powered my cell phone, waiting for it to boot up. Apparently, I'd missed eight calls since turning it off. Six of which had come from Luna. The other two numbers were unknown to me. I suppressed the urge to listen to the voice messages that had been left, and instead, searched the Internet for FedEx, and requested a pickup for a package at the doctor's office next door.

Once that was done, I listened to my voice messages. Two had been from Luna. The first inquiring where I was after waiting another forty-five minutes for me to show up at Rudolfo's. The second, however, sent chills down my spine. She was freaking out. She had indeed been here. Had examined Massey. Even worse, she'd recognized him and suspected I might have somehow been involved. It was the worst possible news I could have received, and for several long minutes, I sat there pondering just how this development would impact everything. After listening to the message at least three more times—each of her words tinged with dread, confusion, and worry—I decided to move onto the third message. Unfortunately, it was even more ominous.

"This is just the beginning, Ryu Nam-gi." The voice on the message—distinctly Asian in accent—knew my name. My *real* name. The name I'd completely abandoned after fleeing Korea and coming to America. "I don't know why you are not dead." The voice wheezed as it drew in a breath. "I paid a considerable amount of money to see you dead, but it doesn't matter. I know you're still alive in that office while the simpletons of the police department walk right past you. Oblivious. But be assured, you will suffer even more now. You will not be able to hide from what I have in store for you."

I couldn't move. Couldn't breathe. Had he just admitted to placing a hit on me? If so, then why hadn't the Peyton brothers shot me and left me for dead? Why the set up? Why kill Massey and make it look like I'd done it instead?

Then, there was the whole *name* thing and everything that represented. I hadn't so much spoken the syllables of my name in nearly twenty-five years. As far as I know, Jerome Jax and Grandma Bernice were the only people this side of the Atlantic that knew it, and there was no doubt that both of them took it with them to their graves. Yet somehow, someone from my past had managed to finally track me down. And they were doing everything they could to flush me out into the open.

I leaned back in the chair, and pondered this new information; working desperately to process it. I struggled to parse the precious data I'd collected from the short, fifteen second message. Then, suddenly, my blood ran ice cold, and I sat up straight.

Luna. If they found me, do they know about her?

I considered calling her…to warn her…but decided it was much more dangerous to contact her right now. In fact, it might be exactly what they were hoping for. I was smarter than that. Acting on impulse and emotion was the quickest way to see both of us dead. No, it was much better to play this one like a Sinanju Master. Cold and calculated. Chiun, if he wasn't a fictional character, would have been proud of my self-restraint and patience. There would be plenty of time to deal with this once I escaped from this office. I glanced down at my watch, wondering how much longer I had to wait before the FedEx truck arrived.

"A trained mind does not need a watch," I heard Chiun's shrill voice from the Remo Williams movie in my mind. "Watches are a confidence trick invented by the Swiss."

Not now, Chiun. I got out of the chair, and crept toward the front entrance of the building.

I spent my time well, carefully removing nails from one board at a time from the empty gap where a glass panel had been the night before. I was careful to ensure the boards themselves remained in place lest the cops outside should notice. When I'd ensured a large enough space to squeeze through, I crouched down on the floor, and waited some more.

I didn't have to wait long. Ten minutes later, I heard the throaty rumble of a large white delivery truck pulling up to the building directly in front of the police cars. Without skipping a beat, I pulled one of the boards aside, and slipped through the opening just in time to hear the cops on the other side of the truck yelling at the poor delivery driver.

With their attention diverted, I strolled casually to the first office on my left, and entered. The receptionist at *Jackson, Pink, and Biggs Attorneys at Law* looked up from her romance novel with a start as I entered.

I gave her a big smile, straightening the lapel of corduroy professor's blazer, and stroking the walrus mustache under my nose. I was nervously pushing the thick glasses up onto the bridge of my nose when she finally regained her composure.

"Um, sorry. With everything going on today, I wasn't really expecting any clients," she said, setting her book down next to the telephone.

"That's okay," I said. "I'm not really a client. What I really need..." I looked out the window as casually as I could to make sure the officers hadn't seen me. "...is a bathroom." I danced an impatient *I-gotta-go* jig. "Haven't been able to go since last night."

CHAPTER 14
AJAX CLEAN

leaned against the bathroom sink, taking deep steady breaths as I willed my mind and body to relax. I was sure Chiun would have had something to say about my quaking limbs, but at the moment, I didn't care. So far, I'd managed to slip from the noose my mysterious caller had strung around my neck, but I wasn't sure how long I'd be able to keep it up. I was sure that the receptionist in the next room was already becoming suspicious. I'd been in the bathroom too long. Calling Yancy, filling him in, getting the latest news from his end of things, and making arrangements for transportation so I can start work at clearing my name.

But the adrenaline rush that had been keeping me going all night was finally beginning to ebb, and the realization of just how desperate my situation really was started to become all too real.

My friend was dead. His throat cut. I was originally a target. Then, somehow, I was supposed to take the fall. Someone from my past was coming after me. The cops were just out in the front parking lot of this office, waiting for me to slip up. And I wasn't entirely sure I'd managed to erase all the evidence of my presence in Hernandez's examination room.

The stress was enough to make even the coolest of cucumbers pickle, and I never liked feeling so out of control. Whoever was behind this mess was going to pay. I swore silently to that, as I turned to the faucet, splashed some water on face, and re-attached the fake mustache.

I moved over to the door and reached for the knob just as someone rapped on it from the other side.

"Sir? Are you all right?" It was the receptionist.

I took one more deep breath, and opened the door with a broad smile. "Right as rain, love. Right as rain." I stepped past her into the narrow hallway of the law firm, looked right, then left, and asked, "I'm sorry to bother you, but mind if I use your back door? I parked on the other side of the complex, and it's a straight shot from here as opposed to walking all the way around this place."

"I...uh..."

As she stammered to come up with an appropriate protest, I strode toward the back of the office confidently.

"I'm sorry, sir. But this area is off limits to anyone who's not a cli..."

"It's quite all right, I'm sure. Biggs won't mind." I craned my head to wink at her. Time to turn on the roguish charm and lie my Asian ass off. "We go all the way back to FSU, ol' Bigglesworth and I did. He'll be fine with me doing this, I'm sure."

I came to a T-section amid a maze of cubicles. The partners at *Jackson, Pink, and Biggs* must have been doing particularly well to have a staff requiring this much office space, though now it was mostly empty. Probably because of all the police activity from earlier.

I turned left and began heading straight back to the rear of the office. My strides were growing longer. Faster.

"Um, I thought Mr. Biggs went to Princeton?"

"Right you are!" I stopped abruptly when I reached the door, and spun around with a hardy laugh. My brain raced. "In fact, he did go to Princeton. But he spent a few years as a Seminole before he did, though he'd never tell anyone about it. Poor guy got booted from school for getting drunk and riding naked on the mascot's horse. Onto the football field. During the homecoming game. It was the talk of campus at the time, let me tell you." I clapped the receptionist on the shoulders and nodded. "Right. I've taken up entirely too much of your time."

"But I..."

"You've been an absolute delight. Thanks so much for the use of the bathroom, and I'll be sure to let Biggsy know what a splendid lady he has working for him."

I turned around before she could say another word, swung up the door, and stepped out into the warm morning light. I counted to three before the door behind me closed, and started walking at a brisk, but nonchalant pace across the back lot and into a nearby alley.

I knew it wouldn't be long before the receptionist went outside to talk to the cops watching the complex. I'd kept her off balance, but she was no idiot. She'd already grown curious about me while I hid in the restroom. The moment I stepped out the backdoor, her curiosity would have hit the stratosphere. The murder the night before. The cops outside keeping watch. A strange man acting so bizarre in the midst of it all. Few people believed in coincidences if they were honest with themselves, and she'd be no different. She'd soon begin to make the connections, if she hadn't already, which meant that I needed to make myself scarce as quickly—and innocuously—as possible.

I walked down the alley, to the next street, and hung a left; away from the office complex. The area in which the office was located was unknown to me. I hadn't spent a great deal of time in Miami—just one night here or there and always within the confines of my cleaning job—so I wasn't entirely certain where to go.

The street appeared to be a small suburban shopping hub. Several mom and pop shops littered both sides of the road, as well as a handful of cafes still serving croissants, bagels, and donuts outside on their open air patios. The throngs of tourists were just beginning to trickle out from their nearby hotels, looking for souvenirs to remember their Miami vacation, without any idea of the horrific murders that had happened during the night just a few blocks away.

A patrol car suddenly appeared at the next intersection and stopped. My heart skipped a single beat when I saw it, but I pressed forward, keeping my head swiveling right and left as if taking in all the wonderful sights, sounds, and smells. Ten steps later, the police car took a right, and patrolled the streets ahead of me. More than likely, the cop was just on his regular beat and not actively looking for the notorious killer of the dentist. My hope was that, at the moment, they still believed Massey's body was John Peyton, and they wouldn't be on the lookout for anyone until I could get myself clear of town. All I had to do was maintain my cool and I might just get out of this in one piece.

I sighed, pulled off my coat and slung it over my shoulder before proceeding down the busy street. I hadn't walked twenty feet when I suddenly knew I was being followed. I hadn't seen anyone or heard them. Hadn't felt the hairs on the back of my neck standing on end. Nothing so dramatic. I simply knew that someone was following me. I stopped, glancing casually around.

Husbands and wives walked hand in hand, window-shopping along the strip of trinket shops. Moms pushed strollers while frantically talking into cell phones. Waiters scurried in and out of the cafes and bakeries, brandishing coffees the size of kiddie pools and great big plates of breakfast Danishes. But as far as someone shadowing me, I saw nothing.

Unnerved, I walked to the next intersection, crossed the street, and strode down the narrow brick-laid road leading to the bay. The street was far too narrow for vehicle traffic larger than a bicycle, and had fewer tourists mucking about on their family vacations. I hoped the decreased traffic would make it easier to catch sight of my shadow. Of course, there was a distinct disadvantage as well. Fewer pedestrians also meant less witnesses, making me a much easier target if things got violent. I just hoped that the benefits of turning down a quieter street would far outweigh the risk.

Unfortunately, my hopes were dashed within seconds when something hard pushed into the small of my back and a deep, raspy voice said, "Mr. Clean, I must ask you to come with me."

The voice had a thick Caribbean accent. I recognized it immediately and I clenched my eyes shut and prayed to the gods above that I'd slipped on a banana peel or something and was only dreaming in a concussion-induced coma. Head trauma was far more preferable to having the hitman Ellis standing behind me with a gun jabbing into my back.

"Ellis? Is that you?"

He didn't respond, which told me everything I needed to know. It was indeed him. And the fact that he was here, now, spoke volumes as well. My mysterious caller must have sent him to finish the job that the failed to do. It was the only thing that made sense. He'd certainly not come here to lend me his support during this time of trial and tribulation. The .45 shoved into my spine was a good indicator my hunch was more than likely correct.

A little bit about Ellis that you might need to know. Although everyone in the business simply knew him as Ellis—we weren't even sure the man actually had a first name—he was also known by another. A nickname that no one dared utter to the Haitian's dark face. *K'ap Ranmase*, the Reaper. Despite his unusually Irish name, Ellis was from Haiti. He was also a high priest of *Palo Mayombe*, a religion originating in the Congo by way of the Cuban slave trade, and known for its macabre death rituals. Because of this, it was said that Ellis was not only brutally efficient at killing for a price, he'd even bring back the soul of his victims for a little bit more. Few clients ever took him up on the offer for souls, however.

Point is, Ellis was not only crazy; he was scary enough to give Freddy Krueger the heebie-jeebies.

"I said you need to come with me." Ellis shoved his weapon hard against the backside of my ribs for emphasis. "Now."

This isn't happening. This isn't happening. This isn't happening.

I opened my eyes and sighed. No matter how badly I'd hoped, this was no dream.

"Look. Can't we talk about this? For old time's sake?" It wasn't like any of our 'old times' were good times or anything, but it never hurt to appeal to someone's sense of nostalgia when you were running out of options.

"Nothing to talk about." Pretty much the reaction I expected. "You be comin' wit me. Now." His accent always seemed to thicken when agitated.

My mind raced. The moment I turned around...the moment I looked Ellis in the eyes and followed him to God only knew where, I was certain I'd be a dead man. Call me a procrastinator if you like, but I had quite a few things left on my to-do list before I'd be ready to meet my Maker.

I had only one option left. Doing my best not to telegraph what I was about to do, I bolted. I ran down the street as fast as my legs would carry me, pushing every bit of speed through my muscles. I was fairly certain Ellis wouldn't risk shooting me in the midst of a busy shopping district—even on a street as isolated as the one I was on. Besides, if he did decide to shoot, it was much more difficult to hit a moving target than a stationary one; and since there was no way I was going to go with him, that's exactly what he would have had to do. Better to run and take my chances, then to just let him shoot me in the back without so much as a fight.

Plus, I was fast. Very fast. It's an advantage of being an Asian with a slight build. Less wind resistance. Long, lean muscles. Plus, I swam regularly, which gave me a pretty impressive endurance threshold. Against anyone else, I would have been gone before they'd run three steps to catch up. But Ellis was exceptionally tall. Nearly seven feet with the long, sinewy legs of an Olympic sprinter. The challenge was to simply outlast him.

I darted to the next street and turned right, running parallel to a high concrete wall surrounding a small little cemetery positioned next door to a quaint whitewashed wooden church. Not breaking stride, I leapt, grabbed hold of the ledge of the wall, and vaulted over it into the cemetery. I then backtracked, heading in between ancient moss-covered tombstones, in the direction of the heavily populated street I'd first stumbled into once leaving the law firm.

The sound of feet landing on soft soil, and a gentle gasped breath told me that Ellis had not given up the pursuit and had followed me over the wall. I risked a glance over my shoulder and confirmed that he was indeed right on my heels. But his typical dark brown face seemed even darker, concentrated along his cheeks and forehead, which told me he was far more winded than I. All I had to do was push myself a little farther, slip through the graveyard's wrought iron gate up ahead, and I'd be home free.

That's what I thought, anyway, until two soft barks of a suppressed pistol sounded behind me, followed immediately by clouds of marble debris from a tombstone to my right.

Son of a…the creep just shot at me. He really shot at me!

I skidded to a halt, raising my hands in the air, and slowly turned to face him.

"You know, it's bad juju to shoot a grave, right?" Maybe it wasn't the best idea to poke the bear when he's pointing a gun at my head, but it's sort of my default setting. A defense mechanism.

I smiled at Ellis. Surprisingly, he was returning the smile and I didn't like it one bit.

He was wearing his typical Havana shirt, unbuttoned a little unfashionably too low to reveal the strange medallion made of human phalange bones hanging from his neck. Although he was unusually tall, he didn't appear to be lanky or clumsy. In fact, he impressively sported pounds of taut, packed-on muscle along his shoulders, arms, and chest which made him all the more intimidating. Even amid the deep shade of the live oak trees cluttering the cemetery, his shaved head seemed to gleam with a death's head radiance. He was pointing his customized Colt 1911 .45 at me as he smiled a Cheshire grin.

"Now, you gonna come wit me or you goin' to force me to shoot you in da leg?"

"Come on, Ellis. Really? You're going to really do this?"

"Gettin' paid to do it. And don't act like we are pals, Clean. I owe you not'ing."

I shifted my weight from one leg to another, preparing for another run, but his sharp eyes caught the gesture and he waggled the gun at me in warning. "Nuh-uh. No more running. Now we walk…to my car."

"Hey!" Shouted a voice coming from the direction of the church. We both turned to see a short rotund black man in a maroon shirt with sharp white collar lumbering our way. The pastor. "What you two doin' in our graveyard?"

Respectfully, Ellis bowed his head ever so slightly in reverence to the man of God, and secreted his weapon in the waistband of his pants. That's when I took off, leaping over gravestones, and beelining directly toward the front gate. I was out of the cemetery —the gate squeaking closed behind me—before Ellis even had a chance to react. Ten minutes later, I was perfectly hidden within the throng of Miami tourists, and heading to the nearest car rental agency.

It was time I visited the home of an old friend and start getting the answers I desperately needed.

CHAPTER 15
AJAX CLEAN

Coral Gables, Florida
Tuesday evening, February 6

I sat in my rental car across the street from Massey's beachside high-rise townhouse complex, watching an attractive middle-aged woman in hot pink spandex jogging gear run past while pushing a stroller. It was a warmer-than-usual February evening in the small beach community just south of Coconut Grove. I'd already seen a number of dog walkers, joggers, and elderly evening strollers walking past as I waited for the last of the Coral Gable police officers to clear out of my old friend's parking lot.

Apparently, Luna had been much more resourceful at identifying Massey's body than I'd given her credit for. According to Yancy, who'd been keeping tabs on all electronic incoming and outgoing correspondence to the medical examiner's office, it had taken less than three hours for her to make a positive I.D, and that was despite the minor thermal damage he'd sustained from my impromptu fire. Then again, after the message she'd left me while I was in hiding, I'd already figured she had indeed recognized him at the office and only needed confirmation through fingerprints or dental records.

She'd also discovered that he had died from a sharp force

injury to the left jugular vein long before I'd placed a bullet into him. Within hours of the discovery, the entire body of Florida law enforcement was on a statewide man-hunt for an unknown killer. There'd even been a composite sketch of my professor persona on TV. I assumed they'd gleaned my appearance from the receptionist at the law office I'd slipped into to affect my escape. I'd just known that woman was going to be trouble for me.

The efficiency in which Luna and the Chief Medical Examiner had identified my old friend concerned me. It's not like the movies. There's not a national database of dental records. In order to use dental x-rays, a medical examiner must first have an inkling as to the identity of the body in which to compare them. Then, they needed to actually find the victim's dentist—something not as easy to do when they have no family like Massey. Granted, the fire wouldn't have caused enough damage to completely incinerate his corpse, so his fingerprints probably would have still be intact. But Massey had been meticulous in his work ethic. He'd never been arrested. Never even been a suspect of any crime. As far as I knew, he'd kept his prints out every database imaginable.

So the question that had been nagging at me ever since had been: what had I missed? Was there some key piece of evidence found on the body? Had my mysterious stalker simply called in a tip? I doubted that, or else my name would have been plastered all over the news casts along with my last mugshot circa 1998.

At the moment, however, I had more important tasks to deal with, such as sneaking into Massey's place, and learning whatever I could about the people who killed him, and set me up. An address and phone number for the Peyton Brothers wouldn't be a bad clue to find either. They had some payback coming, whether they masterminded the operation or not.

When most of the police cars had driven away, I climbed out of the rented Toyota Corolla, and walked casually across the street to the luxury townhome community. The façade was breathtaking with a light peach coloring and white trim along the Corinthian columns that surrounded the twenty-one story building. I avoided entering through the main lobby, made my way around to the eastern side of the building, and stepped into the exterior elevator. I dug into my wallet, found Massey's spare keycard, and swiped at the panel to the right of the doors before pressing the button for the sixteenth floor. When the elevator dinged open, I turned left into the outdoor walkway, and made my way to Massey's apartment. The front door was standing wide open, with a couple of detectives—one of which was wearing a Hawaiian shirt that seemed to offend all five senses—and a uniformed officer conversing inside. From my brief glance, the place appeared like a hurricane had swept through it. It didn't seem to be the work of the police investigating a murder. It looked more like a barroom brawl had broken out inside than anything else. In hindsight, perhaps one had.

The Hawaiian shirt detective spotted me as I walked past the door. I hesitated slightly—a harmless resident, of some Asian descent he wouldn't be able to identify, curious as to what had brought the police to his building. I nodded silently to him with a friendly smile. He nodded back, his eyes stern, as if to say, "Nothing to see here. Move along." So I gladly complied, walked to the very next door down, brought out the keycard once more, and let myself in to the next apartment.

Like me, Ed Massey had several secret places around the United States to lay low when the need arises. A collection of Fortresses of Solitude that only a handful knew about. Whereas my own Floridian hideaway was on a small patch of infertile farm land in Central Florida, Massey's was right next door. Hiding in plain sight.

A few years ago, my friend had been good enough to provide me a key should I ever be nearby and in need of a place to stay. At the moment, it was very fortuitous that he did because I knew that anything work-related would have never been kept in the townhome he paid for under his own name. If there was anything to be discovered, it would be in the rented apartment of Mr. Richard Chesler, Massey's non-existent next door neighbor.

I stepped into the apartment's foyer, slipped on a pair of latex gloves, and closed and locked the door before flicking on the light switch that illuminated the long marble-tiled hallway leading into the living room. A quick visual sweep of the room revealed that Massey's secret clubhouse had been spared the destructive bedlam of the one next door. With the exception of a few moats of dust flitting through the air, the place looked as immaculate as one of Massey's thousand dollar suits.

Of course, it was pretty simple to keep the place clean. There was very little inside it. Unlike his personal townhouse, which was elegant and finely furnished, this was utilitarian to say the least. The two bedrooms upstairs were furnished with one twin bed each, a writing desk, and a lamp. That was it. Nothing more. Just a place to sleep. The master bedroom, downstairs, had been converted into an office, which boasted some of the most state-of-the-art computer and surveillance equipment on the market. The living room was just as sparse as the upstairs bedrooms, with a used pleather sofa and an old 23" cathode ray tube television in the corner of the room. The batteries to the TV's remote had long since died and decomposed to a nasty glob of lime green tarnish, making it utterly useless, and forcing people to actually get up to turn the channel when the need arose. Whenever I stayed there, I just learned to put it on the Cartoon Network and be content with whatever was on.

The only other piece of furnishing in the living room were the built-in white bookshelves that lined the entire northwest wall. The shelves, however, were empty save a handful of Tom Clancy novels, a stack of Guns and Ammo, and three boxes of vintage Playboy magazines dating back to 1968.

I smiled as I thought about his prized collection of skin mags. He'd been so proud of them when he'd won them at that estate auction. He always said he preferred the artistic nuances and soft eroticism of Hugh Hefner's legacy to the raunchy biker chick nastiness of the competition. Personally, I never quite understood the difference.

Focusing once again with a shake of my head, I walked from the foyer, past the kitchen and living room, and moved straight for the office in the master bedroom. I sat down at the desk, pushed the nearly full ashtray aside—ignoring the putrid stench of cigarette smoke still clinging to the air—and set to work turning on the computer and surveillance monitors. I watched the cops inside Massey's home do their thing via hidden security cameras mounted throughout his place. Once the computer finished booting up, it would be a relatively simple thing to see who'd helped to trash it. In the meantime, however, I stared at the screen and played Peeping Tom on the detectives.

They were talking heatedly, that much was for sure. I found the knob on the security panel, and turned up the camera's volume.

"There's got to be something here," Hawaiian Shirt said. "We've backtracked his movements to here. This is the last place anyone remembers seeing him alive."

"Look around, Stan," said the other. "The place is a mess. Pretty big clue there was a struggle here."

Stan the Hawaiian shook his head. "Uh-uh. Nah. This ain't a struggle." His voice was thick with a New England brogue. New Hampshire maybe? "This is someone searchin' for somethin'. It's been tossed. And I bet it was done *after* our guy was dead."

Huh. Stan appears smarter than his shirt would suggest. Though in this case, I had a feeling he was dead wrong.

"We need to look for blood…signs of violence within the house," Stan continued. "Something to show he was killed here."

"Unless he wasn't killed here," the uniformed deputy interjected.

I sat up straight at that. It was very possible whoever was behind this had used another cleaner to remove any evidence of violence from the scene. But that didn't really make a lot of sense. They planned to pin the whole thing on me anyway. Why clean up a mess when they could have just as easily planted more evidence linking me to the kill? Also, if for some reason they did want to cover up a mess in Massey's home, why not straighten up the signs of a struggle?

Unless I'm dealing with two different parties here. I let that process in my head a few minutes before I dismissed it. *Occam's razor, man. Occam's razor.* It was one of the first things Lou, my old mentor, had taught me about forensics. The simplest explanation is usually the correct one. We have the tendency to over-complicate matters. In this line of work, it's essential to keep things as simple as possible unless new evidence develops that allows for a more complex solution.

No, this entire setup screamed out to me that it was orchestrated by a single organized mind. That was the simplest explanation, and it was the one I would build my entire game plan on until something new presented itself to change my mind.

So, the next obvious question is: how did the Peyton's contract go from my execution to setting me up? The simplest route to find that out, would be to discover who'd contracted Massey to begin with. He'd told me Wade 'The Raid' Murphy had contacted him about the hit, but Murphy was simply another middle man. Other than an issue he might still have with my old teacher, he had no real beef with me. Not really, anyway. So all I needed to do was go down the rabbit hole and discovered who'd employed Murphy. That, however, was *not* going to be easy. Especially considering where he was currently spending his evenings.

With the computer now booted up, I began searching through his files, confident that what I was looking for most likely wouldn't be there. Massey was old school. Felt that computers were too unreliable. Too easy to hack. He's right, of course...at least within our circle of friends. But I still had to check for myself. After ten minutes of intense searching, I'd only been able to find a single file related to his business. An Excel spreadsheet—a ledger of some kind. As I'd suspected, it was heavily coded, and without the encryption key, it was completely useless to me. I doubted even Yancy would be able to make heads or tails of the gibberish on the screen, but I sent him a quick email, with the file as an attachment, nonetheless. Just in case.

Slightly dejected, I turned my attention back to the security monitors, and scanned footage for the past week. The last time Massey had been in his apartment was yesterday—around the time he called to say he was coming to see me. The video footage revealed him sitting on the couch in a bathrobe. He was reviewing something on his laptop, scrolling through text I couldn't read. I tried zooming in, but it only made the picture blur.

I gotta find his laptop. I glanced around the room, but it wasn't in his office. I made a mental note to check for it once I'd finished watching the surveillance video.

After Massey had frantically scrolled down the page for several minutes, a nice shapely figure stepped into the room from the corner of the screen and sauntered over to the backside of the couch. A woman. Long, blonde hair. And completely nude. She bent over the back of the couch—I tried to avoid lusting after her amazing heart-shaped ass—and wrapped her arms around my friend's neck before beginning a trail of kisses up and down his neck.

So she was there around the time he died? Who is she? I find her, she might know more about what happened. Discovering her identity might be tricky. Ed Massey wasn't known for his rock solid love of commitment after all. This girl was probably someone he'd picked up only the night before. He probably wouldn't have been able to tell me her name himself.

I kept watching as their kissing became more impassioned. Massey, smiling now, playfully pulled her over the back of the couch and on top of him and soon, I found myself blushing as if Grandma Bernice had caught me taking a peek at a movie on Cinemax in the middle of the night. Out of respect for my friend, I fast forwarded through much of the coitus, watching the action in super-fast motion until a sudden surge of movement caught my eye. I pressed the play button again to bring the video back to normal speed, just in time to see the girl—she'd somehow managed to keep her face away from the camera the entire time—slip something shiny out from behind one of the couch cushions and try to bring it down on Massey's chest.

A knife!

The hot little harpy was Massey's assassin and I was about to watch helplessly as it happened.

CHAPTER 16
AJAX CLEAN

watched, spellbound to the video. The girl, still in the throes of passion...still grinding hard against her target...raised the knife above her head, and brought it down with a violent jerk of her arms. Massey, fortunately, opened his eyes just in time to see the blade sweeping down toward his throat. He jerked to the side, rolling off the couch, and throwing her several feet away from him. He scrambled to his feet just as she lunged again, the knife barely grazing his bicep.

I leaned forward for a better look at the assassin now that she was facing the camera, but her long blonde hair had swung around, impairing the view.

Who is this broad?

I knew almost every hitman or hit-woman throughout the southeast United States. Heck, I knew a large number of them all over the world. And this chick wasn't registering in any of my mental dossiers of wetwork players.

Massey dodged another strike, then spun around in a round-house kick that would have made Jean Claude Van Damme proud. He'd always encouraged me to take martial arts lessons with him. Imagine that. A Korean steeped in the traditions of the criminal underworld, and I didn't know a lick of Kung Fu. But Massey did, and he definitely was using everything he knew to avoid being skewered by the backstabbing hussy's knife. Lamps were thrown. Books, wine glasses, and even pillows—anything he could get his hands around and hurl—flew through the air at the woman, and still she kept coming.

So this explains how his place was trashed anyway.

As I watched, I found myself silently rooting for my friend to win. To overcome this attempt on his life. But I already knew the outcome. Massey was dead. More than likely, it meant she was the one who killed him, and no amount of hope was going to change that. All I could do now was watch and wait for the inevitable, and pray that some new piece of information would come to me as I suffered through the loss of my friend once more.

For nearly another five minutes, the two of them continued their fight. The blonde was good. Better, in fact, than Massey really. He might have been an expert in his own particular field of the martial arts, but she employed moves from a variety of disciplines. Moves that were incredibly difficult to block. After a while, Massey must have realized this too. I watched as his head darted left to right, as if he was searching for something. Then, as she leapt into the air with one powerful kick, he dodged to his right, grabbed the laptop and wallet from the coffee table and dashed off screen toward his front door.

He's making a break for it!

I willed the security camera to pan around so I could see what happened next, but it remained stationary even as the assassin dashed off screen after him.

So what happened? Where'd they go? I watched a few minutes longer, but neither of them returned. Considering they both seemed to run out of the apartment in their birthday suits, I doubted they'd gone too far, which meant…I turned around from the monitors and stared past the office doorway into the living room. *Massey must have come here thinking it would be a safe place. An escape.*

My mind raced, trying to put myself in Massey's shoes as he was chased by his assassin. The priority would be to escape. But he'd grabbed the laptop before he fled. Then, he'd hidden some-where and called me just before he was murdered. Logic said, he'd come here. So could his computer still be here? Whatever was on it seemed important enough to kill him. So would he have tried to hide it, knowing I'd eventually come looking for it?

Knowing my friend, the chances were excellent that he had, which meant I'd need to tear his place apart until I found it. On a hunch, I walked back into the living room, to the bookshelves where the boxes of Playboys were kept, and began rifling through them. Though there were a few odd papers tucked away between the covers—forgotten notations of bygone days—there was no sign of the laptop or anything else that might be useful. Frus-trated, I re-boxed the magazines, placed them in their original spot, and turned around to face the living room with a sigh.

I suddenly found myself nauseated from dense stench of cigarette smoke permeating the carpet and couch. I really wished Massey had refrained from smoking inside. It made the place intolerable until the weekly maid came to add her very special blend of potpourri that always seemed to work magic against the foul stench Marlboros.

Wait a minute. I moved out into the center of the living room, and took a strong whiff. *Maria comes on Monday mornings. Mass would have disappeared later that day. That means…*

I whirled around toward the stairs, and ran up them to the bedroom Massey used when he was here. His suitcase lay on the bed. Opened. A few pieces of clothing thrown in a pile next to it. I rifled through the shirts and pants, but the computer wasn't there either. But at least now I knew this had been precisely where he'd called me from. I moved onto the second bedroom but it was bare of anything of interest to me.

He was here after Maria had cleaned. Just before he was killed. I stepped toward the bathroom in the center of the hallway, and paused. The door was closed. I couldn't see any light coming from the crack at the bottom of the door. Being single, Mass closed the bathroom door about as rarely as he put the toilet seat down.

I tensed as I slowly reached for the knob. A lump grew in my throat, forcing me to breathe through my mouth. My fingers and the palms of my hands inside my gloves were wet from perspiration as I turned my wrist to open the door.

My veins ran cold at the sight that greeted me.

Blood. Dried swirls and splotches of dark red caked the porcelain bathtub. Arterial spray fanned up and outward along the tile wall like some macabre piece of nihilistic modern art. And for the first time in my life, a crime scene brought me to my trembling knees where I immediately threw up the remnants of my hastily eaten fast food lunch.

I'd found Ed Massey's kill room.

CHAPTER 17
AJAX CLEAN

The next two hours were spent examining every inch of that bathroom, and I was becoming more and more perplexed with each sweep. Things weren't adding up.

The majority of the blood was contained within the bathtub. The sliding glass shower door had been pulled closed when Massey's throat had been cut with the killer inside the tub with them. This was a smart move, as it kept the majority of the gore closed off from the rest of the bathroom. There were two distinct cast off patterns that swept up to the ceiling, indicating that the attack had been violent with at least three brutal slashes with the knife. The first slash would have had no blood on it to throw from the blade. Then at least two more slashes where the blood trail indicated.

The arterial spray along the base of the tile wall was consistent with where Massey's head would have been resting. But there was more blood here than I could account for with one man's injuries.

A smile slowly crept up one side of my face. He had continued to fight the knife-wielding strumpet until the very end. Since there were no signs of violence outside of the bathroom, my best guess was that he'd been surprised. Knocked out somehow. Then dragged up to the bathroom, and dropped in the tub. When his killer came in close to finish the job, my old friend must have awakened and fought like a mad man. I made a mental note to collect as many blood samples as I could for DNA analysis later.

I stepped away from the tub and looked down at the tile floor. The bath mat that was usually in front of the tub was nowhere to be seen. No surprise there. Probably got wrapped up with the body when his killer had carted him out of here. Which begged the question—how could that petite waif of an assassin lug Massey's one hundred and eighty pound frame out of the bathroom, down the stairs, and out to whatever vehicle she'd used to transport him?

She had help. My guess, it had been the Peyton brothers. They'd waited outside for her to do the job, then tied him up, dressed him in scrubs, and drove his corpse to Miami to meet with me. It was the best working theory I had at the moment.

I continued my assessment of the bathroom. While there was some dried blood trickling down the outside of the tub, there were only a few drops evident on the floor. The assassin and the Peytons had probably placed plastic down on it prior to moving the body, then rolled Massey up in it to keep the blood from leaking all over the place when they left.

Finished with my examination, I pulled out my cell phone to snap a few pictures of the bathroom. Then reached into my jacket pocket and withdrew a handful of glass microscope slides. Two minutes later, I had a healthy sample of blood to analyze once I found a lab that was friendly toward me in these parts. It was as good a place to continue my investigation than anywhere.

I stepped out of the bathroom and closed the door behind me. I then made my way throughout the entire apartment, searching one more time for the laptop. But if it had been here, the harpy must have taken it. Satisfied I'd learned everything I could, I retraced my steps and wiped down anything I might have touched that could have left trace evidence within the townhouse. I was just wiping the security monitor's volume control when I looked up to see my friend's apartment was now vacant. The detectives and the deputy had apparently left, but I knew there was more than a good chance they'd be back. Even more likely, after canvassing the condo complex, it wouldn't take long for them to discover that their victim rented another unit next door. They'd return soon, and would make the same grisly discovery as I just had.

I decided it was best to clear out of there while the getting was good. But as I made one final sweep of the apartment before leaving, a hundred different quandaries rushed through my mind. Why had Massey been killed? According to my mysterious caller, I was the one being targeted originally for assassination. Then, without his knowledge, the plan suddenly changed. My friend was murdered and I was set up for it. And what had Massey found on his laptop that seemed so important? I pondered the events I'd seen on his security camera. The assassin had been planted in his apartment for the sole purpose of killing him. He would have died whether he'd discovered something important or not. None of this was making sense. Was it revenge or something else entirely?

"Nothing but more questions," I mumbled as I backed out of the apartment and locked the door.

"What kind of questions?" The Haitian-accented voice behind me said.

"Hello, Ellis," I said, not turning around. I wasn't sure whether I refused to look at him out of some sense of courageous defiance, or for fear he'd see just how unnerved I really was by his sudden appearance. The one advantage we Asians have over Westerners is that most people assume we know some form of martial art. It gives us a certain mystique, and many of the toughest goons in the mob tend to give us a wide berth—whether we really know Kung Fu or not. As I've already mentioned, the only martial arts I know came from watching old Bruce Lee and Jackie Chan movies on Kung Fu Theater. But I certainly wasn't going to tell anyone that. Therefore, I'd hoped that my indifferent greeting toward the psychopathic hitman would come across as much warranted confidence in my ability to take him despite how awkwardly I'd handled him earlier that day. "Let me guess. I'm coming with you, eh?"

I withdrew the key from the door's deadbolt, and slowly turned to face him. The good news was that I was still alive, but I knew that my condition might quickly deteriorate if I didn't at least show him the courtesy of looking him in the face.

He nodded at me with a glowering smile. "Undoubtedly."

The suppressed Colt .45 he had pointed at me from his hip helped reinforce his confidence. I could just make out the strange Voodoo-style glyph cut into its muzzle. A warning to all who saw it. Not wise to upset the man with the gun—especially at this range.

"So if you're going to kill me, why not just do it here?" I asked, proud that my voice didn't crack a single time as I uttered the words. "I mean, it's not like you ever care about witnesses or anything."

He holstered his weapon inside his jacket, then lit up a cigarette before answering. He cocked his head to one side, looking me up and down, as he drew in a smoke-filled breath. "Good work on the Muldoon job," Ellis said. He was playing with me. Keeping me off balance. "As always. I could've taken a dump on that floor, and no one would have known. Very professional."

"You went back? To check?"

He nodded.

Gun or no gun, I couldn't help rolling my eyes. "You're not very bright are you?"

His eyebrows furrowed at this, but I didn't care. By this point, I was just a little more than pissed.

"The whole point of a cleanup job is to prevent any trace evidence from showing up. *Your* trace evidence, you bonehead! Showing back up just re-introduced everything to the scene." I turned left, and started making my way down the exterior hall toward the elevator. "Now either shoot me or tell me what you want."

To my astonishment, I didn't receive a hollow point to the back of the head. Instead, Ellis caught up to me with his long, lanky strides. That was the thing about Ellis. The man was like a bean pole on stilts.

"Like I said, I'm here to offer you a ride."

"Have my own car, thanks. Don't need a ride." I pressed the down button on the elevator.

"'The Raid' insists on it."

That stopped me cold as a wave of arctic ice washed down my spine at the mention of the name. I was in worse trouble than I had imagined.

CHAPTER 18
LUNA MAO CHING

Miami-Dade Police Department
Miami, Florida
Tuesday, February 6

"So any luck remembering where you met our mysterious victim before?" Detective Sean Tice asked me as he closed the door to his office and handed me a steaming cup of coffee.

I cradled the mug in both hands, hunching down on the couch across from his desk, and shook my head. "Still nothing. I just remember his face and name, but the context is off. I just cannot place him." I wasn't sure why, but I could not bring myself to mention Remy Williamson to the detective. Something in the pit of my gut rebelled against the notion. My father had taught me long ago to trust my instincts, and that is what I endeavored to do. "Have you been able to learn anything about him?"

Tice sat down in his desk chair and leaned back with an exaggerated sigh. "Not a blessed thing. No criminal record. No prints on file. No family or known associates." I'm sure my face reddened with his last statement, but he seemed not to notice. "If we hadn't lucked out by finding a business card for his dentist in his apartment, I'm not sure we would ever positively identified him. Digging into his background, however, isn't looking to be as easy."

"Are most people that difficult to trace?"

He shook his head. "Not at all. Usually, even if they're not criminals, I can find at least a few things out about them. But this guy has nothing. No known social security number. No bank accounts. No taxes. He's been completely off the grid."

"And what does that tell you about Mr. Massey?" I had my own ideas, but then, I wasn't the detective.

"That he's either a criminal or some sort of government agent." He shrugged. "And since the whole government agent thing is a bit too *Bourne Identity*, I'm guessing he's the former rather than the latter."

Exactly what I thought. And if that was the case, then was my friend Remy also a professional criminal my association? Remy was working on a story about Ajax Clean. Could he have found him in Mr. Massey? Could our victim be the legendary criminal cleaner? The thought intrigued me.

"I'll keep digging though," Tice continued. "For now though, let's talk about why you're here. You said something about some strange phone calls and messages?"

There'd been one more phone call since leaving Dr. Hernandez's office yesterday. The strange, wheezing voice seemed to have nothing to say. More like a semi-polite conversation from a dementia-addled grandparent who forgot who you were for half of the conversation. Do not misunderstand though. The man on the other end of the phone was by no means gripped by the inferior mind of a dementia patient. It was strong, nearly oppressive. Cunning. And by the affect his intrusions were having on my life, he knew precisely what he was doing. I'd become a nervous wreck, which is the reason I finally decided to tell someone about it.

"Yes. It began on my birthday, the other day." I leaned forward in my seat, placing the cup of coffee on the end table, and proceeded to tell him—without giving too much of my own past away—about the flowers and phone conversation. He sat, patiently listening without interruption, until I finished.

"Wow. Yeah, I can see why you might be concerned," he said with a nod.

"That's not the worst part," I said, rifling through files on my phone and holding it out to him once I found what I was looking for. "Last night, he sent me this."

He took it from me and peered at the image on the screen. It was of me, as a little girl. No more than two years old, I guessed. I was being held by a harsh-looking Asian man who I didn't recognize. He had a mustache and goatee, not very common in Korea at the time, and held me in his arms. I was crying. He wasn't smiling. The barest hint of a knife tip could be seen against my shoulder, and a small sliver of blood trickled down the ruffled blue dress I was wearing.

"Geeze," Tice said, handing the phone back to me. "Is that him? Your mysterious caller?"

"I've no idea. I think that's the assumption I'm supposed to make of it, yes."

"Do you have the phone number this guy is using to contact you?"

I shook my head. "He is blocking it, I think. Always reads as UNKNOWN NUMBER."

"Well, write down your service provider and number," he said. "I can always contact them and try to get a record of whoever's been calling you."

I thought of Remy, and for the briefest of moments, I hesitated. If he was somehow involved in the Massey murder, the police might discover him through my own phone. Then, I realized how ludicrous that line of thinking was. There was nothing at all—other than my own testimony—to link Remy to Mr. Massey. Nothing on my phone could possible connect the two of them.

"Sure." I smiled at the detective as I scribbled the carrier service, my phone number, and PIN down on a notepad, and handed it to him. "I would appreciate that a great deal."

"Anything else you can tell me about these calls? Or the caller? Any idea who he is?"

"I think he knew my father." I had to tread carefully here. I didn't dare reveal too much about him to the detective. "I'm not sure how, but they apparently knew each other."

"Could you ask him? Your father, I mean."

"No. He's not in the United States," I said, biting back the well of tears threatening to release. "There's no way to contact him either."

Tice gave me a smile of encouragement. "Well, I'll do some digging and find out who's behind it all. If you'd like, I could talk to the lieutenant about maybe getting you some units to sit outside your home, if that would make you feel better. I know I would definitely feel better with some officers watching your house."

I considered the offer for a few moments, then shook my head. "Thank you, no. I appreciate it, but I can't possibly take up any of the department's resources just to appease my nerves. It wouldn't be right."

"Hey, you're a government official. Medical Examiner's make enemies just as much as cops do. I don't think it would be…"

I smiled and stood from the couch. "I'm fine, Sean. Really. Thank you." I offered my hand. He accepted it and gave it a strong shake. "I might not have had the best of fathers, but he did love me and made sure I knew how to take care of myself. I'd just like you to try to get to the bottom of these calls, if you don't mind."

I walked over to the door and began to open it when he spoke. "Well, just to ease my mind, why don't you talk to your neighbor about all this?"

"You mean Nathaniel?"

He nodded. "Detective Tilg might be retired, but he built his career on crimes involving stalkers and the like. If anyone knows how best to handle this situation, it'd be him. Plus, last time I talked to him, he was bored silly. He could probably use something like this to do."

I considered that, then shook my head. "Thanks for the suggestion. That's a great idea." I opened the door and turned to look at Tice. "It's been a while since Nathaniel and I had a good coffee talk. I'll go see him today."

I then walked out of his office, down the long windy corridor, and out the door of the police station. I was only vaguely aware of the black Crown Victoria parked across the street, that pulled out of its space the moment I got into my car and drove away.

CHAPTER 19
AJAX CLEAN

Florida State Prison
Starke, Florida
Wednesday evening, February 7

I weighed my options as we drove up to the gate of Florida State Prison. As a career criminal, I'd spent my entire life trying to avoid getting into prison, and here I was being hand delivered by one of the nation's most brutal—not to mention, slightly loonie—assassins. Sad thing was, it wasn't the prison that scared me the most about this trip. It was who I was being taken to see.

Wade 'The Raid' Murphy got his name from the bug spray of the same name. The reason was simple. Murphy was the walking poster child for the brand's signature catchphrase. He kills things dead. Plain and simple. And he did it with such grace and style that he'd become something of an idol to even some of law enforcement's elite.

Murphy had been a freelance hitman since the late 60s, and had worked exclusively with my own mentor, Lou Nikopoulos, as his personal cleaner during his entire career. Because of those ties, Murph and I had enjoyed a rather amicable relationship. That is, until he'd gotten caught on a job thanks to a rather unforgiveable mistake Lou had made while cleaning the scene of an assassinated city councilman a few years back. Seems Lou had been slipping for the last few years. The early stages of Alzheimer's. The disease had cost both of them dearly. It had landed Wade Murphy in one of the roughest prisons in the state, and had sent my old mentor into an equally as brutal nursing home where he had spent the remainder of his years in his own filth.

"Um, it's ten-thirty at night," I said, breaking the two hour silence of our car ride since Ocala where we stopped to eat and get me a change of clothes. "Aren't visiting hours over by now?"

Ellis smirked and rolled down the driver's side window to his black 1976 Chevy Camaro. A prison guard walked up to the car, and Ellis handed him a folded sheet of paper. The guard glanced at it, folded it back up, and slipped it into his shirt pocket, before opening the gate without a word.

"There ain't no visiting hours for Mr. Murphy," Ellis said, driving through the gate and following the path to the employee parking lot. "We see him when he wants to be seen. Plain and simple as dat."

He pulled into an empty space near the front entrance, got out of the car, and motioned for me to do the same.

"Er, it's probably not the best idea for me to be here right now," I said, trying to keep up with his long, Ent-like strides. "You know, the whole trying to stay under the cops' radar thing and all. Kind of on the lam here."

"Don't care. I'd just as soon be putting a slug in you, but Mr. Murphy insists on seein' you. You be safe." He clucked his tongue against his teeth twice, then leered at me while rattling a bone necklace tucked under the collar of his shirt. "For now anyway. Cops'll leave you alone in here."

Gee. What a relief.

We entered through the front door, and were met by two correctional officers before quickly being ushered through the labyrinth of corridors and solid steel doors that opened and closed by the will of unseen hands in the security stations. Within minutes, I was hopelessly lost, and felt the not-so-gentle pressure of claustrophobia pressing down on me with each step.

"I take it we're not going to the visitation rooms," I said; my voice echoed down the hall despite its whisper.

"Nope."

Good ol' Ellis. Quite the chatterbox. Can hardly shut him up.

A few minutes later, I found myself in front of a solitary cell. The door opened at the nod of one of the guards to a security camera, and I found myself staring into the smiling face of Wade 'The Raid' Murphy.

He'd aged since I saw him last. The gray of his long hair and beard had spread and whitened, and his usually tall form seemed slightly more stooped than I remembered. But the sinewy muscles of his forearms rippled below the rolled up sleeves of his orange jumpsuit, and I knew with crystal certainty that he was as deadly as he'd ever been.

"Ajax Clean!" he said, spreading his arms in a cheerful greeting. "It's good to see you, boy. It's been too long."

He gave a curt nod to the guards, who disappeared through the hallway doors behind us, leaving me alone with two of the most efficient killers I'd ever met.

"Mr. Murphy." Not the most eloquent of salutations on my part, but given my circumstances, it was the best I could come up with.

"Archie, you can leave us for a while too. Go get some coffee or something. I've got a few things to discuss with our young friend here."

"Archie?" I stood grinning at the gaunt hitman. "Your first name is Archie?"

"That's Archeo to anyone but Mr. Murphy." If Ellis's eyes could shoot lasers, I'd have two pin-prick holes burned into my forehead. Fortunately for me, Ellis was an obedient lap dog, and silently turned around and left us without another word.

Either Murphy didn't see my amusement or he just didn't

care. Instead, he stared appraisingly at me for several uncomfortable seconds.

"Shoot," he suddenly said, making me flinch. "Where are my manners? Come in! Come in!" He motioned for me to enter his prisonly abode, and I immediately obeyed. Considering his obvious influence inside the correctional facility, I was surprised to see his cell was as sparse as most I'd seen before. I'd half expected to find the place decked out in wall to wall carpeting, wood paneling, and a fully stocked bar. Instead, the twenty by twenty foot cubicle was little more than concrete floors and four cinderblock walls. Though, I must confess, it did boast a pretty impressive assortment of alcohol packed in wooden crates in one corner of the cell.

"Whiskey?" Murphy asked, motioning for me to take a seat on the sole metal folding chair in the corner of the room. He eyed me up and down before I could answer. "Or are you more a wine guy?"

"Whiskey's fine," I said. I knew it would be a mistake to drink it. I hadn't had anything but a half-dozen Krispy Kream donuts and a gallon of coffee since this entire debacle had started. But at that precise moment, I could just really use a drink. He poured me a three fingered glass, and handed it to me before pouring his own and taking a seat on his bunk.

"Been hearing great things about you, boy. Making quite a reputation for yourself. Ol' Lou would be mighty proud of you, I think."

I downed the glass in two gulps, and waited for the burn to settle from my throat before I responded. "Thank you, sir." I pondered the best way to ask the question weighing on my mind, then decided the direct approach would work better on someone like The Raid. "Is that the reason for the setup in Miami? My reputation? Or was it my relationship with Lou?"

The old man stared at me for several long seconds before chuckling gleefully. "You think that was me, kid?" He poured himself another glass, but ignored my own. "Maybe you aren't as bright as I first gave you credit for."

I wasn't sure if it was the whiskey or my own ever-growing frustration that gave me such courage, but I returned his gaze without blinking. "Why else would you send that psycho goon to collect me so soon after Mass was murdered? I figured you were subcontracting or something."

Murphy finished the glass, reached into his jumpsuit pocket, and withdrew a fresh cigar. "I know you have some sort of vendetta against Archie, but I can promise you, not every vile deed you come across is his fault. There *are* other killers out there, after all." He bit off the tip of the cigar, and lit it with a propane lighter. "As for me, what possible reason would I have to kill you or Massey? Both of you are too invaluable to my little operation here."

He made some excellent points, but I still had my reservations. "All right. If you're not involved in setting me up, then who is?"

"Now that's the question, isn't it? Why were you so certain it was me?"

I took a moment to think about my answer. Until Ellis had shown up at Massey's, the thought had never really occurred to me. "Revenge? You couldn't get back at Lou, so you decided to take it out on me instead."

He laughed at this before taking another pull on his cigar and expelling the smoke in my direction. "Why would I do that, kid? I've never had ill-will toward the Greek, and way too much respect for Bernice to ever go after her little 'grandson'." He chuckled again, his eyes glazing over in deep thought. "Shoot, that old woman was mean enough that she'd likely rise up from the grave to tan my hide if I ever did harm to you."

"Maybe. But Lou put you in here. His mistake cost you your freedom."

"And who said it was a 'mistake'?" he asked with a wink.

That floored me. I opened my mouth to speak, but couldn't find the words.

"That's right kid. Lou did exactly what I asked him to do. He left that print on the mirror on purpose."

"But...but why?"

"Doesn't matter why. All that matters is that I asked him to do it, and he followed through even though it would mean forced retirement, and a lifetime of ridicule from his peers. I owe that man a debt. And that, Ajax Clean, is why I had Archie bring you here. It's high time I start repaying that debt."

I stood up, and walked over to the liquor crates. "I think I could use another drink."

He waited until I was back in my seat before continuing. "Kid, I can't tell you who the man behind Ed Massey's murder and your frame job *is*, but I can tell you who he was." I cocked my head, letting his words sink in. "Jung Ki-yeol."

The name wasn't new to me. I'd been running from the man most of my life. He'd been a former South Korean army colonel who was arrested for spying for the North.

"Last I heard, he was still in prison. And if that's not enough, he supposedly developed COPD or something like that anyway. I doubt the guy has strength left to plan a trip to the bathroom, much less a job like this." I thought about the phone message I'd received while hiding in Hernandez's office. The haggard, labored breathing on the other end. Undeniable symptoms of chronic obstructive pulmonary disease. *Crap*.

"He escaped prison a long time ago—easily managed in such a corrupt system," Murphy said. "Went on to develop ties to the *Kkangpae*."

"*Kkangpae*?" I asked. My grasp of the Korean language had long since dwindled to a few four-letter words. Now, I would have been lucky to ask for directions to the nearest bathroom in the language.

"It's what they call their criminal underworld. Mostly, they're little more than unorganized thugs—which is what the word literally means—but Jung Ki-yeol was an enforcer for the *Jopok*, the South Korean mafioso."

"But what does this Jung Ki-yeol want with me? I was only twelve when I left Korea."

Murphy gave me a knowing gaze. "Who says he's after you?"

I tried to swallow, but couldn't overcome the lump building in my throat. I didn't like where this was going.

"Ever heard of someone named Ryu Nam-seon?"

My throat became even dryer as he spoke. Luna's...father.

"I reckon you know that tasty little number at the Medical Examiner's Office in Miami too, eh?"

His grin was almost lascivious. *He knows about Luna.*

CHAPTER 20
AJAX CLEAN

"Leave Luna out of it." The moment the words had left my lips, I bit down on my tongue. Had I just gave The Raid a command?

He simply laughed it off and continued. "It was her father who discovered Jung's treason and arrested him thirty years ago," he continued. "My guess is he's looking for this Ryu Nam-seon, and is using her to get to him."

"I...I don't know how." It was a bold faced lie. "Luna hasn't seen him in several years. And me? Geeze. I can't even begin to think that far back to when I last spoke with him. It's been nearly twenty-five years at least. Besides that, this Jung guy told me he'd put a contract out on my head. He was as surprised as I was about the setup. If he wanted me to help him find the old man, he wouldn't have hired the Peytons to kill me."

"You don't get it yet, do you boy?"

I cocked my head, not quite understanding the question. "Enlighten me."

He drew in a deep plume of smoke from his cigar, then exhaled. "Jung only needs one of you. By your own admission, the medical examiner has seen her father more recently than you. Stands to reason, he only needs her.

"You, however, are a variable he can't account for. Maybe he doesn't quite know who you are to Ryu Nam-seon. He definitely doesn't understand your relationship with the girl—no one really does, by the way. Therefore, best remove you from the picture altogether."

I thought about it a moment, and shrugged. "So let me ask you...how do you know any of this? If you aren't the one who facilitated the hit or the setup, how do you know about Jung Ki-yeol?"

He leaned back on his bunk, prompting himself up with his hands as he stared up at the ceiling as if in thought. "I was approached, yes. But when I learned you were the target, I refused. I honestly had no idea the man had co-opted the Hernandez hit. If I'd known, I would have warned you. That, I promise you."

The steady gaze he gave me convinced me he was telling the truth. "Well, what about the setup? Know anything about that?"

He shook his head. "No. Whoever did it though, must have paid the Peytons a God-awful amount of money to betray this Korean dude. That means, they have resources."

"And Massey? I saw who killed him in a security video. A blonde female. Playing the seductress to get into his apartment. Sound familiar?"

"Nope. She doesn't sound local, I can tell you that much. Whoever killed Mr. Massey must have recruited an out-of-towner."

I sighed, leaning back in my chair. Once again, I was at a dead end. The one person with his finger on the pulse of almost every criminal enterprise through Florida knew nothing more than the name of the man who wanted me dead. It wasn't enough.

"There's got to be something else you can tell me. Something to point me in the right direction."

He gave me a sad smile and shrugged. "Sorry, boy. No can do. But I can give you some advice to consider. Something that might set you on the right course to find those answers you're looking for."

Three loud tones suddenly burst from the overhead loud speakers, followed by a hollow-sound voice. "Cell Block One. Lights Out. Cell Block Two. Lights Out. Cell Block Three. Lights Out."

Murphy looked up at the speakers. "Don't worry about that. They don't apply to me. I'm too old to have a bedtime." He chuckled over this, then looked back at me. "Here's the thing, Ajax. You're still a target. But unlike that pretty thing in Miami, you're like a ghost. The cops can't find you. Neither can he. So if he wants you dead, what does he do?"

I pondered the puzzle quietly for several seconds before bolting up from the chair, nearly tipping over from the effects of too much alcohol. "Holy crap! I need to go."

He beamed. "Now ya get it. He'll go after her to get you to come out into the open. Exactly."

I looked over at him, then at the cell door. "Can I leave?"

"That depends. How dead do you want her to be when you find her?"

"Huh?"

"If you go after her now, you're doing exactly what he wants you to do. You play it cool. Detached. Travel to Fiji or something, and he might just leave her alone. You try to make contact with her and he'll pounce. He might need her alive to tell him where her old man is, but that doesn't mean she can't be the victim of collateral damage."

"There's no way I'm going to let her go through this alone," I said, moving over to the cell door and awaiting his permission to leave. He was, after all, in control of the guards, who were in control of the doors. If he didn't authorize it, I wasn't going anywhere. "She's not part of this world. Not equipped to deal with someone like Jung."

"And you are?"

I stood my ground. "I'm going to have to be, aren't I?"

He chuckled with a nod, then stood from his bunk, placed the stub of his cigar in an ashtray resting on a small table, and stepped over to within inches of my face.

"You're going to need help on this kid. You can't find Jung alone, and no matter what you think, you certainly aren't prepared to deal with him if you do. I want you to take Archie with you. He'll help you in anyway you—"

"No way!" I growled. "Look, I appreciate it, but there's no way I'm going to work with that voodoo-spouting psychopath."

The old man took a step back, his eyes narrowing. "I've never understood your distaste for the man. Granted, he's not the most traditional assassin on the market, but he certainly gets the job done, and I can't think of anyone I'd rather have watching my back than him."

I shrugged. "I stopped working with him after the Stanelli job."

"I'm aware of this, but the question is why."

"Because he...he..."

"Yes?"

"He not only killed the target, he also killed Ranger, the Stanelli family dog."

Murphy burst out laughing. "The dog? Really?"

"I don't do dog kills, and he knows it. He did it on purpose. One of his crazy death sacrifices."

He reined in his laughter, placed a hand on my shoulder, and nodded. "Anton." He intentionally used the name Bernice had given me back when she first took me in. "You're in over your head here. If you plan to survive this—if you want the girl to survive this—you'll accept my gift to you. Take Archeo Ellis. Use him. For something like this, you'll need a man who's not squeamish about putting down a dog when the need arises. Trust me."

With that, he looked up at the security camera, and nodded. Less than a minute later, Ellis and two guards entered the room once more, and escorted me out of the prison.

CHAPTER 21
AJAX CLEAN

Greenlawn Subdivision
Miami, Florida
Thursday morning, February 8

Ellis pulled the Camaro up to the curb at the corner of Brisbane Court and Beardon Street, and put it in park. We'd driven straight for the last five and a half hours and the both of us were exhausted, irritated, and ready to take each other's heads off at the drop of a hat.

And I'd still not had anything decent to eat in two days—giving me the slight edge over my Haitian bodyguard/chauffer.

"I still think you are making a mistake," he said with a scowl.

"I can't leave her here. If Jung Ki-yeol is after her, I need to get her to safety before it's too late."

The hitman shrugged. "Or you could be leading him right to her doorstep. It's a bad move…strategically. It'd be better if I went in, grabbed her, and brought her to you."

"Uh-uh. No way. You'd probably shoot her goldfish as a sacrifice to the spirits of the sea or something." I unbuckled my seatbelt, and opened the door. "I need to do this. On my own."

Ellis rolled his eyes, and sighed. "It's your op. If you blow it, and get yourself and the girl killed, I won't be held responsible."

He then reached into his jacket, and pulled out a gun. "You might need this."

I shook my head. I had left my Ruger in my car back at Massey's place, thinking it unwise to carry a weapon with so many cops searching the townhouse. My circumstances hadn't improved, so I opted for the same wisdom here. "No thanks. Just be ready to roll once you see us, okay?"

"Well, at least take this." He holstered the gun, and pulled out a capped syringe. "She might give you a tough time. This will sedate her."

I looked down at the syringe, contemplating my options. Then, almost reflexively, I took it from him, and climbed out of the car. "You've got my number. Warn me if there's any sign of trouble," I said, gently closing the passenger side door, and began strolling down the sidewalk of the middle class suburban neighborhood where Luna lived. It was approaching three in the morning, and a thick blanket of fog rolled in from the sea to smother the air in its cold, wet embrace. Perfect cover for a night time stroll in which I hoped to stay hidden. Of course, it was equally as perfect for any would-be assassins lying in wait for Luna and me.

But whether I was falling into a trap or not, it couldn't be helped now. I had to do what I could to get Luna as far away from this mess as I possibly could. The only thing I was concerned about was keeping her safe, even at the expense of my own life.

I slipped through the shadows between one street lamp post to the next, making my way to Luna's modest little single-story starter home. Once it was in view, I scurried around one side of the house, and over the privacy fence where I tried opening the gate with a gentle click of the latch. But it was apparently locked on the other side and wouldn't budge.

Pressed for time, I stood, took a deep breath, and clambered over the fence with a well-timed vault. Being only five foot six inches tall and of slight build, I'd always been rather agile, and had even studied gymnastics during my brief stint as a high school student before dropping out. The skills learned in that class had saved my hide on more occasions than I could count.

Once I was safely out of sight in the tiny backyard, I crept up to the sliding glass door, crouched down, and peered through the vertical blinds for a glimpse inside. I was looking into the living room. Various shades of blue strobed in the otherwise dark room, revealing Luna reclining on the couch watching television. Her Persian cat, Muffin, rested sleepily on Luna's shoulder; fidgeting only when her human would take a sip of wine from her glass. The rest of the house appeared dark, and devoid of life. Luna was alone.

It wasn't unusual for her to be up at this hour on her days off. Like me, she was a night owl and preferred the solitude of the night to the brutal harshness of the burning light of the sun. It was peaceful in the early hours of the morning. There was a sense that you were the only one alive on the entire planet when the rest of the world sleeps, and that always brought a certain comfort to me. I assumed it was the same for her as well. Plus, she always said, the classic monster movies were on late at night, which always tempted her away from her bed.

I stood, clinched my fist, and prepared to knock. There was no way around this. No one expects a knock to come from their back-yard sliding glass door in the witching hours of the night. There was no way to know what her reaction would be. Thinking better of it, I pulled out my cell phone, and flipped through my contacts until I found her name. Calling her first would be the best move, and even if the bad guys were monitoring my phone, we'd be long gone before they traced the call here. Of course, according the messages she'd left after missing our coffee date the other night, she wasn't exactly going to welcome me with open arms. In fact, with my connection to Massey, I'm sure she was going to want to discuss my involvement in his murder. This, of course, was a conversation I couldn't afford at the moment. Either way, a courtesy phone call would at least be better than just tapping at her window in the middle of the night.

I put the phone to my ear, and it rang twice before being answered.

"H-hello?" Luna spoke quietly into the phone. She sounded nervous. No, more than nervous. Downright scared was more like it.

The flashing blue light from the TV stopped as she placed her program on pause.

"Luna? It's me. Remy."

There was an uncomfortable pause. "Remy? Where have you been? I've been trying to…"

"I'm sorry. I'll explain everything, but right now, I need to talk to you. It's urgent." I took a deep breath. "I'm right outside your back door now."

A choir of frogs could be heard off in the distance, croaking away despite the unusually cool Florida winter temperature. I could imagine what was going through her mind at the moment. Although I knew Luna better than anyone else in the entire world, I was still little more than a casual acquaintance to her. An occasional friend with a common interest in a legendary criminal named Ajax Clean. We'd only spent a few days together every year since she'd 'known' me, and to her knowledge, I'd never even been to her house. The fact that I was there now, in the middle of the night, must have been quite unnerving.

"Luna? You still there?"

A second later, one of the vertical blinds shifted to the side, and the back porch light flicked on. I watched as one almond-shaped brown eye stared back at me from inside. A glint of silver caught my eye, and I looked down to see that she was holding a revolver tight in her hand.

Sheepishly, I gave her a shrugging wave, and an assuring nod. "It really is important or I wouldn't be here," I said aloud, hoping she could hear me past the glass door.

She straightened up, unlocked the door, and slid it open about two inches wide. She adjusted her robe, brushed a strand of hair behind her ear, and leaned toward the crack. She also pointed the barrel of the .357 revolver directly at my head. "I think you owe me an explanation about a few things."

"Really? Right now? Out here?"

"It's as good a place as any. Tell me about Edward Massey. Tell me you didn't have anything to do with his murder."

Still eyeing the gun, I held up both hands. "I swear. I swear. He was my friend. One of my closest. I would never have hurt him."

She squinted at me, her eyebrows furrowing.

"Why shouldn't I just call the police now? Let them sort it out."

My mind raced, trying to find the best answer to that question. She was understandably suspicious. I'd expected it. What I hadn't expected with the Inquisition. There was no way she was going to trust me enough to let me explain the danger she was in. No way, unless...

"Because I'm your brother. Ryu Nam-gi. I swear it."

Her eyes widened almost as much as her gaping mouth. The barrel of the gun tilted toward the ground as she stood there in silence processing the news.

"I'm not lying to you, Luna. I'm your brother. And I'm here because you're in danger. If it takes me telling you everything... everything about me...in order to convince you, then so be it." My eyes narrowed. "It's time I tell you what happened to me after father put me on that boat to America. It's time I tell you the truth about Ajax Clean."

CHAPTER 22
LUNA MAO CHING

wasn't sure I'd heard Remy right. Had he just told me he was my brother, Nam-gi? Had he also said he was about to tell me about Ajax Clean?

"Um, what did you just say?" I asked. My entire body had numbed. My ears rung as the blood rushed to my head with every thunderous pump of my heart.

The man who was supposed to be my brother fidgeted where he stood. His head turned from side to side, keeping his eyes fixed in as many places as possible as if expecting to be ambushed any second. "Look, can we discuss this inside? I'm not sure how safe it is out here. I promise, I'll try to explain everything as soon as I can."

I backed away from the door, and gestured for him to enter. The moment he was inside, he stuck his head out the door once more for another peak, then slid the door closed, and shut the blinds before turning to look at me with a nervous grin.

"Sorry to spring that on you so suddenly," he said. "It's just that we really don't have a lot of time. You need to pack some things, and we need to go."

I pointed to the couch. "Sit."

"But I'm serious. We need to…"

"Not until I know what's going on. Things have been insane

the last few days. First the birthday flowers with the strange, threatening note…then the double homicide and the…"

"Wait," he said. "Hold up. What note?"

"If you'd check your email every once in a while, you'd already know." I nodded to the couch. "Now sit. It's three-thirty in morning. Nothing's going to happen here. We're safe."

I suddenly remembered the gun still in my hand. Embarrassed, I tucked in back in the waistband of my pajamas and sat down on one side of the couch. I then pointed to the other side and glared at him.

With his usual boyish charm, Remy rolled his eyes and did as he was told.

"Now," I said. "Tell me everything. I need to know before I can trust you." I sense he was about to protest when he opened his mouth, and I shook my head. "I'm not going anywhere with you until I have some answers. That is a fact. So, the longer you take, the longer we will remain here."

"Fine. You already know about dad sending me here to America. When things got weird—when he was forced to go on the run —he knew he couldn't take both of his children with him. He sent me to a man he'd met during the Korean War. An American soldier named Jerome Jax."

"I remember father telling stories about the man. How he'd saved the American's life."

He nodded. "Yes. Jerome owed dad big time. So I went to live with him and his wife, Bernice. Now, Jerome was a hard man. Brutal even. But he was honorable. He took me in, but we never really saw eye to eye. In his mind, his job was merely to put a roof over my head and feed me until I was old enough to go out on my own. This sentiment wasn't shared by his wife, however. She grew to love me as her own son. Our age difference, however, made me more like her grandson of course."

I was confused. I didn't know how any of this factored into our current situation. Apparently, he'd sensed my bewilderment, and smiled.

"Don't worry. It'll all become clear soon enough."

"Okay." I stood from the couch, and moved toward the kitchen. "Keep talking. I'm going to make us some tea, but I can still hear you."

As I prepared the kettle, he continued with his story.

"The thing is, both Jerome and Bernice weren't your average American citizens. They both had mob ties." Remy coughed. Perhaps he was nervous about finally coming clean about who he really was. Maybe his mouth had simply gone dry. I wasn't certain. "Long story short, I found myself in the family business at an early age."

I poked my head around the corner. "Seriously? You are in the mafia?"

He shook his head, smiling. "Nah. It's nothing quite that definitive. I just learned a trade that was very useful to enterprising criminals. A very specialized trade."

The kettle began to howl, but I didn't hear it. Everything, as he had promised, was becoming clearer and my mind struggled to process the full scope of what I was being told.

"Specialized?" I was almost afraid to voice the question. Afraid of what the answer was going to be.

He nodded past me. "You might want to get that," he said. "The kettle, I mean."

I blushed, and ducked back into the kitchen. I scooped up the kettle, poured the scalding water into a couple of cups, and began steeping the teabags as I carried them back into the living room. "Please, go on."

I handed him a cup and saucer, and he carefully took a sip.

"Yeah. I think you pretty much figured it out," he said. "I'm a cleaner. And yes, I go by Ajax Clean."

My cup of tea slipped from my fingers, splashing all over the area rug at my feet. Muffin, startled by the sudden splash dashed off from the living room to find refuge within my bedroom.

"But why? Why did you...I mean, I do not understand the..."

"The deception?" He stood from the couch, walked into the

kitchen and returned with the roll of paper towels. He then picked up the cup, placing it on the table, and began dabbing at the tea stained rug. "Honestly, I just wanted to be part of your life. But dad had made me promise—before, ya know—he made me promise that I would stay away from you. He was afraid that if we reconnected, it would make it easier for those searching for him to get to us. He wanted me to watch out for you, but the two of us were never supposed to actually meet." He shrugged. "With all that's going on, I guess he was right."

I left the paper towels on the floor to soak up the remaining liquid, and returned to his seat. He proceeded to tell me about his last job—the job that resulted in the death of his friend, Ed Massey. His frame up. And the discovery of the man named Jung Ki-yeol, who apparently was the one hunting the both of us down.

For my part, I told him about the flowers, the card, and the strange phone calls. I showed him the photo that had been sent to me as well, which seemed to agitate him more than I'd anticipated.

"That must have been taken sometime just after I left," he said; his voice a near growl. "I should have been there."

"For you to do what? I don't know what was happening in this photo, but apparently, not even father had been able to prevent it. What could you have done that he could not?"

He sat there, staring at the photo for several minutes in silence. Then, he handed the phone back to me, stood up, and held out his hand. "Look, we really do need to get going. I promise you, we can talk all you want, but for now, let's…"

His phone buzzed in his jacket pocket. Holding up a finger, he answered it in a hushed whisper. I could just make out the sound of the voice on the other end of the line.

"We've got trouble," the voice said. "Looks like a freakin' tactical unit…like S.W.A.T. or the Feds. You've got three minutes, tops."

The line went dead, and my brother stared down at the phone in his hand as if in shock.

"What? What is it?" I asked.

"I expected trouble, but not this kind of trouble," he finally said. "The cops are on their way."

"Why would they be coming here? They couldn't know you're here with me." I paused as another thought struck me. "And even if they did, how could they possibly know who you are?"

"Don't know. All I know is that they're heading our way. Now." He reached out to me, took me by the hand, and attempted to pull me from the couch. "Come on. We've got to go."

I recoiled from his grip. I really didn't like being manhandled by men—even if they *were* my own flesh and blood. "Why? There's no need to worry about the police. I work with them. I can talk to them. Explain things. You didn't kill those two people."

He shifted the weight of one foot to the next, alternating his gaze between me and the back door.

"Now's not really the time to discuss this. It's kind of my nature to avoid the cops at all costs, if possible." He glanced at his watch. "Just come with me, please. I'm not sure what's going on, but I can't leave you here. Not with Jung after the both of us."

I sat there, looking up at him while I considered his proposal, then shook my head. "Look Remy…or, what exactly should I call you anyway?"

"Ajax works fine," he said. "That's what my friends call me anyway."

"Okay. Fine. Look, Ajax. I'm sorry. I'm just a little confused here. Despite the fact that you're my brother, I hardly know you. Or at least, the *real* you." She finally stood up from the couch, and walked over to the back door. "I think I'll take my chances with the police. At least I know them. Trust them. I think they can help us with Jung Ki-yeol. They can offer us protection, anyway."

The glare of multiple headlights shone through the curtains in the front of the house. As Ajax's friend had predicted, the police had arrived. I wasn't certain why, but their presence did little to ease my mind. Something deep within me screamed that I should go with my brother. But the other, more rational self, demanded I not listen. Slowly, he approached me with a very sad expression across his face.

"Alright," he said with a shrug. "I'll go. But first, I need to apologize."

"About wha—"

Before I could finish the question, he withdrew a syringe from his jacket pocket, and lunged. I felt the needle slide into my neck before the powerful sedative rushed into my system. I felt my legs go numb just before my peripheral vision began to cloud up. I struggled to stand, and felt his arms wrap around me, offering his support to keep me upright.

I tried to speak. To curse him. But no words would come. I didn't care who he was, Ajax Clean was going to pay for this. I vowed that as the rest of my vision began to grow dark. I felt myself being lifted onto his shoulders. Heard the sliding glass door open and the cool February night air bite into my skin. Then, everything went dark and I was no longer aware of anything.

CHAPTER 23
AJAX CLEAN

I heard them before I saw them—their boots shuffling in the sodded grass on the other side of the fence. From the sound of it, there were at least four of them coming, while I was trapped crouching in the middle of the tiny back yard with a kidnapped woman on my shoulder, and few places to hide.

Fortunately for me, the fog had gotten thicker in the short amount of time I'd been inside Luna's house. But it wouldn't obscure me from view when the cops searched the yard with their Stinger high-powered flashlights. I needed a blind. Something to hide me from their sweep long enough to clear out before they brought in the dogs.

I scanned my surroundings, and my heart quickly sank deep into the pit of my gut. There was a small vegetable garden—the plants withered from either neglect or the winter chill—against the fence on the southwest edge of the fence. An old rusted-over swing set sat unused for years off to my left. The slide looked as if it would crumble away from the swing's frame with the slightest gust of wind. And then, there was the small shed, presumably where Luna kept her lawnmower and gardening tools, rested next to the garden, a few feet away. But A) it was locked tight with a combination pad lock, and B) it would be one of the first places the cops would look once they searched the interior of the house.

The latch at the gate clicked and shook. They were trying to open it. Since cops typically didn't want to announce their arrival on a bust, I figured they wouldn't force the gate open. Instead, they'd take their cue from my own playbook, and climb over. Any minute now, actually.

Already starting to feel burdened by Luna's dead weight on my shoulder, I moved as fast as I could to the shed, and slipped around to the back. There was barely a foot of space between the shed's rear wall and the privacy fence, but it was enough to squeeze through once I lowered my captive to the ground, and dragged her from under her armpits. Once I felt reasonably concealed, I allowed myself a brief moment to catch my breath, pulled out my cell phone, and sent Ellis a quick text as to what was happening.

No sooner had I sent the message, than I heard the sound of boots hitting the ground on the other side.

"Red One to Team Leader," I heard one of them whisper into his radio. "We're in back. The back door's standing wide open. Awaiting orders."

"10-4, Red One. Clear it. Now."

There was a sound like a small crash coming from the direction of the house. I risked a quick peek around the corner of the shed to see five black clad figures shuffling in through the back door, while five more swept in from the now doorless front entrance. They'd smashed their way inside with a battering ram, and were now busy clearing the house. The beams of their flashlights zigged and zagged through the windows, creating a strange disco ball effect from the outside.

But I wasn't concentrating on that at the moment. Instead, I couldn't take my eyes off the bright yellow block letters on the backs of each agent's body armor. The letters that read: D.E.A.

The Drug Enforcement Agency? What on earth are they doing here? What do they have to do with all this?

I had first assumed the cops were coming for me, but despite all my crimes, I avoided drugs and drug trafficking like the freakin' plague. I knew Luna did as well. So what had prompted this raid?

In the end, it didn't matter. The coincidence was just too huge not to imagine that Jung Ki-yeol had something to do with it, and sitting here pondering the complexities of it would only get me caught. I needed to move now, while they were searching the house.

"I'm not sssure why the shorse is eating the nyechins," Luna slurred deliriously. "Ish just a purple lodop." Instantly, I crouched, covering her mouth with my hand and glanced around the corner of the shed again. The DEA agents hadn't seemed to have heard her mumblings and were still focused on the interior. I was certain there were still a few of them out front, but for the moment, it looked as though now was the best shot I had of getting out of here.

Taking my cell phone, I sent Ellis another text, informing him to be ready. I then grabbed Luna by the arms and pulled her out from behind the shed before slipping her onto my shoulder again. I crouched there, on the side of the work shed, and watched the movement from inside. Relatively certain there were no eyes looking my way, I crept over to the gate, unlocked the bolt, and cracked it open a few inches. From my position, I couldn't see the DEA vehicles in front of the house, which meant they probably couldn't see me either.

I hope.

There was no way to be certain there wasn't a thermal scope-equipped sniper perched in some tree nearby, watching everything like some famished hawk. However, at the moment, I really had little choice.

I squeezed through the gate, and pressed myself as close to the side of the house as I could with Luna still across my shoulder. Slowly, I crept to the front corner, and peered around. Two black vans with D.E.A. stenciled on their sides angled across Luna's front lawn. Five men in full paramilitary gear crouched nearby, their automatic rifles pressed against their shoulders as they aimed toward the house.

A sixth agent, and a large German shepherd, leapt out from the back of one of the vans, and began making their way toward the front door. When they were midway, the dog suddenly stopped, and turned in my direction before letting out a low growl.

Crap. Crap. Crap. "Just move along, puppy. Nothing to see here," I whisper as I scanned all potential escape routes. From my vantage point, I couldn't see Ellis's Camaro anywhere. *Jerk better not have ditched me.*

The dog took another step toward me, and the agent's flashlight shot my way. I ducked back behind cover, and watched peripherally as the beam swept back and forth. It was at this precise point that I suddenly realized Luna was growing heavier in my grip. My shoulders ached from the prolonged pressure, and I knew a full-on sprint would be impossible with her in tow. *Idiot! What were you thinking drugging her with the cops outside?*

Yeah, it probably was not my brightest move. But let's face it…I panicked. I'm not ashamed to admit it either. No matter what you see in heist or hitman movies, the cops show up with their shock and awe, the real criminals' brains just seem to leak out their ears, and they react almost entirely on instinct. And in the cops and robbers business, instinct is one of the quickest ways to find yourself doing twenty-five to life, or just plain dead. With Cujo and his trusty DEA handler sniffing me out just around the corner, I figured it was high time I scooped my brains back into my noggin, and start using it for more than just a scratching post for a change.

The beam of light began bouncing rhythmically, widening as it drew closer. The agent and dog were heading my way. I could hear the dog snuffling at the ground, trying to pinpoint my scent.

Carefully, I shifted Luna to my other shoulder, eased out my cell phone, and tapped out another frantic text to Ellis.

"Out in open. Do something. Now," I typed.

The roar of a V-8 350 engine, and the screech of tires suddenly shattered the evening silence, and the hitman's black Camaro coupe sped into view from down the street. Shouts erupted from the direction of the vans, and I risked a quick glance around the corner to see all eyes firmly planted in the car's direction.

Smiling at the distraction, I bolted from my hiding place—still keeping the house between me and the DEA agents—and lumbered the twenty-five yards into the neighbor's property before ducking behind a minivan parked in the driveway. With the girl's additional weight, I hadn't been nearly as quick as I'd hoped, but it was fast enough to move me out of sight before being spotted at least.

I laid Luna on the driveway—gently cradling her head as I lowered it to the concrete—then crawled over to the front of the van, and looked around the bumper to see the DEA agents now standing in the middle of the street. They were aiming their rifles at Ellis's car as it drove mercilessly in their direction.

Don't kill them, you idiot. The last thing we needed right now was to be labeled cop killers along with all my other offenses. Fortunately, Ellis had sense enough to swerve just as they opened fire on the car, then shoot past them, and head for the next street over. Lights in houses from all over the neighborhood began flipping on as three of the agents scrambled to the nearest van, climbed in, and quickly gave chase. That left two to watch the exterior of the house, the K-9 unit, and the two teams inside while curious neighbors poked their heads out doors and windows to see what the commotion was outside.

"Who the heck are you?" came a rough, scratchy voice from behind me.

I turned my head to see a gray-haired old black man, brandishing a baseball bat, stepping off his front porch in his pajamas and slippers. A red ember of a cigarette butte hung from his lip.

"Shhhhhhh," I hissed; my eyes widening with the sudden intrusion.

"Don't you shush me, boy. Why don't you tell me what yer

doin' on my property." He nodded next door to the DEA agents. "You hidin' from them Feds or something?"

"Please." My voice was barely audible. "I'm not going to hurt you. I just…"

"I sure as hell know you ain't gonna hurt me." He raised the bat higher in the air, as he took another step closer. He didn't seem to have the same concern about his volume as I did. "Now start talkin' or so help me…"

I glanced over at Luna, and hoped she had a good relationship with her neighbors. "Luna's a…a friend. She's in trouble. I'm trying to help her."

The old man eyed her sleeping form suspiciously. "Looks like yer kidnappin' her to me, boy. That pretty little thing ain't done nothin' to warrant so many Feds. I figure it's you what brought 'em."

I shook my head. "It's not like that at all. Luna hasn't done anything wrong," I whispered. "But some bad people are trying to—"

"Excuse me, sir." It was a voice from the other side of the van. A distinctly authoritative voice. "You're going to need to go back inside. We're conducting an investigation here, and…"

"Don't you go tellin' me what to do on my own property, ya fascist!" The old man was no longer looking at me. Instead, his gaze was fixed past his van's front end. "Yer all makin' a racket. Keepin' an old man awake with yer guns and whatnot. Why don't you go arrest some really bad people…like them idiots in Congress or somethin'."

"Sir, I must insist that…"

"I don't care what you insist. I ain't budgin' until I'm good and ready."

There was pause, then the agent mumbled something into his radio. There was a sharp response from someone else—presumably his supervisor. "Alright, sir. Have it your way. Just don't get in our way."

"Wouldn't dream of it, kid." I heard the sound of the agent

walking away, then the old man laughed and looked down at me again. "Goose-steppin' bastards. Shootin' up our neighborhood in the dead of night." He pointed to Luna. "Well, don't just sit there gawkin', boy. Grab Ms. Luna up, and get yer ass inside where it's safe."

CHAPTER 24
AJAX CLEAN

After scooping up Luna, the old man led us to the back of the house—well beyond the view of the agents—and through the back door. We immediately stepped into a small kitchen, moved past the breakfast bar, and into a cozy living room. A small television blared a late night talk show host laughing hysterically as a chimpanzee danced across the studio floor in a tutu and top hat.

The house was a bit warmer than I would have preferred, and I felt a trickle of sweat beading across my forehead as I surveyed the rest of the room. My nostrils burned at the stench of stale cigarette smoke, mildew, and just a hint of ammonia. I figured the man probably had a pet that was prone to urinating inside, and a careful inspection of the carpet proved me right. Tuffs of animal hair—presumably a cat—coated the fabric of an area rug in the center of the room. On the wall to my left, I saw a large shadow box containing a set of handcuffs, a badge, and an empty space that looked suspiciously like where a handgun might have once hung.

Is this guy a cop?

Our host quickly turned the TV off, then gestured toward the couch. "Might want to put her down there for a bit. Probably a bit more comfortable than yer shoulder."

I did as I was told, then turned to face the old man, who was now holding a .38 caliber snub-nose revolver in my direction.

"Why didn't you pull that on me outside? Why threaten me with a baseball bat?"

Keeping his eyes trained on me, he snubbed out his cigarette in an ashtray resting next to an old, patched-up Laz-E-Boy recliner, and chuckled. "Seriously? A black man rushes out in the middle of the night, holding a gun within pissing distance of a bunch of trigger-happy *federales*? How dumb do you think I am, boy?"

"Good point." I slowly moved over to the armrest next to Luna's head, and sat down. I honestly didn't think the act was putting her in any danger. On the contrary, it might just prevent the old man's trigger finger from getting itchy. At least, that's what I was banking on anyway. "So now what?"

"What do you mean?" He cocked his head, genuinely puzzled at the question.

I gave a quick shrug. "Well, you lured us into your house, and pulled a gun on me." I nodded toward the shadow box. "I figure you're a cop or something. You planning on arresting us or just shooting us and saying we broke into your place?"

He looked to be pondering the question for several seconds before returning my own shrug, and lowering himself down into the recliner. The gun never waivered in its aim for a second. No matter how old the man was, his nerves appeared to be made of solid steel.

"Ain't really thought it through all that much," he said, finally laying the weapon on his lap. "Guess that'll be entirely up to you and the story you're about to tell me. All I know for sure is, I'm sitting on my front porch, enjoying the cool air with a cigarette, when some chink scitters through the fog and into sweet Luna's backyard."

"Chink? Really?"

"What?"

"'What?' You, of all people, are really going to ask me that?"

He continued to stare blankly at me, obviously not getting my question.

"First of all, I'm Korean, not Chinese."

"Same difference."

I leapt from my seat, prompting him to grab his gun again. His reflexes were amazing to be so aged. "Same difference? You're basically saying we 'all look the same'!"

He squinted a little at this, like a young child trying to decipher the meaning of advanced Calculus. "Well...um, ya'll kind of do."

"Oh. My. God! Really? This? Coming from an African American?"

"What's my race got to do with anything? I mean, can even *you* tell the difference between Chinese and Korean?"

He actually had a point. Forensic anthropologists could, by looking at a skull, distinguish between Caucasian, African, and Asian descent, but that was as far as they could take it. Truth was, there weren't that many quantifiable differences to identify in the Asian race. We aren't so much divided by nationality as we are regions. There were the Northern Asians, and there were Southern Asians. And an infinite number of variables in between. Geography, more than anything else dictated our physical features. It's precisely why my father was able to live for so long in Hong Kong pretending to be Chinese. Still, despite the anthropological argument, I wasn't quite ready to concede just yet.

"As a matter of fact, I—"

"Oh don't get into such a tizzy. We'll be here all night arguing. The point I was trying to make was, I saw you sneak into Luna's backyard, so I decided to keep an eye on things."

"So are you the one who called the DEA on us?"

"Now why the heck would I do somethin' as asinine as that? You dealing dope or somethin'?"

"Well, no. I'm just trying to figure out why they were there? Trying to figure out how they play into all this?"

He reached into his pajama shirt pocket, withdrew a cigarette from a crumpled pack, and lit it. "Play into what, exactly?" He took a puff, then dashed an ember into the ashtray with a tap. "I'm just trying to piece all this together. See, I look over at Luna there, and I see a woman that's been drugged. Looks to me like she's being kidnapped when the fuzz arrives." *Fuzz? Did he really just say 'the fuzz'?* "I know she's been having some issues...strange notes and unwanted phone calls at all hours of the night. A stalker, maybe?

"Then, I watch as you sneak into my yard, and ever so gently, mind you, lay her head down on my carport. I mean, the way you cradled that girl's head just screamed that you cared about her. So, there goes my kidnapping theory, right? Problem is, I can't quite figure out what's goin' on, and I don't feel all that comfortable with letting you just go rendezvous with your little partner in that shiny black car while Ms. Luna is in the condition she's in. I'd rather wait 'til she can make the decision for herself."

I looked down at her, and brushed a strand of hair from her face. I could only imagine how ticked off at me she was going to be when she came to, but for now, she was that little girl I remembered from so long ago.

"She's my little sister," I said. It was barely audible. I hadn't uttered those words to a single human being in more than twenty-four years, yet I'd already done so twice tonight. "She just found out about it herself. We were split up when we were kids." My brain screamed at me to shut up. It couldn't understand why I was doing this...why I was betraying the promise I'd made to my father a lifetime ago. Part of me, I suppose, felt I could trust the racially insensitive stranger sitting across from me with a .38 in his lap. Another part just felt really good to hear the words. I couldn't bring myself to stop. "I recently found out some pretty bad people are looking for my dad. Luna is the only one who knew...knows where he is. I knew she was in danger, so I came here to save her."

The old man sat in silence, processing the information. It

suddenly occurred to me that I didn't even know his name, and a sudden surge of panic welled up in my gut.

"I'm going to find the man responsible, and take him down. But first, I have to get her to safety."

He nodded in understanding as he took another pull on his cigarette, but he still didn't say a word.

I kept going to ease the awkward silence. "My father was a cop back in Korea. A good one, from what I hear. Apparently, he made a few enemies—that's why he sent me to America to stay with an old friend of his. Why he and Luna moved to Hong Kong. But I guess his past has finally caught up with us."

The old man rocked back and forth in his chair, his eyes staring blankly at the ceiling.

"Um, that's it. The whole story." My nerves were now on over-drive. "You going to say something or are we going to sit here like this 'til dawn?"

His gaze fell to meet my own. "I don't think that's the 'whole story', but close enough, I suppose," he finally said. Then he smiled, revealing one dead tooth amid several yellow stained ones. "Alright, I'll help you."

The proclamation stunned me. I hadn't been expecting a response like that at all.

"Help? How?"

"Well, I suppose, I can help you however an old homicide detective forced into retirement can help anyone wrapped up in a criminal conspiracy. Call in a few favors and see what happens."

CHAPTER 25
AJAX CLEAN

We talked through the rest of the night, discussing our strategy, making plans, and setting up the game pieces necessary to see it all come together while the red-orange ribbon of the sun began to creep through his window shades. I wasn't entirely sure why I so readily trusted the old man. Perhaps it was his obvious affection for Luna—how protective he was toward her. Maybe I just sensed something good in him. Something akin to the relationship I'd had with Lou back when he was showing me the ropes. Then again, it could have been simply because I was stuck in his house as long as the Feds continued to process Luna's house next door. I simply had nowhere else to go.

Of course, the old man had opened up to me as well. His name was Nathaniel Tilg, and he'd been born and raised in the swamps of Louisiana. He'd joined the Army in 1968 when he was only seventeen, fought in Vietnam, and had come to Miami when he was discharged four years later. With no real skills other than killing people, he'd taken a job as a cop, and rose up in the ranks until he became lieutenant of Homicide with Metro-Dade Police. He'd been forced into retirement two years ago, and hadn't quite managed to find his place in the world since.

Tilg had developed a liking for the young Chinese pathology

student interning at the Medical Examiner's Office, and had taken to mentoring her before his retirement. When the house had become vacant next door, he'd told Luna about it, and even helped her get a mortgage to buy it.

"I reckon them Feds will be wrapping up soon," Tilg said, putting out yet another cigarette, and ambling to the kitchen. "Want some coffee?"

"Sure. Thanks."

My phone chirped, and I glanced at it to find a text from Ellis. "I'M CLEAR. MEET AT RENDEZVOUS. 9:30."

I confirmed the meet with a few taps on the screen, and looked over at Luna. Her head shifted against her pillow, and I watched as her right leg stiffened in a stretch. She was waking up.

"Nathaniel?"

I heard the clinking of dishes from the kitchen, then his head peaked around the corner. "Yeah?"

"She's coming to."

"And?"

I stared at him blankly. For a former homicide lieutenant, he could be kind of dense. "And, she probably isn't going to be very happy when she sees me," I said. "I *did* inject her with a pretty powerful sedative, after all. Not to mention the fact that her house is now a wreck because of those DEA goons."

He bit at his lower lip for a second, then nodded. "I see your point." He disappeared back into the kitchen for a few minutes, then returned with two steaming cups of coffee. He put a cup down next to me. "Sorry. Don't use cream or sugar. You'll have to drink it black."

I shrugged, then looked back over at Luna. A sudden surge of panic grew in my chest, and I felt my hands begin to shake as she slowly began to regain consciousness.

"I assume you need to meet up with your friend in the black car?" Tilg asked.

"Yeah. Nine-thirty."

He looked from me to Luna, then back at me again.

"Then why don't you go? Meet your partner, and start looking into this Jung character. I'll watch over the girl...try to explain things to her, and work on my own investigation until you get back."

"Why are you doing this?" I asked.

He squinted at me. "What do you mean?"

"Helping me. You don't even know me. In my world, people just don't help complete strangers in these kind of situations." The panic suddenly intensified. What had I done? How could I have been so careless as to share the secret with this complete stranger? What had I been thinking? *Can I really leave Luna with him? Helpless and alone? For all I knew, he's working for Jung Ki-yeol.*

He chuckled at this. "Well, who the hell knows? Maybe one day, you'll be able to return the favor for me." He took a swig of his coffee, winced, then pulled out a metal flask from his robe and poured a finger of whiskey into it before taking another sip. "Besides, I ain't helpin' you. I'm helpin' that lil' darlin' there." He nodded over at Luna, then moved over to a desk on the other side of the room, opened one of the drawers, and withdrew a set of keys. "Now, here. Take my car. It's in the garage. You can back out, and drive away without those federal pigs being any the wiser. Then, come back for yer sister when everything's ready." He dropped the keys into my open palm, and smiled. "We'll be here waiting. Promise."

I stood there, staring at the keys, trying to decide whether I could trust this stranger. He was a cop. An ex-cop, but a cop nonetheless. Though I respected most of them, I'd never trusted a single one. We were, after all, on opposite ends of the law. In my experience, none of them would think twice about arresting me if they thought it would bolster their career. And Tilg hadn't seemed very pleased about being forced to retire. He missed it. He could see this as his big chance.

After a while, I looked up at him and smiled. "Could I have a few minutes alone with her? Just to say goodbye and let her know what's going on?"

He glanced down at her and shrugged. "Not sure what good it'll do. She may be comin' to, but she's still too far gone to hear anythin' you have to say."

"Still. I'd like a moment, if that's okay."

"Sure thing, kid. Sure thing." He picked up his cup of coffee and disappeared back into the other side of the house.

I counted to ten, then knelt down beside Luna and began whispering in her ear. "Don't react. I know you're awake," I said. She'd been the worst pretender at sleep as far back as when she was two. "Just remain still and listen to what I have to tell you. Then, please…please, do as you're told. I can't hope to find Jung if I'm constantly worried about your safety. I promise you…if you follow my plan to the letter, I'll let you be part of taking that bastard down."

I proceeded to give her instructions, laying out the skeleton of a plan that had already begun to develop in my head. I wasn't certain how I was going to pull all of the plan's aspects off, but I figured opportunities would come around. For other aspects, I'd just have to *make* them come around. Something I was very good at it. One way or another, all this would be over very soon.

Once finished with my instructions, I stood up, took Tilg's keys and his 1985 Crown Victoria, and left my sister behind wondering if I'd ever see her again.

CHAPTER 26
LUNA MAO CHING

Nathaniel Tilg's House
Miami, Florida
Thursday morning, February 8

The moment my brother—I was still having trouble accepting the fact that the man I'd known as Remy Williamson was actually my brother, who was also the notorious Ajax Clean—left Nathaniel's house, I sat up from the couch and looked around the room. I wasn't entirely sure how long I'd been out, but I could just make out the purple-orange haze of the rising sun through the living room blinds. I'd been asleep for a while. Fortunately, I'd awakened and feigned sleep long enough to be caught up on everything that had happened since Ajax had drugged me.

He and I are going to have a long talk about that one.

"Oh, good. You're awake." I looked up to see Nathaniel walking from his bedroom, holding his orange tabby, Roscoe, in his arms. "I'd wondered how long you were going to pretend to be knocked out."

"You knew?"

He chuckled. "Of course, I knew. I caught you peeking every

now and then." He sat down in his recliner and kicked the footrest up. "So how much did you hear?"

I stretched my arms and back, but managed to stifle a yawn. Despite the strength the sedative had had, my repose had apparently not been very restful. "Enough."

"And what did your brother say before he left?"

I merely shrugged. "Just that I needed to stay safe and he asked me to go to Eustis to hideout until he contacted me."

The old man nodded. "I suppose he has friends there he can trust?"

I'd known Nathaniel for as long as I'd worked at the Medical Examiner's Office. He'd been my mentor and friend for most of that time. I trusted him without reservation. But something in the tone of his voice concerned me. The questions he was asking seemed beyond mere concern for a friend. I suddenly regretted telling him about Eustis, but I wasn't certain why. Then again, in the last few days, my life had been turned upside down. I was being stalked by an enemy of my father's that I'd been running from since I was two. Federal agents had raided my home. And I'm been abducted from a brother I hadn't seen in almost twenty-four years. A girl has a right to be suspicious at times like these.

"I suppose," I said. "He just gave me an address to go to and told me someone would meet me there and take me to a safe place."

"And you trust him? This brother of yours?"

There was his questions again. But I had to admit, it was a good one to consider. My brother was Ajax Clean, a world class criminal, skilled in the art of manipulation and deceit. Could I trust him? Blood, after all, did not make someone family, and this man had not been part of my family in decades. With Jung Ki-yeol having me in his crosshairs, could I place my faith in this brother I really knew nothing about?

In answer to his question, I just shrugged.

Nathaniel's eyes narrowed. Then, he let Roscoe down from his lap, got up from his chapter, and limped over to the window of his living room to look outside. "Looks like the Feds are gone." He turned to face me. "I've got a second set of wheels in my garage. I'll drive ya to Eustis if you want. Ya know, for safety sake."

My head had been throbbing since I awoke, but I only now began to notice. I pinched at my temples, massaging them with my index fingers, then carefully shook my head. "Thank you. I appreciate the offer," I said. "But I can't ask that. You've already stuck your neck out for me far more than you should."

"Nonsense! Young pretty thing like you...someone needs to look out for ya." He meandered into the kitchen and returned with a couple of Advil's and a large glass of water and handed them to me. "Not that you can't take care of yourself, mind you. It's just always good to have a friend for backup every now and again."

Gratefully, I swallowed the pills, then carefully stood up from the couch. "May I use your phone?"

He nodded toward an old wireless phone with a retractable antenna sitting beside his recliner. I picked up the phone and dialed a number from memory. After a few rings, Gerald Jimenez answered the phone.

"Hello?"

"Gerald, this is Luna."

"Luna! What's going on? Some Federal agents came by the office a few minutes ago. They were looking for..."

"Gerald, listen. I need your help."

"Sure. Anything! Are you in some kind of trouble?"

"Not at all. The agents just want to talk to me about the double homicide at the dentist's office the other day. No big deal." I hated lying to him, but I could see no way around it. Gerald deserved better. But for the moment, it was the only choice I could think of. "My car broke down. I need to drive to meet a friend in Jacksonville. I was hoping I could borrow your station wagon."

"Absolutely. I'll swing by your house later tonight and..."

"It can't wait, Gerald. And I'm not at my house. Can you meet me at Lindsay's? Say, around noon?"

There was a pause. "Um, sure. Yeah. I'll take the car to you during my lunch."

"Thank you so much! You are a true friend and I owe you a great deal for this."

We said our goodbyes, and I turned around to thank my neighbor, only to find him pointing his revolver at me.

"Nathaniel?"

"I'm sorry 'bout this, Ms. Luna," he said. His eyebrows crinkled as he spoke the words and pulled back the hammer of his weapon. "But you won't be harmed none. As long as that brother of yours does his part anyway."

"What's going on? I don't understand."

"You're not supposed to understand." He let out a sad sigh and shrugged. "Look, Ms. Luna. I'm not the bad guy here. But I do have a job to do. And I need both you and your brother to see that job completed. So, if you'll just follow me into the garage, you and I are going to take a little drive. I promise you, I ain't going to hurt you."

My head felt as though it was stuffed with cotton balls, the remaining effects of the sedative. I could hear the pounding of my own pulse within my ears as my heart began to race at the betrayal playing out before me. I needed to move. Needed to act. But my legs and arms would not budge.

"Why?" It was the only word my trembling lips could manage.

"Everything'll become clear soon enough, sweetie." He waved the gun, gesturing toward the kitchen and the door that led into his garage. "Now let's go."

My brain whirled to life, calculating all the various scenarios and their inevitable outcomes I could come up with in seconds. It did not look good. The way I saw it, I had only one option for escaping and it was very risky. Still, considering the alternative, it was a risk well worth taking.

I stepped toward Nathaniel, who, upon seeing me comply

with his demands, relaxed the grip on his gun. When he did, I leapt into the air, and spun around, striking the older man's jaw with the heel of my foot. My startled than injured, Nathaniel tumbled backwards toward the couch. Landing on my feet, I lunged forward, grabbed his right wrist, and twisted. Unable to counter, and trying to avoid having his arm broken at the elbow, the former homicide detective dropped the gun, and spun in the direction I twisted his arm. When the gun hit the floor, I raised my foot and slammed him face first into the couch before scooping up the weapon and dashing out the front door.

Leaping from the front porch steps, I nearly stumbled onto the brick sidewalk, but managed to regain my balance just in time. Unsure of which direction to go, I opted for the one I knew best and ran directly toward my house. If I was going on the run, I needed a few supplies to help me. Since none of the police vehicles were still parked outside my house, I figured it was safe enough. Nathaniel was old. It would take him a while to recover from my assault, hopefully giving me enough time to throw a small bag together and escape.

I sprinted to my front door, which now lay wide open after being kicked in. It seemed odd to me that there was no police tape blocking my path, but I did not have time to wonder about it at the moment. I tucked Nathaniel's gun into my robe pockets, then ran inside, going directly to my bedroom closet, and withdrew a small piece of carry-on luggage.

After throwing the bag on the bed, I changed into some clothes more appropriate for being out in public and slid the revolver into waistband of my jeans. Once fully dressed, I began rummaging through my chest of drawers for some fresh changes of clothes, my passport, and spare cash I kept in a safe in my closet. I'd have to leave my cell phone and credit cards behind. They were too easy to trace.

My heart raced as I threw the most necessary of items into the bag and zipped it shut. I glanced at the clock on my nightstand.

About ten minutes had passed since fleeing Nathaniel's house. I needed to move.

A sudden thought struck me.

Muffin.

I looked around my bedroom for my cat, but there was no sign of her. I looked under the bed, then went into the utility room to check behind the dryer, where she liked to hide when she was upset. But nothing. She wasn't anywhere to be found.

"Muffin? Sweetie? Are you here?"

Silence. Not even the bell I'd placed on her collar jingled when I called.

"Muffin?"

"She's not here."

I spun around at the voice and nearly screamed when I saw the sight of a large blonde man dressed all in black, and leveling a very fierce looking assault weapon at me. A badge hung around his neck, and I could just make out the embossed letters D.E.A. etched into the metal. A sudden wave of relief washed over me. He was a police officer. Or the federal equivalent anyway.

"Oh, thank God!" I said, stepping toward him, which prompted him to steady his aim. "Thank you. This is my home. A man, my neighbor, was trying to kidnap me and…"

"Be quiet," the agent said. He then pressed the pads of a throat mic with two fingers, and spoke. "Yeah, I've got eyes on her. She returned home. Orders?"

I couldn't hear the response, but judging by the coiled wire leading up to the agent's ear, I assumed he had an earpiece that his superiors could speak to him with. A few seconds later, he nodded. "Copy that. We'll be enroute in five."

When I figured he had finished with his dialog, I spoke up once more. "I'm Dr. Luna Mao Ching. I work for the Medical Examiner's Office and…"

The agent shook his head. "I don't care. I've got my orders. I've got to take you in."

"What? On what charges? I've done nothing wrong."

"Once again. Don't care." He reached behind him and removed a pair of zip-tie handcuffs, and tossed them to the floor next to my feet. "Now, put those on."

Warily, I bent down and picked the plastic cuffs up. "I don't know what's going on. I'm not a criminal. I've broken no…"

"Just put the damned cuffs on, lady." He waggled his weapon, attempting to hurry me along.

"But I…"

Pfft. Pfft.

Two barks burst from behind the agent and he dropped to the floor, blood pooling around his face and head. I stood there, looking down at him, unable to process just what had happened.

"Don't worry. He was dirty," the familiar voice of Nathaniel Tilg said. I tore my eyes away from the dead agent to see the retired homicide detective a few feet away. He was holding a suppressed semi-automatic handgun that I couldn't quite identify. "He was taking you to Jung. If you want to avoid becoming a prisoner to the man who wants to take his revenge against your father out on you, I suggest you come with me." He flashed me an insincere grin. "Now."

CHAPTER 27
AJAX CLEAN

Brewster Meadows Trailer Park
Ocala, Florida
Friday morning, February 9

Ellis and I sat in the car in silence, watching the rusted out, single wide trailer sitting on cinder blocks on Lot 47. Ellis crunched down on a Cheese Puff; an orange film of powdered cheese-like substance coating his fingers.

"So how you want to play this?" he asked.

I reached into the glovebox, removed a packet of moist towelettes, and handed him a few. "First, clean yourself up." I pointed to his hands. "You look a five-year old."

He scowled at me, but complied, then rolled the snack bag up, and set it on the seat next to him.

"Are you sure this is where they live?" I asked. "We've been here for two hours, and haven't seen so much as a pimple from them."

"They're in there. Trust me."

I sighed. "Okay. Way I see it, we only need one of them. The one with hair preferably. The shaved one is too stupid to do us any good."

Ellis smiled as he screwed on a suppressor to his pistol.

"Can we try not to kill anyone? Please? I'm already in enough hot water as it is."

"It's what I do." The hitman's eyes narrowed at me.

"Yeah. When you're paid to do it. Last I checked, I'm not paying you for this. You're only helping me because the Raid asked you to."

He responded to this with a grunt, then tucked the pistol into a modified shoulder holster.

"We'll play it just like we talked about on the way here. You take the back of the trailer," I said, withdrawing my Ruger LC9 and chambering a round. Just because I didn't want Ellis to kill anyone didn't mean I was going to approach our targets unprepared. "Make sure they don't run. I'll take the front door."

Ellis looked at my gun with a contemptuous sneer, then opened the center console, rummaged through its contents, and came up with another suppressor. He handed it to me. "This'll fit your girley gun. Don't want to wake the neighbors, do ya?"

I took the suppressor, and nervously screwed it into my piece. I then opened the passenger door, and climbed out. Ellis followed suit, then immediately dipped into the shadows underneath a stand of trees, and made his way toward the back of the trailer. I watched him until he completely disappeared from sight, then tucked my gun into the back of my jeans, and walked boldly up to the front door. I counted to twenty, giving my companion enough time to get into position, and knocked loudly. I then pressed my back up against the trailer, to the right side of the door, opposite the window.

It was twenty minutes past one in the morning, but the lights and television were on, so I figured they were still awake. After about thirty seconds, I knocked again. This time, I heard some shuffling inside. A female voice, followed by the hushed whisper of a man.

"Who's there?" came the female voice, sounding very nervous from behind the door.

"Wade Murphy sent me," I growled, deepening my voice to make it more foreboding, while adding just a dash of a New York accent in the mix. "He wants I should have a word with dem. Now."

More rustling. Another hushed voice joined the others. Then, a large crash from inside, the sound of the backdoor being forced open. The girl screamed, followed by the sound of two muffled pistols shots.

Geeze! What is that nutball doing?

I moved in front of the door, raised my boot, and slammed it against the door. The metal frame bent under the impact, but the door didn't budge. Another shot erupted inside, then more crashing. Glass shattered. Men yelled.

I grabbed my pistol from my waistband, aimed at the doorknob and fired. The 9 mm slug tore through the lock, and the door swung open. I rushed in in time to see Ellis slamming John Peyton's shaved head down on a coffee table. His brother, James, lay curled in a fetal position in the kitchen area, next to the refrigerator. He rolled back and forth, holding his groin tight with both hands, but blood was quickly pooling underneath him. There was no sign of the girl anywhere.

"Ellis, stop!" I shouted as the hitman's fist slammed down on John's right ear with a cartilage-popping crunch. I lunged, grabbing his arm before he could land another blow. His head whipped up, and he glared at me with maniacal death-filled eyes. Then, he took a deep breath, and relaxed. "What are you thinking?" I pointed over at James. "I said we needed the one with hair. He's got hair! And you shot him! I thought I told you no killing."

He took another deep breath. "They not dead. Yet." He turned to look down the hallway to the other side of the mobile home. "Well, the hooker might be. Not sure."

I brought my palm to my face, and shook my head in disbelief. "You were supposed to wait until I was inside."

"I got impatient. You were takin' too long."

James Peyton struggled on the coffee table, pinned down by Ellis's powerful arm.

"It's the dog all over again. See? This is why I refuse to work with you." I turned my attention to the skin head Peyton brother, who was now hurling a string of curses at us as Ellis continued to pin him down. "As for you, you're going to tell me everything we need to know." I withdrew a syringe filled with the same sedative I'd used on Luna, bent down, and injected it into his neck. Within seconds, he was unconscious.

I straightened, and took in the trailer's interior. To call it a mess would be like calling Godzilla a chunky iguana. The kitchen table was turned onto its side, spilling heaping portions of tacos, ground beef, vegetables, and cheese all over the floor. Beer cans had been sent flying during the fracas, and the filthy shag carpet was soaked in places with the tangy stench of beer. Although the television was still mounted on the wall, the brothers' Xbox and a slew of games were scattered throughout the room, as were several kitchen knives. I chuckled to myself when I realized that among the chaos, there wasn't a single book anywhere to be seen.

Sounds about right.

Eventually, my eyes landed once more on the younger brother, James, still clutching his groin and moaning.

"John will be out for a while," I said to Ellis. "Go check on the girl. Oh, and if she's not dead, don't kill her, okay?"

He grunted before moving off toward the other end of the trailer. I then stepped into the kitchen, and crouched down on one knee to take a look at James's injury. "Hold on," I said. "I just need to take a look." He winced as I placed my hand on his leg, and tried to straighten him out. "Seriously dude. We need to get that bullet wound looked at."

Now sweating profusely, his teeth chattering, James nodded, rolled onto his back, and tried to relax. Lifting his shirt, my eyes swept back and forth over the beer-gut of his abdomen, tracking the trail of blood that seemed to originate a bit further south of his pants.

"Geeze, Ellis. Why'd you have to shoot him there?"

But the hitman didn't respond, and I didn't care. The sooner I could get away from that voodoo nutball, the simpler my life would become. I just knew it. Pushing the thought from my mind, I carefully unbuckled Peyton's belt, and pulled his jeans down just above the swell of hip to reveal a single gunshot wound to the pelvis—high and just barely to the right of his, um, junk.

"Okay. I think we're going to need Doc Kane for this one," I shouted to my companion. "It's, uh, entirely too sensitive for me to try to patch him up myself."

Still no response from him.

"Ellis?" Silence. I decided to try a different tact. "Archie?"

When he didn't respond to that, I knew something was wrong. Slowly, I eased my Ruger out again, and crept over to the corner leading to the hallway with my back against the cupboard. I strained my ears in the disquieting silence, but the only thing I could hear was the sound of my own pulse.

"Don't try anything stupid," came a sultry female voice at the other end of the hall. "Or I'll put a bullet in the back of your friend's head."

"That's okay," I said, gripping the gun tighter in my hand. "We're not that close. Go ahead and shoot him." There was a sudden gasp, and I wasn't certain whether it had come from the girl or Ellis. "Seriously though, this has nothing to do with you. We're just here for the Peytons. You're free to leave whenever you like."

"Can't. Job's not finished."

"Uh, darling…I have a feeling neither of these guys are in any condition to finish what they started with you. If you need money for your pimp, I'm sure Archie in there's got a few bills he'd be happy to hand over."

The moment I'd said the words, I realized my mistake. Ellis was a trained assassin. And one of the very best. Stories I'd heard said he'd learned his trade in some black ops outfit that had specialized in taking down entire governments. He was the kind of guy who could stab a man in the spleen with a spork if he needed to. There was no way a hooker—as I'd assumed she was—would have been able to get the drop on him, which meant only one thing...

"I'm here for *you*, Ajax Clean."

"Um, sorry. I'm not all that fond of hookers. You never know where they've been." Why is it that in the worst possible moments of my life, I just can't keep my big mouth shut? I've always got to antagonize the big bad hitmen—or hit persons, whatever the case may be—in my life.

"You know as well as I do that's not what I'm talking about," she said. Her voice sounded closer. Was she moving up the hallway toward me? I was sent here to kill the Peyton brothers. You were next on my list. I ought to thank you. You just saved me a trip."

I glanced around the floor, spotting a pair of mirrored sunglasses that had been knocked off during the tussle with Ellis. The glass from one eye was missing, but it still had the left side. I scooped it up, lowered it to my waist, and held it just past the corner. Sure enough, a rough-looking, though potentially attractive bleach-blonde was inching her way toward me. Ellis was held tight around the neck with one arm, forced to bend backwards to match her shorter height. She held a Glock semi-automatic against his temple as they inched forward. I took a second look, and noticed something surprising about her. The blonde hair had initially thrown me, but she was Asian. Chinese or Korean descent, more than likely—I guess we really *do* all look alike. But I figured it was a good bet she was the latter, rather than the former.

"Look, we don't need to do this," I said. "I just want the brothers. You leave now and you can walk away. Your employer doesn't have to know."

As they approached the corner, I pulled the glasses away, stepped away from the wall, and brought my aim up. A moment later, Ellis's bent frame stepped into view, followed immediately by the female assassin.

She shifted from one leg to the other, repositioning her gun to the other side of Ellis' head. Her left arm was bandaged, the telltale signs of bruises edging out from under the white gauze. Another set of bruises could be seen along her thigh and leg. My eyes followed the injuries down to her petite, bare feet. So small. Almost like a child's. My eyes shot up to her face, and began working back down once more. It was hard to see her nude body behind Ellis' lean frame, but I could see enough to know that she'd been battered pretty recently. Cuts. Scrapes. And they were already healing, so I knew the Peystons hadn't been playing rough with her.

And her hair. Blonde straight out of a bottle. Just like the woman from the surveillance video at...

Massey's. She's the one who killed Mass.

The realization sent my blood to a slow boil, but I held my temper in check for the moment. Instead, I stared down the barrel of the Ruger, sighting her up for a clear shot. With a tug of the neck, she jerked Ellis backwards, blocking my aim. "Uh-uh-uh," she said with a fake pout. "Don't even think about it."

"You killed my friend."

She winked at me. "Not yet. But I will." She pushed Ellis further into the kitchen.

I adjusted my aim. "I really think you're underestimating my indifference toward Ellis there." I shifted slightly to my left, keeping my eyes squarely fixed on hers. "If you haven't heard, the dude likes to sacrifice dogs for voodoo."

"Oh, for the last time, I don't practice voodoo!" Ellis hissed. "It's *Palo Mayombe*. There's a difference."

"Uh, yeah. An *evil* difference. You kill dogs, remember?"

The female assassin laughed at this, then slowly squared off with me. This, of course, was exactly what I was hoping for with the banter.

Keep her off guard, Anton. Keep her off guard.

"But I'm talking about Ed Massey," I said to the woman. "I saw his security feed. Saw you attack him. Saw the fight you two had."

Her eyes narrowed, then she shrugged. "Then he ran," she said. "I couldn't find him. So I left. He wasn't a hard target anyway."

"You're lying. Something tells me you're not the type to give up so easily."

"He was only worth a few grand." She smirked. "Not really worth my time."

"So if you didn't kill him, then who did? He ended up in the Peytons' van, for crying out loud!" My voice was steadily escalating and I struggled to keep it down. "With you here, with them now, you really expect me to believe it's all a coincidence?"

Another shrug. "Don't care if you believe me or not. You're going to be dead in a few seconds anyway." She shifted her weight from one foot to the other. "And unlike these idiots, my payday for you is going to make everything worthwhile."

I watched her grip on her own gun shift ever so slightly. The tendon along her forearm flexed. She was about to switch targets. About to aim at me.

I squeezed the trigger, and a muted explosion of gunpowder ripped through the suppressed barrel of the Ruger, unleashing a plume of fire and smoke. A millisecond later, the blonde Asian woman developed a third eye, directly center in her forehead. She stood staring blankly at me, her mouth twisted in a mask of confusion. Then she collapsed to the linoleum floor in a heap.

Ellis stiffened, his mouth twisted in the exact same shape as our would-be assassin's, just before she went down. "You...you could have hit me!" he shouted. "...da hell were you thinking, man?"

I slid the pistol back into my pants, and glared down at the woman who might not have killed Ed Massey after all. "Just because I'm not a big fan of killing doesn't mean I'm not an ace shot." I motioned toward John, still unconscious on the coffee table in the living room. "Now get Bubba over there, and put him in the trunk of your car. I'll get his brother. Then it's time we finally get some answers." I stopped and turned toward the assassin again before a sly grin stretched up my face. "Oh, and I think we need to bring her along for the ride as well."

CHAPTER 28
AJAX CLEAN

Shamrock Motel
Ocala, Florida
Friday morning, February 9

watched John Peyton slowly drift toward consciousness as he lay, bound by duct tape at the hands and feet, in the pay-by-the-hour motel room's bathtub. He was naked except for a pair of stained tighty-whiteys and two mismatched socks. His eyelids fluttered wildly as a low moan hissed from behind several strips of more duct tape covering his mouth.

"Up and at 'em, sunshine," I said, hurling water from a glass into his face. Instantly, his eyes shot open, and he squirmed violently inside the wet tub. I'd been sure to run the shower into the tub to keep the fiberglass nice and slick, and I chuckled to myself as my captive's head slammed down hard each time he tried to rise up from his spot. "Shhhhh. Shhhhh. We don't want to wake our nice neighbors, do we?"

I was in the bathroom with him, seated on the lid of a large rubber trash can. Two other cans, fifty gallons each, rested on either side of me. The bathroom door was closed, and with no window, the only light inside the small space came from the dim forty watt bulb mounted without a shade into the ceiling.

"Now before we begin, I want to set your mind at ease." I climbed down from my perch, and onto my knees to look him squarely in his wide, frightened eyes. "Your brother should be okay. Yes, Ellis did shoot him in the groin. He's really sorry about that, by the way. But we called in Doc Kane. He's working on him even as we speak." Dr. Gil Kane had been chief of surgery at a very prominent hospital in Tallahassee until it was discovered that he'd been making a little extra money on the side selling organs to unsavory types. Disgraced, and in all kinds of legal problems, he found himself seeking out help from a certain mafia don, who in turn, recruited him as Florida's premiere underworld physician. I knew that John Peyton would understand that having Kane looking after his brother meant the finest care possible, which would go a long way in obtaining his cooperation.

Of course, with the contents of the garbage cans at my disposal, I honestly didn't think cooperation was going to be much of an issue. But every little bit helped. It was well-known about me that I was a pretty easy going guy under most circumstances. But threaten me. Or someone I care about. And I could be downright ruthless.

Skinhead Peyton was about to learn firsthand just how much that reputation was justified.

"Now, I'm going to take that tape off your mouth there, and you're not going to shout out or anything, right?" I drew my suppressed pistol from my waistband, and placed it on the toilet seat next to me. His eyes followed the gun's movement, then locked onto mine with a slow nod. "Good."

I carefully pulled the tape from his face, trying my hardest to avoid ripping the bristling five o'clock shadow as I did so. Once removed, he squirmed a bit more to gain more purchase in the tub, then glowered at me. "You know, when this is over, I'm going to enjoy killing you, right gook?" he said.

I was sincerely impressed. The way he'd said it was so calm. Calculated. Even genuine. I'd expected him to hurl every cuss word and threat in the book at me, forcing me to re-tape his mouth shut. But he was keeping an uncharacteristic level head about him.

"You know, I might have been wrong about you." I gave him a pat on the shoulder. "I wanted Ellis to spare your brother because I thought he was the brains of your operation. Thought you were the dumb hothead who just liked killing people. But I think you're going to do much better than I'd originally thought. Now, let's begin. First things first, where's Jung Ki-yeol?"

The skinhead rolled his eyes, and leaned back in the tub.

"Let me ask that again. Where's Jung Ki-yeol?"

"You're barkin' up the wrong tree, gook."

I clenched my fist, and slammed it hard across his face. "You call me that again, I'll put a bullet in your head and move on to your brother. Got it?"

He sneered, spat a glob of blood onto the floor next to me, and nodded.

"Good. Now for the third and final time, Jung Ki-yeol. Where is he?"

Staring up at the ceiling, John Peyton shrugged. "I really don't know who you're talkin' about. I ain't ever heard of no Jun Key-yowel."

"Then who hired you for the Hernandez hit?"

He laughed. "Same as you. His wife."

I raised my fist again, but he jerked his head away. "I'm serious, man. His wife hired us to do him. Paid us five grand each."

This was kind of a surprise. I had wondered how the dentist had come into play in the whole thing, but figured he'd either pissed Jung off too, or he'd simply been a victim of some elaborate scheme. It had never occurred to me that his hit had been legitimate, and that my set up had merely ridden piggyback on it.

"So how did I get involved in all this? Who paid you to set me up?"

He laughed harder at this, but didn't answer.

"Who told you to set me up?"

"I ain't sayin' another word." He grinned maniacally at me.

I nodded, smiling back. "That's fine. Completely understandable." I took the tape, and placed it firmly over his mouth again. I then stood, grabbed hold of the trash can lid, and lifted it off. Immediately, the room was filled with a disturbing series of clicks, whirrs, and buzzing. "Know what's in here?" I pointed to the can. He shook his head, his eyes wider than when he'd first awakened. "In this drum alone, there's something close to twenty solid gallons of *Dermestes Maculatus*. Know what that is?"

He shook his head again, very nervously.

"It's better known as the 'hide beetle'. A buddy of mine in Homosassa raises them. Give me a discounted rate on bulk jobs like this."

He groaned at the revelation.

"I use them quite frequently in my line of work. They're great at stripping the flesh off a cadaver. It's a rather slow and meticulous process, but it gets the job done." I glanced down at the trash can and whistled. "You should be thankful. These cans hold fifty gallons, but they were just too heavy to lift with that many bugs in them." I tilted the trash can forward, and let it land on the tub's lip. Instantly, Peyton started screaming behind his tape gag. "Oh, it's too late for that. You wanted to play games. So this is a cleaner playing games."

I bent down, grabbed the bottom of the can, and tilted it up, spilling the beetles into the tub. Peyton's screams turned frantic, but fortunately the tape held. Once the can was empty, I moved it aside, moved to the next can, and repeated the process. The skinhead writhed inside the tub, trying desperately to stand up, and falling backwards each time he did. I repeated for a third time, and the beetles now were spilling over the sides of the tub, climbing up my captive's neck, and inching toward his nose and eyes.

"Look at me John." His wide eyes would not focus. They darted left and right, watching the flesh-eating insects scurrying all over his body. "John." My voice was stern, yet soothing. "Look at me." He finally garnered enough will power to comply. "Good.

Now listen. *Dermestes Maculatus* typically only eat dead things. I've never heard of them eating living tissue. But honestly, it's an experiment I've always wanted to try. So this is me..." I paused, letting my words sink into his frazzled brain. "...experimenting. The sooner you tell me what I want to know, the sooner I'll pull you out of there, okay?"

He nodded with quick, jerky motions.

"No screaming, remember?"

He nodded again, frantically.

"Good." This time, I ripped the tape from his face fast, and he bit down on his lip to keep from shouting. "Now. Who hired you to frame me?"

He looked at me, his entire body shaking uncontrollably as the millions of insects scurried around his near naked body. "Th-that's just it," John said. There was a distinct quiver in his voice. "The original contract wasn't to frame you. It was to kill you. Supposed to leave you in the dentist's office, and make it look like a mob hit gone wrong."

I opened my mouth to speak, but no sound would come out. So Jung hadn't lied to me. He really had expected me to take a bullet in Hernandez's office. Hearing it now, from my would-be killer's mouth, unnerved me more than anything else I'd learned within my investigation. Finally garnering my wits, I pressed for more information.

"Who hired you for the hit then?"

"Uuuuhhhh, get them off me. Please. Get them off me!"

A single beetle was crawling above his upper lip; its head penetrating his left nostril.

"Soon. Now who contracted you?"

"You ain't gonna like the answer."

"Humor me."

"It was some cop." Tears were running down his cheeks now. "A Fed. Not sure what agency. He said some Asian high roller was footing the bill. Was going to pay us a cool hundred grand each for knocking you off."

"Okay, so it was a Fed." The words wouldn't pass the grape-fruit-sized lump in my throat. That was the second time the Feds popped up in this little mess of mine and John Peyton had been right. I didn't like it one bit. I'd done everything I could to steer clear of them my entire career and now this. "But he's looking for my father. Why does he even care whether I live or die?"

"You know how it works man! I don't ask questions. Just do the job and collect the money. That's all."

I knew he was right. There was only so much that John or James would know when it came to the job they'd been hired to do. "So tell me this. How did the set up come into play then? If you were supposed to kill me, how did Massey end up dead and me getting framed for it?"

Peyton sneezed, expelling the insect from his nose. "They're freakin' biting me, man! They're biting me!"

"Nah. I don't think so. It's just your mind playing tricks on you." I nodded. I'd lost any sense of amusement for his ordeal five minutes ago. "Now tell me."

His body convulsed as he struggled to free himself from the duct tape. To stand and run. Anything that would help him escape the sea of creeping insects swarming every inch of his skin.

"John, you need to focus. Tell me what I want to know."

"Okay. Okay. Some black dude showed up at our hotel room in Miami an hour before we were supposed to meet you. He said the plans had changed. Offered us double what we were origi-nally offered, and gave us Massey's body for the job." Tears continued streaming down his face. "We didn't know it was Massey though. Not until we saw the news. Just thought it was some schlub."

"Did you recognize him? The black man?"

He shook his head, and a sudden rush of dread filled my veins.

"Was he older? Gray hair? Yellow teeth?"

"Nah. Well, more middle aged, I guess. Dressed all sharp like. Expensive suit. Gator-skin shoes. Gold tie-pin with a star on it."

"Did he at least give a name? Say who he was working for?"

"No. But James kept sayin' how the dude stunk like a pig. Another Fed, maybe." He twisted his neck, trying to dislodge one of the insects trying to crawl into his ear. "But I ain't ever seen a Fed dress that good."

Another Fed? What the hell is going on here?

"What about a way to contact him?"

He squirmed once more. "Man, come on! They're hurting me. They've crawled up my shorts!"

"Don't worry. They'll come out soon from starvation. Now tell me…did he give you a way to contact him."

"No. He just wired the money into our accounts. I don't know nothin' else about him."

I thought about all I'd learned so far. As usual, for each answer I got, ten more questions popped up. But I had a feeling I was running out of options with the Peytons. Whoever had orchestrated all this was way beyond their pay grade. I doubted either of them knew much more than I'd already gleaned.

"One more thing, and we're done." He looked up at me with hopeful eyes. "I realize we're not friends. Realize we owe each other nothing. But why on God's green earth did you ever think I'd ever let you get away with putting my sister in danger?"

His mouth gaped. "Your sister…but I…"

"Oh, I realize you may not know anything about her. You only had eyes on me. But putting your sights on me, you've inadvertently placed my baby sis in danger. Put her in the crosshairs too. After all, if I'm dead or running from the law, I can't protect her. Can't keep her safe."

He cleared his throat. I could tell the strain of the beetles were taking their toll on him. "But you were just a job, man." A slow, pathetic squeal eked out from somewhere deep inside his throat as the insects continued to swarm around his naked body. "It was nothing personal. You know how it is. We didn't know nothin' about a sister."

I nodded at this. "Like I said, I know. I know." I leaned down, and slapped the tape over his mouth for the third time, and gently brushed a handful of insects off his shoulder. I then reached over to the toilet seat and picked up my Ruger. "Now, John. You know my reputation, right? How I'm a pretty nice guy. Loyal. Easy to get along with. How I loathe violence. Would rather leave that kind of stuff for the movies…or, for guys like you. You know all that right?"

He gave a short nod. Tears streaked his dirty face as he silently pleaded with me behind the tape.

"So, if you know my reputation, you also know I have two uncompromising rules for anyone I work with or work for." I lowered the gun's barrel, and pressed the suppressor against Peyton's left temple, before sliding the shower curtain closed around my gun arm. He clenched his eyes shut. "Rule One. Don't betray my trust." I pulled the slide back, chambering a round and eliciting another whimper. "Rule Two. Never ever threaten the people I love." His body shuddered with sobs as I continued to talk. I didn't fault him for it. He was seeing a side to me that very few people ever witnessed. It was a side that even I was afraid of, if I had to be perfectly honest with myself. I was about to do something that grated against every fiber of my conscience. But it was going to definitely be done and I wasn't going to lose a single hour of sleep over it.

"You and your brother broke both of those rules, John. You might not have been aware of breaking Rule Two, but it doesn't matter. Someone I love dearly is a target in someone's scheme. Someone you were employed by and helped to set in motion. I can't abide that. Can't abide it at all."

I pulled the shower curtain as tight as I could, and squeezed the trigger. The gun barked, and I found something hot and wet splash around my hand. I withdrew my arm, wiped my hand and gun off with a motel towel, and moved into the next room to have a similar chat with a dead man's brother.

CHAPTER 29
AJAX CLEAN

"**H**ow's he doing, Doc?" I asked as I stepped out from the bathroom into the motel suite.

Doc Kane, hovering over his patient with a needle and sutures, looked up at me. He then looked over at the bathroom door I'd closed behind me. I knew he and Ellis had heard the gunshot.

Unlike the movies, there is no such thing as a 'silencer'. Suppressed pistol shots didn't sound like little puffs of air. Suppressors were designed to suppress the sound caused by the expulsion of gasses out of the barrel. They couldn't stop the sonic boom of the bullet itself, therefore, they couldn't mute them entirely. It was the difference between a gunshot and an M40 fire-cracker.

It wasn't for reasons of stealth that most hitters used them anyway. In a closed space—like say, a small bathroom—the sound of a gunshot echoing against all four walls and bouncing back at the shooter could cause serious hearing damage. It was simply pragmatic, especially in the heat of the moment, when being able to hear potential danger was critical.

But I wasn't concerned about anyone in the motel overhearing the noise. I knew from the moment we checked in, that there was no one occupying any of the rooms on this side of the motel. It's why I'd asked for the room by number.

"He's still unconscious," Dr. Kane said, now eyeing the blood stains on my right hand. "I've managed to remove the slug, and stem the flow of blood, but I think he's going to probably need a transfusion. He's lost a lot of…"

"Never mind that." I looked over at Ellis, who was reclining in the other bed, watching a muted television with Closed Captioning on. "We need to start cleaning up. I need to get back to my place and have a friend of mine start doing a little…um, online research. Whatever's going on has something to do with one or more federal law enforcement agencies, and I need to find out which ones before making any other moves."

"Why do you think the Feds are involved?" The hitman's eyes never left the television screen.

"Because every time I turn around, they keep popping up in this fiasco. It's the only thing that makes sense right now." I shrugged. "From what that female hit, um, person said, it also sounds like we've got two different parties screwin' with my life. If she didn't kill Massey, then someone else did. Then, there's the whole issue with the Peytons originally being contracted to kill me, then someone doubling their fee to simply set me up. I'd kind of like to know who all the players are in this. Yancy's the guy for the job."

"You trust him? This Yancy fellow?"

"Absolutely. He's not much use, but he's a friend and knows his way around a computer."

"When are you going to learn, Clean. There're no such ting as friends in dis business."

I paused, thinking about that for a moment. In many ways, he was right. I was being played by someone. I wasn't entirely sure if the few people in my life weren't part of it. After all, Jung seemed to know an awful lot about me. I couldn't help but wonder where he was getting his information from.

But it wasn't something I could easily accept. Lou had been

my friend. Murphy had apparently been Lou's friend. And Grandma had been friends to many in our line of work. It just wasn't in my nature or the way I was brought up to admit Ellis was right. "Well, I..."

"Um, excuse me." I glanced back at Doc. "I'm serious, Ajax. I need to get him to my place. He needs a transfusion, or he's not going to make it."

"So?" Ellis asked, picking up the remote and changing to a different channel.

"You guys brought me hear to keep him alive. It's my duty to do just that. No matter who I work for or how I make my money, I'm still a good doctor." He stopped for a moment, then nodded as if coming to some internal decision. "No matter what some people might say. I can't stand by and let him die."

"Funny. I did not see you runnin' in to save his brother when Clean shot him," Ellis said, chuckling.

"I assumed there was little I could do for him," Kane said. "But James here has a decent chance."

I shook my head. "You know who your patient is, right, Doc?"

"Of course. But I see them as no different from the numerous others I've treated over the years." He glanced over at Ellis. "Including you, Mr. Ellis."

"No, you don't understand. You don't *really* know who this is." I walked over to the bed, gently moved the doctor aside, and pointed down at James Peyton with the barrel of my pistol. "This man...and his brother...were hired to kill me." I thumped the barrel against Peyton's unconscious forehead hard. "That the nature of the biz. I get it. I accept it. No harm, no foul."

I turned to face the doctor as my blood cascaded into a slow simmer. "But like I explained to Mr. Skinhead in there, they made it personal. Because of them, I'm not only the target of a crazy Korean who's got a grudge against my family, but I'm apparently also in the crosshairs of some weird Federal conspiracy. And to top it all off, their actions have done the unforgiveable...something that I simply wouldn't abide from the best of my *friends*." I glared at Ellis as I uttered that last word. "They've side with someone who's threatening a person I care more about than anything in the universe. That alone, as far as I'm concerned, is reason enough to put a bullet in their brains."

"Hey, Clean," Ellis said.

"Not now, I'm not finished." I tapped the barrel harder against James's forehead. "But if that's not enough for you, consider this...these creeps are sociopaths. They don't kill for principle. They don't even really kill for money. They kill because it's how they get their kicks. And we've just given them some rather nasty black eyes to their reputation. We let James here go, especially after I just whacked his brother, he'll be coming after us. And don't think for a minute he won't come after you, Doc. As far as he'll see it, you were party to the whole..."

"Seriously, Clean. You need to see this."

"What!"

Ellis pointed toward the television set before turning the volume on.

I glanced at the screen to see a spray-tanned, middle-aged news anchor. His neatly groomed hair sat atop his head perfectly glistening in the bright studio lights, and his crystal blue eyes swept from left to right as he read from the teleprompter in front of him.

"There has been new developments in the grisly double murder of a Miami dentist and another man from four nights ago," the morning anchor said. "Reporter Cheryl Dalton has the story."

"Thanks, Mike," said a pretty young blonde who beamed rather inappropriately into the camera. "It was at this failing dental office behind me that this small suburban community on the outskirts of Miami was shocked to discover a gruesome double homicide had been committed. The case, bizarre in the fact that..."

"Oh, just get on with it!" I shouted at the TV, as I absently sat down on the foot of the bed occupied by Peyton.

"Shhhhh." Ellis hissed. "She's pretty. Don't interrupt her."

"Up until last night, the police have been completely stumped regarding the identity of the unknown man who apparently hid away inside the office while investigators processed the crime scene." Cheryl Dalton gripped her microphone tighter in her hand as she prepared for the big reveal. "That is, until a secret cubbyhole—believed to have been utilized by Dr. Hernandez as a panic room—was discovered. With the discovery, came two key pieces of evidence that looks to break the case wide open."

The screen cut to a pre-recorded interview with a tall, overweight police officer with a gold-colored badge. The caption underneath his face revealed he was Commander Richard Steeves, Public Information Officer for the Metro-Dade Police Department.

"Well Cheryl, I can't go too specific on this, but we definitely need the public's help in apprehending our suspect, so I can share these two things. First, upon entering the panic room, we discovered a secondary security camera system. The primary system had been shut down by someone...presumably our suspect. Even though we believe he actually hid inside the room, we think he had no idea he was being recorded the entire time."

The scene shifted again to a grainy, black and white video—time stamped—showing a small, middle-aged Asian male in a tweed blazer and long, salt and pepper hair tied up in a pony tail.

"Ha! You look like some nerdy professor," Ellis laughed. "Ya nerd."

I rolled my eyes. "Kind of the point," I replied. My mind raced, trying to remember exactly what I did while holed up in the panic room. *Did I ever remove my wig? My glasses? Do anything at all to reveal my true appearance?*

I kept watching. The video fast forwarded, blanked out a couple of times, and finally ended with my crawling out the way I'd entered with my disguise fully intact. I sighed in relief.

The TV switched back to the interview with the police captain. "We believe our suspect was wearing some type of disguise, and is probably considerably younger than he appears in the video. As a matter of fact, that leads us to the next piece of evidence we found that is the actual key piece of evidence we're excited to share with the public. Our crime scene unit, in conjunction with the Florida Department of Law Enforcement, managed to obtain a single fingerprint inside the room."

"What?" I shouted. My heart pounded hard against my chest. It wasn't possible. I'd just seen the security feed. I'd been wearing latex gloves the entire time. How on earth had they managed to...*Ah, crap*. There was only one explanation. The same people who'd co-opted the Peyton's hit and turned it into a frame-up had obviously planted the print somehow. It was the only possibility.

The TV returned to reporter Cheryl Dalton, still smiling as pretty as you please. "Captain Steeves went on to say that the print belongs to an Anton Jax of Pensacola." Well, at least they only had my public address. As far as I knew, they didn't know about grandma's place in Eustis. "Little is known about Jax at this time. According to the police, he's only had one arrest when he was eighteen years old for grand theft auto." My mug shot taken eighteen years before materialized on the screen. I grimaced at the spikey-haired mullet and soul patch I was sporting, and Ellis burst out with a guffaw at the sight.

"Not a word," I growled.

"An age-progression composite has been provided by the police department." Cheryl Dalton said as the mug shot transitioned to a computer generated composite sketch that bore an uncanny—if not unnerving—similarity to the thirty-six year old me. My jaw nearly dropped as I studied the image, though I silently thanked God above that I had much more hair still than the computer had predicted. "If anyone in the public has any information regarding the whereabouts of..."

"Turn it off," I said.

Ellis complied, then sat up in bed. "So what now, *Kemosabe*?"

I ignored the question. My mind raged, trying to decipher exactly what these new developments meant. Naturally, we'd have to be doubly more careful while out in public. But there was something even more disturbing brewing in the back of my mind. Something I was missing. Something important that my subconscious was screaming at me to consider.

"Ajax?" Doc Kane placed a hand on my shoulder. "What will you do now?"

There was something screaming at me from the darkest corners of my brain, but I just couldn't place it.

"Uh, I think he's in full-on meltdown mode," Ellis told the doctor.

Something that nagged and…

"Oh, God." I sat up from the bed with a jolt, and pulled my phone from my pocket. "Luna."

Kane looked curiously at Ellis, who simply shrugged, and said, "Don't ask. It's not worth da heartache of havin' to listen to him whine."

I ignored them as my fingers fumbled over my contacts until they came to Luna's. Something had been bothering me since leaving her with Nathaniel Tilg. Something I hadn't been able to put my finger on until I saw the age progression photos and the video footage of me wearing my disguise. I've said it before. It's all about disguises in this business.

I pressed the CALL button and after four rings, someone finally answered.

"Son, you got yerself some mighty fine troubles," Nathaniel Tilg said the moment he answered the phone.

"Where's Luna? Why didn't she answer?"

"Take it easy, boy. She's fine." He paused and I heard him take a puff from his cigarette. "She just left her phone here. Thought she'd be safer if they couldn't track her by her phone."

"Where'd she go?"

"No idea. But then, I'm pretty sure you have a good idea on that one."

His responses were too pat. Too prepared. Something strange was going on, but I couldn't quite pick up why I felt that way.

"You saw the news?" I asked. I wasn't sure where to direct my next set of questions. I had a hunch, and I wanted to see if my suspicions were warranted.

"Of course, I did. Everyone did. Heck, I bet even those tribesmen in the Amazon jungles saw it. It's the talk of the town." I heard the old man *tsk* into the phone.

"And Luna? Was she still there? Did she see it?"

"Oh yeah. She most definitely saw it. It's been hard enough to convince her to stay put 'til we heard from you before. Once she saw the news, she went ballistic. I couldn't hold her here any more. She just took off, and I haven't been able to find her since."

Lie. That was an out and out lie. I knew my sister had very little reason to trust me, but I had no doubt she would have carried out my instructions and head to grandma's house the moment I was gone. I'd warned her not to stay there any longer than she had to. I hadn't heard from Yancy yet, telling me she'd arrived, but I'd been a little too busy to notice. Uncertainty was beginning to nest like a pack of diseased rats in the back of my mind.

"Son, why didn't you tell me about that Hernandez business? You told me everything, but that I suppose?"

"Yeah." *How much do I want to play along with this guy?* I wanted to reach in through the phone and wring his neck until he told me what happened to Luna. But I'd played this pretty smart up until now. I couldn't lose my head just yet. At least, not until I knew more about this Detective Tilg. "Something like that," I continued, pretty much already forgetting the question he'd just asked. My mind was spinning. "I mean, if I'd told you...could you honestly say you wouldn't have turned me over to those DEA goons?"

"Nah. I reckon it was a smart move on your part." He let out a little cough before continuing. "So, um, did ya do it?"

"Of course not! No. I didn't do it." *Something tells me you already know that though.*

"Had to ask, ya know?"

I decided to change the subject and maybe fish for some new information. "Any idea where Luna is now?" I couldn't let on that I had caught on to his game. For my sister's sake. He had to believe I was buying his yarn. "Think she's safe?"

"Yeah. I've been keepin' tabs on her...whether she likes it or not. She's good. Went to hide out at a friend's place for a while. Someone named Lindsay. Lindsay Hogan."

Luna's sparring partner at the dojo. I doubted she was really there, but it told me Tilg had done his homework on my sister and her associates.

"Good." I tried sounding cheerful. "Look, I'm going to be incognito for a while longer. Still working on trying to find who set me up. Not sure how long that's going to take." I needed to put his mind at ease for the next phase of my plan. Nathaniel Tilg had answers. I planned to get those answers and surprise needed to be on my side for that to happen. "The moment I know more, I'll pass the info onto you, so you can relay it to Luna. Okay?"

"Sure thing. I'll try to reel her back in for ya. You just stay safe and get all this straightened out. That sweet sister of yours isn't cut out to be on the run. She's too special."

I bit my lip. I could be barking up the wrong tree about the man. Luna might have chosen to disregard my instructions entirely. He could be telling the truth and could really care about her. Still, I didn't think so. There was definitely something very wrong with the former detective. I just wished I'd realized it sooner.

"Thanks. I truly appreciate it." I tasted bile as I uttered the words. "Talk to you soon."

He said his goodbyes and we hung up.

Then, I stood in the middle of the hotel room for several quiet seconds, letting everything soak in—processing everything—before walking back over to James Peyton's bed once more, lowering the barrel of my Ruger against his temple, and pulling the trigger. Three times.

"Holy shit!" Dr. Kane shouted, grabbing my arm, slinging me aside, and darting to his patient. "...the hell are you doing?"

"Don't sweat it, Doc." I nodded to Ellis, who'd moved from his bed to the window since seeing the news report, keeping his eyes peeled outside. Understanding my silent command, he got up from his seat, and started packing up the doctor's bag. "We're done here. Have to assume we've been compromised." With my clean hand, I handed Kane a folded slip of paper with some scribbling on it. "Get this to Wade Murphy. He'll see to it that you get paid."

Ellis slapped the medicine bag into the doctor's hands, and shoved him out the door. He then turned to me. "So seriously. What now?"

I pondered the question, counting backwards from ten to let myself cool off, then looked down at the dead man next to me. "Well, first I need to make a call to Yancy." I waved my hand around the motel room. "Then, we take care of this mess, then finally go on the offensive for a change."

CHAPTER 30
AJAX CLEAN

Greenlawn Subdivision
Miami, Florida
Saturday, February 10

peddled the stolen bicycle down Glade's Cove Lane, and stopped at the first house on the right. Climbing off, I glanced down the street, counting the houses until I'd reach Nathaniel Tilg's place. Just five more stops. Of course, that's when things were going to get tricky. I wasn't sure whether Tilg was home or not, but I needed to do some spywork to find out just what the retired detective was up to. In order to do that, I was going to have be really sneaky, which was why I was beginning my ingress into the neighborhood at the first house on the street.

Earlier this morning, after arranging the Peyton double murder scene just the way I wanted it, I'd made a series of phone calls, setting a very loose plan in motion. It hadn't been easy, but I'd eventually got everyone involved to be ready at a moment's notice. Ellis and I had then split up. I'd sent him to Grandma's house work with Yancy on the research we needed and to collect some supplies for the plan I'd devised. After that, he was supposed to head to Home Depot and pick up a decent sized refrigeration unit, before heading back to Miami and be ready to act when I called him.

For my part, I had no other priority than to find Luna and get her to safety before my entire world went up in flames, which meant starting at the last place I'd seen her. Tilg's place.

Problem was, my age-progressed composite sketch was posted in almost every police car computer screen all over south Florida. They were airing it morning, noon, and night on every TV station with a local news broadcast. Anton Jax was the literal talk of the town, though fortunately, I'd done a good enough job keeping my life as under the radar as possible. There weren't a whole lot of facts about me known publicly, and only a handful of the shadiest people in Florida new my connection to Ajax Clean. So far, the police were grasping at straws, and I was only happy enough to let them keep doing that.

So with the prospect of being identified by some Gertrude S. Busybody in Luna's neighborhood—or in case the DEA were maintaining surveillance on her house—I decided the best option was to employ another disguise. Once again, the more visible, the better. Pizza or UPS delivery guy was out of the question. Thanks to almost every spy or buddy-cop comedy thriller movie ever made, those two options were the most obvious. I'd considered going for the local ice cream man option, but it would have required A) an ice cream truck, and B) actually selling ice cream to every pre-diabetic child in the neighborhood. So, I opted for the next best thing on the list.

I walked up to the door of 34 Glade's Cove Lane, and knocked. A few seconds later, the door opened to reveal a bent-over, elderly Hispanic woman in a bathrobe and slippers.

"Excuse me, ma'am. Could I have a moment of your time to talk about the Church of Jesus Christ of Latter Day Saints?"

The door slammed immediately in my face, and I straightened my tie as I breathed a quick sigh of relief. I knew next to nothing about Mormonism, and if any of the residents between me and Tilg was actually interested in hearing the sales pitch, I wasn't entirely certain what I'd say. All I know is that I had a white button-down short sleeve shirt, black tie, black pants, and just so happened to have a little black missionary name tag engraved with the words 'Geoffrey Kafer' on it—it's kind of amazing what handy little items one comes across when cleaning up crime scenes for a living. Anyway, where an ice cream truck isn't exactly the easiest thing to come by, bicycles were a dime a dozen and easy enough to steal in a pinch. So, I had figured that 'Geoffrey Kafer, LDS Missionary' was the best way for moving unnoticed in Luna's neighborhood. After all, most people who see Mormon missionaries riding around on their bicycles usually lock their doors, shut off the lights, and hope their house will be passed by. I was counting on that very attitude for my little gauntlet.

I got onto the bike, and meticulously completed the circuit of houses in case the Feds were watching. The only thing my getup couldn't hide was the fact that I was Asian. Dark sunglasses helped with that, but that was just one more example of how little I knew about the Mormon religion—were they allowed to wear sunglasses while on mission? In the end, I figured it didn't matter. After all, if I didn't know the answer to that, it was a good chance that your typical cop or G-Man would be equally as clueless about it.

Finally, after twenty-three minutes, four slammed doors, one semi-curious octogenarian, and one big pile of dog crap all over my loafers, I made it to the edge of Tilg's driveway. I parked the bike behind a row of hedges on his neighbor's property, and was just about to creep around the backyard, when something shining in the setting sun caught my eye from over in Luna's yard. I glanced around, hoping Tilg wasn't peeking out of his blinds to spot me and praying I was only being paranoid about the house being watched, and jogged over near a potted spider plant resting against the railing of her porch.

Next to the pot, I found what had caught my eye. It was a single, unspent high velocity bullet laying in the unmowed grass. I figured one of the DEA agents must have dropped it the other night, and picked it up to give it a quick once over. I turned the round over to look at the base, and read the engraving: 300 BLK.

I gave it a little toss in the palm of my hand, feeling the weight of the bullet while trying to work out just why the ammo type was causing the hairs on the back of my neck to stand. There was something off about it, but for some reason, I couldn't quite put my finger on it. Then, I remembered where I was—the potential eyes on me—and slipped the projectile into my pants pocket as I stood.

Not wanting to blow my cover as a missionary, I moved up onto the front porch, and prepared to knock on the door, only to discover several strips of yellow police tape symbolically blocking the entrance into the house. The door itself, it appeared, had already been repaired, and I assumed it had been at the expense of the United States taxpayer considering it had been a U.S. agency that had demolished it to begin with.

I feigned a nervous glance around, doing my best to imitate a bewildered Mormon on mission, then stepped off of the porch and straightened my tie while I took in a much deeper sweep of the neighborhood behind my dark sunglasses. Three houses could easily be seen directly opposite Luna's. To my right, sat her next door neighbor. To my left, was Nathaniel Tilg's place. I could just make out the outline of a very extravagant tree house in the back-yard of one of the houses across the street. The entire block seemed to be connected by one continuous privacy fence that skirted each piece of property like an unbreakable chain. It was the precise picture of American suburbia and I could easily imagine the sound of splashing from nearby swimming pools and the rich smell of barbecue cooking in just a few more months. No matter where I looked, however, I couldn't imagine a single place where law enforcement or anyone else for that matter would be lurking, watching my every step.

But I hadn't survived this long by allowing myself to be lulled into a false sense of safety. It wasn't coincidence that the DEA showed up at Luna's house less than thirty minutes after I arrived the other night. They'd been tipped off. Or they'd anticipated I'd go there, and were laying in wait for me. My bet was on the former, and until I knew otherwise, I'd lay odds on it being Tilg who'd called in the Feds despite his protestations.

Either way, I was only increasing the possibility of getting caught if I continued loitering in Luna's front yard. I turned and began walking toward Tilg's house, when a gentle shuffle from behind my sister's fence caught my attention. I stiffened, listening for the sound to repeat, but I heard nothing else.

Crap. I took another step forward, using my peripheral vision to survey the gate, but caught no movement. My nerves were on edge. To most people, a single rustle of leaves or sound of movement would be no cause for alarm. Common sense said that it would be multiple noises in quick succession that should breed concern as it was most likely something being done intentionally. But this was one of the rare instances that common sense should be issued a dunce's cap, because a savvy stalker knows when they have possibly given their location away and will do whatever they can to regain the element of surprise.

Slowly, I turned to look at the gate, wishing, not for the first time, that I had actually sent off for those x-ray specs in the back of the comic books as a kid. I looked back over at Tilg's house, less than fifty yards away. I knew I should just keep walking. Resume my mission to sneak inside the retired detective's house and learn whatever I could. But the soft shuffle I'd heard beckoned to me like a big red button with the words 'DON'T PUSH' stenciled on it. It was just impossible to resist.

Taking a breath, I turned once more, walked up to the gate, and reached for the handle. The moment my fingers touched the rusted metal, the gate swung inward, and a black-clad figure lunged, throwing me backward onto the grass. I recovered quickly; letting my momentum carry me further backward until I rolled back onto my feet to face my assailant.

He was dressed in black fatigues and body armor, a rifle slung over his left shoulder. The man was nearly six feet tall, with short cropped blonde hair and a neatly trimmed mustache and beard. An earpiece was nestled inside his ear, and I could just make out the vague round shapes of a throat-mic pressed on both sides of his neck. He said nothing. Didn't make so much as a grunt as he pulled a six-inch blade from his belt, and leapt at me again.

I dove to my right a fraction of a second too late, and the blade sliced through the flesh of my left arm. I hit the ground, rolled, and came up to my feet again in a single motion. Instinctively, my hand slapped against my injured arm, trying to stave off the flow of blood.

"Whoa, whoa!" I shouted, taking a step back. "I'm just trying to share the good news of Joseph Smith here, man! No need to get violent." Outwardly, I might have seemed flippant to my situation, but inwardly I was once again silently cursing myself for never taking martial arts like a good Asian-American boy should. *Why couldn't Sinanju be a real thing? I so would have studied that.*

The blonde man grinned ominously, his eyes shifting to follow the trail of blood down my arm. His gaze returned to my own, and without warning, he jumped into the air, wheeling his left leg around in a roundhouse kick that slammed against my jaw. I heard a crunch as I tumbled backwards, but didn't think anything was broken. I would, however, have a nasty bruise tomorrow.

Before he could press the attack, my ears literally ringing from the last blow, I scrambled to my feet, and lunged; tackling him around the waist and driving him backwards. My body, slight as it is, crashed down on top of him, and I slammed my fist hard against his face with one blow after another. But if he felt any pain, he didn't show it as he rolled out of the path of my final blow, and bucked me off of him with a powerful thrust of his legs. I landed on my injured arm, sending a lightning bolt of searing pain up my shoulder. I cried out, cursing uncontrollably as I rolled onto my back in agony.

The man was now standing directly over me, his assault rifle now pulled from his shoulder, and aimed directly at me. I recognized the weapon immediately. A *Fabrique Nationale* SCAR-H rifle, an advanced modular assault weapon used by SOCOM, and a match for the 300 Blackout round I'd found near Luna's front porch.

"Nothing personal, Clean." It was the first words my assailant had uttered since our altercation began. His voice was rich and deep, but contained not even the slightest trace of an accent. "Standing orders are to kill you on sight."

"Wh-whose orders?"

The man just shrugged in response. As he did so, I caught my first glimpse of a piece of shiny silver tucked away under his body armor. A badge. I'd seen several just like a few days earlier. A DEA badge. That's when I realized what had been bugging me about the ammo I'd discovered. The DEA's standard tactical rifle was a 5.56 mm LAR-15, and while agents could qualify to use their own personal handguns, the agency was very particular on what shoulder-fired weapons were allowed to be used. A SCAR-H was nowhere close to being on that list. Heck, it wasn't close to being on anyone's list accept for black ops guys.

"Who do you work for? You're not really DEA."

He gave me that same infuriating smile he'd blessed me with during our fight, and pressed his weapon tighter against his shoulder.

"You can't shoot me here." I sat up, propping myself on my elbows and casting a glance around the neighborhood. "Our fight's been pretty loud. I'm sure the neighbors have already called the police."

He stepped around me, his back to Tilg's house where he could gain a better view of the neighborhood, and paused.

"Is that the sound of sirens I hear?" It wasn't, but I was hoping I would unnerve him enough to plant a suggestive seed in his mind.

He listened for a few seconds more, shook his head, and then returned his attention to me. "I still have time to carry out my mission, and be well away from here before…"

CLICK-CLICK. The sound of a revolver hammer being pulled back could be heard just behind the assassin's head.

"Don't even think about it, fella," Nathaniel Tilg whispered in the man's ear. I stared at the old man, unable to move. *What is he doing here? Is he actually trying to save me? And if so, why?* I'd already pegged him to be working for the bad guys. "This here's a .357. You're obviously good with guns. You know what mine will do to that pig brain of yours, right?"

The man nodded slowly, raising the barrel of his SCAR-H up along with his left hand.

"Good," Tilg said. "Now I want you to drop that plastic pop gun of yours and scurry out of here before I turn your head into a pun'kin six days after Halloween. Got it?"

Another nod, then the assassin slowly lowered the rifle to the ground, and allowed his right hand to join his left in the air. "You know you're making a big mistake, right pops?"

Tilg shoved him away with a powerful forearm. "Let me worry about my mistakes," he growled. "Now get!" Without another word, my assailant took off running and we both watched until he'd disappeared around the corner of the next street over. When he was gone, Tilg reached down and helped me to my feet. "Come on, boy. We need to get that arm taken care of quick. Then, we'll get down to business."

CHAPTER 31
AJAX CLEAN

T ilg led me into his kitchen, pulled out a chair from the table, and sat me down with a grunt. He then went to the faucet, and poured a huge glass of water, and sat it down in front of me. "Drink this. With your blood loss, you don't want to get dehydrated." I picked up the glass, and gulped it down as quickly as I could. "Good," he said, smiling. "Now just a sec. Gotta get a few things to fix you up." Without another word, he left the kitchen, and disappeared from view.

I sat there, holding my arm and wondering if I'd been wrong about him. He seemed genuinely concerned about me and there was no doubt that I would have been bleeding out, a gunshot wound to my head in Luna's yard, if he hadn't come to my rescue. I'd been so certain before. So sure that Luna would have followed my instructions to the letter. Why wouldn't she have listened to me and fled to Grandma's place in Eustis?

Then again, why on earth would she, you Bozo. She doesn't really know you. And the man she thought you were turned out to be a lie. I wouldn't have listened to me either.

As I pondered all this, I took in the kitchen, and the pile of unwashed pots and dishes jutting up from the sink. Dried, nasty remnants of old food still stained the dishes, and I caught the faintest trace of something sour in the air. I pulled away from the sight, and glanced to my right where an old Frigidaire refrigerator, with a pull-latch handle hummed against the wall. Above the refrigerator, hanging on the wall, was a tom cat clock with swinging tail and roving eyes. I glanced at my watch, and realized the old man hadn't reset it since the last time change.

Not exactly the digs of some sort of master criminal.

"All right," Tilg said, startling me as he shuffled back into the room holding a first aid kit. "Take your shirt off. Let's have a look at you."

I removed my shirt, as he pulled another chair up to me, and began cleaning the cut on my arm with a wet towel.

"Have you heard from Luna?" I asked as he worked. I wasn't sure whether I was still trying to trick him into revealing himself or if I sincerely wanted the truth.

Grimacing, he shook his head, and I noticed the pressure increased as he brushed the cloth over my skin.

"But she's okay? I mean, she's still with her friend Lindsay, right?"

He pulled the bloody cloth away, pushed his glasses up onto the bridge of his nose, and leaned in for a better look at my wound.

"Tilg? Answer me."

"Yeah, yeah, yeah," he said, nodding as he concentrated on my arm. He clucked as if unsatisfied with the cleaning, pulled out a fresh cloth, and resumed his attention to the cut. "I sent a buddy with the department over to her friend's to check on them. No one was home." He stopped to look at me, and smiled. "Now, don't get too worried. There weren't no signs of forced entry or violence or anything like that. They just weren't there. Good chance, the two of 'em got in their car and found some place to hide out for a couple of days."

If he was lying, he was damned good at it. And, it made a certain kind of sense. I hated to admit it, but I had only recently begun to get to know my little sister. I didn't know her well enough to know how savvy she was at being on the run. Granted, after the life she'd lived with my father, I should have had more faith in her. But she was alone now. Without his guidance. Or mine. And I didn't like it one bit.

"So, have your contacts come up with any news about Jung Ki-ye-OW!" I winced as he poured a monsoon of hydrogen peroxide down my arm. The wound fizzed and popped with the effervescent liquid. "I mean, Ki-yeol."

Tilg dabbed at the bubbles, and applied a little more of the stuff. "Oh yeah. That." He turned to the first aid kit, and rifled through it for supplies. "First of all, that's not his name. At least, it's not his name anymore. I found out he's going by Karl Johns now. Apparently, he thinks it sounds more American, which he believes makes doing business here easier."

"Okay," I said, leaning back in the kitchen chair. I couldn't help but wonder how he'd come by that piece of information. After all, your average cop isn't privy to the comings and goings of international crime lords. But my head had started to swim, and I couldn't quite gather my thoughts enough to question him about his sources. I wasn't sure whether it was from the pain or loss of blood, but either way, I was having to force myself to stay awake. "So he's doing business here in America? You know... know where?"

"This might need stitches, but we'll see if these work." He unwrapped three butterfly bandages, and began applying them to the injury. "As to where Johns is, that's where we run into a snag."

I blinked at him. It was becoming more difficult to speak, but by the look on his face, he understood my unspoken question.

"Oh, I know, all right. As a matter of fact, he's not even trying to hide. He runs his U.S. operations in Tampa, though he spends an equal amount of time tending to his international interests in Hong Kong."

"So that's the snag? He's in Hong Kong?"

Tilg shook his head. "Why would I call Hong Kong a snag? You're practically Chinese anyway, right?"

I rolled my eyes at him, then motioned for him to continue.

"Nah. The problem is that Karl Johns has apparently gotten himself some pretty powerful people to protect him."

The lightbulb suddenly went off in my head. "You don't mean..."

He nodded. "Yeah. Seems a few years ago, he made a deal with the Feds. The D.E.A. actually. From what I've gathered, they pretty much turn a blind eye to his operations and head any official investigations off at the pass under two conditions. First, he's got to keep them apprised of incoming drug trafficking within the United States, and second, he can't run any drug operations within their jurisdiction. International, is fine. Just not here."

"You've gotta be kidding me." My jaw felt like a lead brick glued to a brick wall with molasses. Why was it so difficult to speak? I shook my head, trying to clear the cobwebs that were starting to clog up the gears. I then turned my attention to my arm. It felt better. Carefully, I swiveled my shoulder at the rotator cuff to test it out. The bandages seemed to be holding. Now I could focus more on my thoughts. On the words I needed to speak. "So this guy basically gets a 'Get Out of Jail Free' card for anything he does as long as he agrees not to be part of the domestic drug trade?"

"And as long as he continues being an informant for them. Yeah. That's basically the situation."

"And Wash...Washington is okay with thish?"

Am I starting to slur?

Tilg shrugged. "I got no idea. My source tells me Johns' DEA deal is being handled by a scumbag agent who's had some shady dealings himself in the past. It's possible it's a rogue op, but no one seems to know for sure."

"So the DEA showing up at Luna's house the other night..."

"Was probably orchestrated by this agent. That's what I think anyway. He's obviously caught on to what his buddy Karl is doing with you and your sister, and wants to stop you before you ruin his sweet deal with an international crime boss."

I thought about this for a few seconds, then shook my head. It still didn't explain everything. Didn't explain who had co-opted the Peytons into setting me up or who had killed Massey to do it. It was all backwards. At first, I thought maybe they had been the ones who had co-opted the Peyton's hit to a frame job. But if they wanted me out of the way, why co-opt it to begin with? Why not just let it go down as planned, and then they wouldn't have to worry about me at all. Unless they hoped that by sparing my life, I'd leave things well enough alone.

Which was incredibly stupid.

No, it just didn't add up. I still had another shady government operation involved in all this. The fake DEA agent that had just tried to kill me a few minutes ago was proof of that.

Then again, if he'd actually been intent on killing me, his actions were not those of an able hitman. As a matter of fact, he was rather inept. His SCAR-H had a suppressor. He could have easily shot me, and been long gone before anyone even bothered to look out their windows to identify the strange noise they might have heard. His knife play had bothered me as well. He'd handled the knife expertly enough, but his attacks had been…*What? What had they been?*

It was so difficult to concentrate. To focus. My eyes kept shutting on their own. I hadn't slept a solid night since all this started. Had eaten only donuts and Ho-Ho's since leaving Hernandez's office. I was tired. But I didn't remember ever being so tired that my mind began to shut down.

So, what had the attacks been like, Ajax? Think.

In my line of work, associating myself with everyone from the lowest echelons to the highest of organized crime, I'd seen my share of thrown boxing matches. I'd seen enough to know when a fight had been choreographed. Rehearsed. The more I thought about it, the more I realized the fake DEA agent's attacks had been just as false as his Cracker Jack badge.

"What is going on here?" I mumbled to myself.

"Excuse me?"

His question brought me back to the present, and I reached

into my pocket and pulled out the bullet I'd discovered in Luna's front yard.

"This is a setup, isn't? That...that DEA goon. He'ssh workin' for you, ishn't he?" I was definitely slurring now, and my eyelids were growing heavier by the second. "It was all a lie to get me to trusht you." I stood from the table, and instantly regretted it. The entire kitchen began to spin uncontrollably, and the floor swelled liked a tempest-tossed sea. My knees buckled underneath me, and I felt myself teetering to the floor. Firmly planted on solid ground, I rolled onto my back to see the old black man standing over me. A strange grin planted across his face.

I looked from him to the table where my empty glass still sat, and I groaned. My dizziness had nothing to do with either the pain of the knife wound, blood loss, or lack of sleep. It had been the water. It had been drugged. Tilg had put something in the water, and I'd gulped it down like a thirsty man in the desert.

"You...you...bast..." But the words wouldn't come.

"Now don't you be worryin' none, Mr. Jax," Tilg said, still smiling as he reached up and seemed to tear the very flesh from his face before everything started going black. I was about to drift off into unwilling slumber any second. Before I did, I heard him reassure me. "No harm will come to you. Or your sister. Not yet anyway. Right now, Uncle Sam needs your services, and he ain't gonna take no for an answer."

CHAPTER 32
AJAX CLEAN

Unknown Location
Unknown Day and Time

When I finally began to regain consciousness, I was aware of only three things. First was the fact that I was resting on an old aluminum and canvas cot that creaked with even the slightest movement of my body. Second, from the dank odor of mildew, I was being kept in a room or building that wasn't regularly occupied—a building that had recently been flooded, I guessed. And finally, the last thing I knew was that I couldn't be certain of any of this as my eyes were securely blindfolded with a thick strip of felt.

I tried lifting my hand to remove the blind, only to discover a fourth fact I thought I knew. Apparently, my arms had been bound with zip ties behind my back. They felt numb underneath me, and my shoulder ached from bearing my weight for however long I'd been resting here.

A door opened, and the dank tang in the air was immediately replaced by the smell of something rich, and savory that wafted from the door. Something distinctly salty. Perhaps even spicy.

"I figure you ain't had much sleep since this little fiasco started." It was Tilg's voice, only it sounded different. Not as gravelly. "You're welcome for the little nap, by the way." I heard something drag across the floor toward me, then something flat and metallic was placed near my ear. "Guess you haven't eaten much either." Suddenly, my blindfold was pulled from my face, and the first thing I saw was a small table next to the bed with a steaming bowl of...something. I couldn't quite place what the strange concoction that appeared to be made up mostly of rice, meat, and various vegetable bits. "Hope you like jambalaya, kid. It's pretty much all I know how to make."

He helped me sit up, and nodded toward the bowl.

"Where's Luna," I growled.

"She's safe. Trust me. Thinks she's being placed into our own little version of witness protection until this whole thing plays out."

"I want to see her. Talk to her."

His mouth pursed, then he shook his head. "Don't think so. At least, not yet anyway. Not until you do me a little favor, that is."

The door to my cell opened once more, and a black clad, blonde-headed figure walked in carrying a pitcher of ice water and a glass. His rugged features were instantly recognizable to me and I shook my head with a disgusted chuckle. "Your 'DEA' agent and would-be assassin."

I looked up at Tilg, who seemed to have found the Fountain of Youth and cut his age down by at least twenty years. I suddenly remembered the sight of his ripping his face off as I blacked out, and understood. He'd been wearing latex prosthetics to give himself the appearance of being much older than he was.

Tilg glanced at his accomplice and scowled. "Yeah. That's Agent Moore. Ms. Luna thinks I killed him, which helped gain her trust and made it far easier to get her to cooperate. You, on the other hand, were another matter. I knew you'd see through such an obvious ploy." He paused and looked me square in the eye. "You'd already begun suspectin' me, hadn't you?"

I scowled at him, crossing my arms in defiance.

"Yeah, you had. I can see it in your eyes." He nodded at the bowl of jambalaya. "Now eat, son. You need to regain your strength. Then, we'll get down to business." He leaned behind me, and cut the zip ties from my wrist, then gestured toward Agent Moore. "He may be an idiot, but he's watching you like a hawk. Don't try anything funny while you're unbound, and we'll see about letting you stay unbound. So eat up. It's my own grand-daddy's recipe."

No matter how angry I was with the man, he was right about one thing. I was starving. And though I'd never eaten jambalaya before, it smelled exquisite. I picked up the bowl, and spooned out a mouthful of the steaming food. I prepared myself to spit it out immediately. I had very little tolerance for spicy foods, and I'd always heard of the lava-esque appeal of gumbo and jambalaya. But I was pleasantly surprised. Though it was indeed spicy, the proportions had been prepared just right, and I could easily stomach the Creole delicacy with little effort.

I used the time while I ate to take in my new digs. It was a small room comprised mostly of cinder block. The few areas where dry wall still hung showed signs of severe water damage, and mold colonies pocked every surface of the room. There was a single window off to my left that allowed light into the room, but was barred with wrought iron from the outside. Other than the cot I was sitting on, the small table, and a couple of folding chairs in the corner, there were no furnishings. I considered all this as I took another bite.

Tilg smiled warmly at me as I ate. Despite our current situation, he appeared genuinely hoping that I would enjoy his cuisine. As I ate, he took the pitcher of water and poured a glass full. "Sorry," the black man said. "Almost forgot. You might be thirsty."

I looked back at him suspiciously, a thick portion of the delicacy still in one side of my mouth.

"Don't worry. I ain't gonna use the same trick twice. The

water's clean." He chuckled. "Besides, I already got ya where I need you. There ain't no need to drug you any more."

I rolled my eyes as I finished off the bowl and downed the water in three gulps before leaning back on the stone wall that my cot was resting against. "Thanks for the meal." And I meant it. "But how about you tell me what I'm doing here. What's all this about? And most importantly, where the hell is Luna?"

Nathaniel Tilg picked up the empty bowl, and handed them to Agent Moore. He then pulled up a rusted metal folding chair, and sat it next to my cot. "What I'm about to tell you is classified Top Secret. Actually, it's more than that. Probably only a handful of people in the world know anything of what I'm about to tell you. Heck, even Moore out there doesn't even know what we're really doing here. He's on loan from a special ops unit. Just following orders like all soldiers do...without question."

I sat up straighter as I stared at him. "So you're saying that if you tell me, and I don't play ball—or I blab about it—what? You'll arrest me?" He cocked his head at me, gracing me with a chilling smile. "Kill me?" He inclined his head at me in the affirmative. "Then don't tell me. I don't want to know. You can drop me and my sister off at the nearest gas station, and we'll get a ride, and be on our way."

Tilg stood up, and lit a cigarette. "That's the problem, Anton. You don't get a choice in the matter." He took a pull of smoke, then blew it up above his head where it was immediately sucked into some kind of vent near the ceiling. "You've already been selected for this, and we don't accept volunteers."

Warily, I clambered out of the cot, and shook my head. "This is ludicrous. This is the United States of America. You can't just..."

"America has used the draft to boost military enlistment for most of its existence, kid. Don't tell me what America can or can't do. Think of this as just a more complex kind of draft. You either accept it, or we'll be paying one of your cleaner colleagues to clean up your own mess when you're gone." His eyebrows furrowed and he gave me a sad shrug. "And if that ain't enough, that's precisely why we've taken your sister. So you will, as you say, 'play ball'."

"You son of a bitch. If you touch one hair on her head…"

"Trust me, boy. There's nothin' I'd hate more than to hurt that precious little thing." He took a pull on his cigarette and exhaled. "I didn't lie about how I felt about her. She's a special kind of lady. Sweet as molasses. There ain't many like her out there. But yeah, for the job, I'd do whatever it took to see it done."

"You had Massey killed, didn't you?" I knew the answer already, so when he didn't respond, I was ready to go with another. "Why?"

He looked up at the ceiling as if reflecting on the question. "It ain't something I'm proud of. Mr. Massey wasn't really a bad guy, though I don't approve of the way he made his living. But he'd stumbled on something—something about Jung—that threatened everything we were working toward. If he ended up getting word to you, everything would have been lost.

"We thought we weren't going to have to dirty our hands with that one. The Asian woman almost had him. She just didn't know about his hideout next door. Unfortunately for Mr. Massey, our agent did."

"He was my friend."

"And I'm truly sorry for that."

"You will be. I'll see to that personally."

He smiled sadly. "Perhaps. Only time will tell on that."

Trust me, buddy. You will. It may take years, but you'll pay for Massey's murder. But I decided to let the threats go for now. I was finally getting answers I'd been looking for since last Monday.

"So why the setup? Why hire the Peyton clowns to set me up?"

"Better that than their original contract, don't you think?"

I glanced around my dank cell. "I'm not so sure. Why don't you tell me what I'm doing here and I'll let you know the answer to that one."

"All right. If you're ready, let's clear the air on this, so you can get started with your new job."

I let out a disgusted laugh. "Job? I've already got one of those. And, believe it or not, I do have scruples when it comes to who I work for."

"No. You really don't. Don't kid yourself on that. You're little more than a highly intelligent, sociopath. Your psych profile reads like a damn Thomas Harris novel." He glared at me with disdain. The look in his eyes—the utter contempt he had for me—told me everything I needed to know. If I refused to do what he said, he'd kill me without a second thought. So I decided it was time to stop taunting him. Take in his proposal and play everything by ear until I could find a way to rescue Luna and get the hell out of there. He leaned forward in his chair with his elbows on his knees, and waited until he was sure he had my full attention. "I work for an agency that doesn't officially exist. As a matter of fact, we're so non-existent that we don't even have our own budget."

"If that's true, who pays your salary?"

"Why do you think I've worked the last thirty years with the Miami-Dade Police Department? They provided my livelihood while letting me do what needed to be done within the organization. The six other full-timers work in their prospective fields as well, as a means to make a living. And just like us, you'll be allowed to continue working your...um, particular profession... yes, we'll turn a blind eye to your criminal activities...in exchange for occasionally working for us from time to time." He gave me a knowing wink. His earlier anger had seemed to have dissipated. "But don't be fooled. Even though we don't have our own budget, we have the unlimited resources of the United States government to handle anything that's thrown our way."

I stared at him in disbelief. It was the most ridiculous thing I'd ever heard of...a federal agency without a budget, whose employees were essentially unpaid volunteers. It sounded more like some black ops version of the Salvation Army than anything else.

I was just about to voice my skepticism when he held up a hand and continued. "This group, as I've said, is beyond covert. We were established back in 1985, and were commissioned with a very specific task."

"Let me guess, you kill people the government doesn't particularly like."

"This? Coming from a man who helps people get away with murder as a profession?"

"I told you. It doesn't mean I don't have scruples."

"I'm well aware of your *scruples*, Anton. The Peyton brothers saw your *scruples* first hand last night, didn't they?"

He already knows about that?

"Sociopath. Remember?" he said. "You may play the charmer to those around you, but when it comes right down to it, you're as brutal as that Haitian hitman you're always going on about."

My mind whirred. Not about his claims of me being a sociopath. That wasn't exactly new to me. You can't do what I do for a living and not be. No, what I was trying to figure out was whether there'd been anything at all I'd left at the scene that might pin the Peytons' murders to me. In the end, I couldn't think of a single thing. All Tilg had was mere speculation. My word versus his. Of course, if he really was a government man, his word was way more believable than mine in a court of law.

"Getting back to your original question, assassination isn't our objective. Well, not as a first resort anyway. And we don't choose our targets based on popularity either. Believe it or not, there is a very rigorous vetting process that occurs before we choose a mark. If we tag someone for an operation, I can guarantee you they deserve it."

"You mean, like Massey? Or me?"

Tilg shrugged. "You were never a target. You are a tool. A very impressive, and useful tool. The setup was simply to ensure you had no alternative but to do as we say."

"A bullet to the head is a good incentive too. You didn't have to sic the entire Florida law enforcement bulldogs on me. I mean, come on! I've kept my private and professional personas separated for years without a hitch. Very few people believed Ajax Clean even existed, and no one freakin' knew who Anton Jax even was. And you blow it all with a single, planted fingerprint in Hernandez's office."

"And if you agree to work for us, everything will go back to normal just as easily." Tilg lit another cigarette. "Of course, Anton Jax will have to disappear, but Ajax Clean, or Remy Williamson, or…" He looked at the Mormon nametag on my shirt. "Geoffrey Kafer, if you choose, can live a long, and peaceful life without interference from any law enforcement."

"So what would I have to do to earn all this? Remember, I'm not an assassin."

"You could have fooled the Peytons." His smile was almost lascivious. "But don't worry. We have someone special for those kinds of operations. No, you'd be part of our primary objective branch."

"And that is?"

"It's exactly what you already do, Mr. *Clean*. It's exactly what you already do."

He glanced back at Agent Moore, who stepped forward, handing Tilg a manila envelope and a laptop computer. The detective, in turn, handed envelope to me. I looked at it, and read the words:

TOP SECRET
TARGET: JUNG KI-YEOL
A.K.A. JOHNS, KARL

I looked from the envelope to my captor. "Go on," he said. "Open it. Read." He stood from his chair and placed the laptop down on the table before walking over to the door. "I'll give you some time to study the file." He nodded at the computer. "And I believe you might recognize that."

I glanced at it and I nearly choked. It was Massey's computer.

The one he'd been looking at when the Asian hit woman had attacked him.

"Once you're finished, we'll get down to the nuts and bolts," he said with a nicotine-stained smile. "I'm sure you'll make the right decision, kid."

Then, he walked out the door, closing it behind him.

CHAPTER 33
LUNA MAO CHING

Unknown Location
Unknown Day

"Hello?" I shouted, banging on the door to my cell. I wasn't sure how long it had been since Nathaniel Tilg had brought me to his secret facility and tossed me into the small cell to seemingly be forgotten. "Is anyone out there?"

No one answered, of course. No one had answered since I first began beating on the wooden door earlier that morning. If memory served me, I'd been here for at least two mornings. But the small slit of a window near the ceiling offered very little outside lighting. It was difficult to establish how many dawns I'd actually seen here.

Then again, I'd counted the meals that had been shoved through a slot at the bottom of the door since first coming here. Five. From the level of hunger I was currently feeling, I'd say my feeding time came twice a day. One in the morning, the other at night, making it two and a half days.

I slammed the side of my fist against the door again. "Someone answer me!"

When no one did after another ten seconds, I whirled around

and stalked over to the bunk on the other side of the room and sat down.

What is happening? What are they going to do to me? To Remy?

I knew worrying about things wasn't going to help my cause any. If I hoped to get out of these deplorable circumstances, I knew I would have to keep my wits about me. Stay focused. And act when the opportunity arose. Playing the helpless damsel was not an option I could afford.

Though I suspected that Remy—or Ajax, whatever he was called—was doing everything within his power to find me, I could not rely on either him or his associates to see me out of this. I would have to take measures into my own hands.

I glanced around the room, maybe for the fiftieth time, with the same results. There was nothing inside my cell that would help me escape. Growing up in China, we'd had limited television options. But a friend of my father's ran a video pirating business in a back alley of Hong Kong. As a child, I'd been given a DVD of the American television show, MacGyver and had fallen in love with the dashing Richard Dean Anderson and his uncanny ability of thinking his way out of almost any situation. Unfortunately, I was afraid that not even MacGyver could have rigged a device to get me out of this cell.

Though the door wasn't particularly formidable, it was solid enough that I knew I could not break it down. Furthermore, one of the few skills my father had never bothered to teach me during our sojourn through China was the ability to pick locks—even if I had something strong and slender enough to be used as picks.

No, for the moment, I was stuck here. Waiting. I knew, from experience, that an opportunity would arise. A chance to escape and free myself of…of whatever organization Nathaniel really worked for.

I sighed. Nathaniel. I still couldn't believe he'd betrayed me. Betrayed my brother. He'd eventually told me about the shadow government agency he worked for and their mission. Filled me in on the plans he had for my brother, and how I was being used as leverage to keep him in line.

Nathaniel, how could you have done this? You were my friend. A mentor to me.

Only now, I knew better. Whether he truly cared about me or not, I now knew I'd been an assignment to him. They'd discovered my identity almost immediately upon my arrival to America. Because of that, they'd discovered Remy via our emails and phone calls we'd made to each other. They'd been able to connect the dots much easier than I and realized that Remy was none other than Ajax Clean and my brother all rolled into one useful package. They'd known from the beginning that our relationship would one day come in handy, so Nathaniel had been assigned to me. To watch over me. Protect me. And even guide me when the need arose.

I ran my fingers through my hair, then leaned back against the wall with another sigh. I jumped when the slot in the door slid open and a cell phone was shoved through the hole.

"He wants to talk to you," said a man on the other side of the door.

I sat there, looking at the phone as if it were a filet mignon and I was starving from hunger. It was a lifeline. A way to call for help. All I had to do was hang up on whoever was on the other line and dial 911. The police could trace the call. Triangulate to wherever I was being kept. And they'd be here to free me in no time.

As if sensing my thoughts, the man spoke again. "Don't even think about it. The phone can't dial out. Just talk to Agent Tilg like a good little girl, okay?"

Though my plans had gone up in flames, I realized a few important pieces of information from this phone call without even having to speak. One, Nathaniel was obviously not here. In the facility. Probably not even nearby, otherwise he would have waited to speak with me in person. Second, something important must be happening in order for him to call here. Was it news of Remy? Was he okay?

Slowly, I slid from the bunk and walked over to pick up the phone. "H-hello?"

"Ms. Luna," Nathaniel said. He sounded genuinely pleased to hear my voice. "I hope they've been treating you well."

"Why are you doing this? Why won't you let me go?"

"We've already been over this. It's as much for your protection that you stay there as anything else. I'm just watchin' out for you. That's all."

My fingernails suddenly bit deep into the flesh of my palm and I realized I'd formed my free hand into a tight fist since the conversation began. "You're going to regret this, Nathaniel."

"So your brother keeps saying," he said with a half-chuckle. "Speaking of…he's here. He wants to speak with you. Hold on a second."

There was a rustle as the phone was passed from one person to the next, then I heard someone clear their throat, and a familiar voice soon spoke on the other end of the line.

"Luna, are you okay?"

"Remy! I'm fine. I'm fine. What about you?"

He paused, then made a strange sound with his throat. "I'm okay. Just worried about you. That's all."

"Remy, whatever they want you to do, don't do it! They don't care about you or me. They'll probably just kil…"

"I know. But I have to do what I can. Whether we're involved with these guys or not, we won't be safe until Jung Ki-yeol is taken care of. He'll keep coming after us for the rest of our lives." Someone spoke in the background, but I couldn't quite make out what was said. "You've worked too hard to get where you are now to go on the run again. I won't let that happen."

The same voice—I thought it might be Nathaniel Tilg—mumbled something again.

"Hey, Luna. I have to go. But don't worry. I've got a plan. This is going to work and you'll be safe once and for all. Never have to run again. I promise."

A lump had formed in my throat as I struggled to hold back the tears. I'd never known what it was like to have a brother before. Oh, I knew of his existence, certainly. But I'd never had an actual older brother who looked out for me. Protected me. Cared so much for me that he'd risk so much. Though I hadn't exactly trusted him when he'd revealed his true identity to me a few days before, I certainly did so now. With my very life, in fact.

"Remy, wait...before you go, I..."

But the phone had gone dead and I was alone in my cell once more.

CHAPTER 34
AJAX CLEAN

Interstate 95, Miami, Florida
Monday, February 12

stared out the window as the black SUV I was in pulled onto I-95, and headed south, on its way to the Miami International Airport. Even at four in the morning, I was amazed at how much traffic was still buzzing about the city. I was reflecting on this when a caravan of police cruisers and rescue vehicles, their flashing lights cutting through the night, raced past to some emergency down the road.

I sighed, and looked over at Tilg, who sat next to me with a grim expression on his face.

"So?" he asked. "What do you think?"

I turned back to the window, and gazed up at the rich orange glow of the sodium street lights. "Does it really matter? I honestly don't have much of a choice, do I?"

After the Fed had told me their plan, I hadn't quite managed to get a full grasp of what I'd heard. As far as shady government operations go, Tilg's organization—if it really existed anyway—was about as black as an apple seed under the shade of an oak at midnight during a full lunar eclipse. Supposedly established during the Reagan Administration, the unnamed organization had been set up with one goal in mind: justice for those who had a nasty habit of avoiding justice. While the organization wasn't beyond your basic assassination of certain targets, they're first response was something, in my opinion, even more illegal and reprehensible. As a matter of fact, I'd experienced what they could do first hand—orchestrate a crime scene that undeniably pins a crime on a subject of their choosing.

It seemed that Jung Ki-yeol, or Karl Johns as Tilg insisted on calling him, now had his own target on his head, and I was the sniper rifle the organization intended to use against him. The manila envelope I'd been given had detailed the plan to the second, leaving very little to chance. I, and a team of my choosing, were to meet in Hong Kong, locate Jung's office, and orchestrate a crime scene that the Chinese authorities could not ignore. The idea was that the organization would see the man's day in court, and justice would finally be served without the interference of the Drug Enforcement Agency's crooked agent. I'd immediately told the Fed how stupid his plan was, but he'd hear none of it. Instead, he'd handed me a government credit card, requested a list of names for a crew that would best be able to handle the operation, then threw me into the back of the government issue SUV before heading to the airport.

The former detective shrugged at the question I'd just asked. "We all have a choice. Granted, with some choices, neither option is really preferable. You either do your job, send Johns to a Chinese prison, and you and your sister walk away with a target no longer on your backs or..."

"Or either you or Jung's goons will kills us and you'll just find another way to put him down."

"Precisely. All you can do is make the most out of the lesser of two evils, I suppose."

I was in no mood to discuss semantics with the man who had my nards in a vice grip. "And the crew I asked for?"

"Everyone as you requested." He pulled out a cigarette from a pack. "Though I'm not quite certain about some of your choices. Rob Jenkins? Really?"

I shrugged. "From what I hear, he's an excellent security specialist. Comes highly recommended."

"You've never worked with him before? Isn't that dangerous?"

"For something like this, I think it's better to avoid my normal associates. It'll be a lot harder to anticipate what we're up to if Jung gets word of our movements."

Tilg nodded at the wisdom of this. "So why not ask for Archeo Ellis? Up until this week, you've always refused to work with him. Seems to me he'd be the perfect person for…"

"No! I've had to rely on him through this, but I've never trusted him. The guy's seriously nuts. I'd rather take my chances with Toufic Boulos as our team hitter. He's not as experienced, but at least he follows orders…if the money's good enough anyway."

"Fair enough." He started to light the cigarette, but before his thumb could strike the cheap Bic lighter's spark wheel, my left hand lowered the passenger side window a crack while my right shot out, grabbed it, and tossed it out.

"Okay, I'm absolutely sick of being subjected to this smoking crap from every other person I run into in this business. When you were just an old geezer, I was willing to let it go. Now that you're blackmailing me, all bets are off." I rolled the window back up. "Also, keep in mind, I'm only agreeing to your little cloak-and-dagger operation for one reason…Luna. If I'm going to Hong Kong, you better keep her safe until I get back. Got it?"

He started to protest to waste of a cigarette, but I cut him off by holding up my index finger for silence.

"Choices, remember? We all have choices. You want the job done? You want the job done right? Keep Luna safe and release her when it's over. You want to do the job yourself? Just put a bullet in my head and be done with it." I grinned at him. "Those are *your* choices. Choose wisely, Tubbs."

He didn't answer right away. He just leaned back in the plush, leather backseat of the organization's exceptionally extravagant

SUV, and took a sip of his brandy. I was willing to let him stew on it for a little while too. It gave me more time to reflect on everything I'd learned, as well as cement the plans I'd devised on my own since being press-ganged into Tilg's service.

If Tilg hadn't finally agreed to let me speak to Luna, I wouldn't even be considering my current plan. Wouldn't even be in this blasted SUV. More than likely, I'd be face down in a shallow grave in the Okeechobee National Forest somewhere. But he had agreed to let me talk to her, so I'd agreed to go along. For now. Despite what I'd learned about the reason for Ed Massey's murder.

When I'd booted up Massey's laptop, I'd gone directly to his email app and discovered a thread of correspondence from Don Kim, a colleague of his out of Singapore. From what I gathered, for the last eighteen months, a feeler had been sent out everywhere requesting any information regarding the whereabouts of Ryu Nam-seon and his two adult children. A reward had been offered. A damn big reward, actually. Then, three weeks ago, the mysterious inquirer had put the word out that the reward had been collected.

The last email Don Kim had sent Massey was to let him know that a rumor was circulating that the one searching for my father was reportedly in the United States. In Florida, in particular. Massey had stumbled on the danger I was in and he was killed before he could warn me.

I glanced over at Tilg, who pulled another cigarette from his pack and stuck it in his mouth. To his credit, he didn't light it. The darker part of me imagined the cigarette lighter catching on fire and sending the government spook responsible for my friend's murder up in flames. But no. I had other plans for him. I'd be patient. Bide my time. But he would eventually get what was coming to him. I vowed that much as I continued to glare.

He caught me staring. "What?"

"Just plotting your future torment." I flashed him a smile.

He shrugged. "Good luck with that." And he lit his cigarette before cracking the window on his side of the vehicle to let the smoke vent away from me.

Ignoring him, I pulled out a mirror, and took a look at my new 'disguise' in silence. As disguises go, this was one of my more subtle ones. The only difference being that I'd bleached my hair blonde. After all, as the female assassin I'd killed knew all too well, blonde Asians kind of stick out like a sore thumb. It figured that law enforcement couldn't imagine a fugitive being so brazen as to draw such attention to himself, therefore, it was the perfect cover for a busy airport filled with cops of all types. I primped and teased my spikey hair until the driver pulled up to the departure terminal. Once we'd come to a complete stop, I opened the door to exit, but was stopped by a strong grip on my arm. I turned to look at the G-man, who was holding a United States passport with his free hand.

"Don't let me down, *Ryu Nam-gi*," he said, using my Korean name. I tried to take the passport from his hand, but he gripped it tighter. "If you do, don't bother coming back. There won't be anything for you worth coming back for."

I understood the unspoken threat loud and clear. I don't succeed, my sister wouldn't survive. I was really beginning to hate this bastard.

"Just remember," I said. "You touch her, and you'll wish to God I would do to you what I did to the Peytons. Trust me on that."

Tilg chuckled. "Oh, I don't have any doubt. Then again, if you don't succeed, I'm thinkin' you ain't going to be in any shape to carry through with those threats of yours." He released his grip, and the passport slipped easily into my possession. I glared at him for six seething heartbeats, then ducked out the door. I met Agent Moore, our driver at the open trunk, where he handed me a suitcase and a carry-on bag before watching me disappear into the airport's terminal, and make a bee-line to the payphone bank.

CHAPTER 35
AJAX CLEAN

Miami International Airport
Miami, Florida
Monday, February 12

"Y ou get all that?" I said into the payphone's receiver. I had no idea who might be listening on my cell phone, so I thought a payphone would be the best way to make the arrangements I'd been reluctant to share with Tilg. The response on the other end was garbled, the noise of early-rising travelers scurrying back and forth through the terminal nearly drowned out the phone call completely. "What was that? I couldn't hear you."

"I said, you worry too much." Yancy sounded a bit miffed on the other end of the line. About a great many things. And if I was honest with myself, it was extremely justified. "It's a good plan. It'll work. We're all set on this end. I've got the equipment ready and the others are ready to go. Everyone is just waiting on your word."

"And by everyone...?"

"Yes. I'm pretty sure I know where they're keeping her. When the time comes, Tilg will be notified and I guarantee, he'll bring her to watch. Once it's over, there's no reason for him to keep her, right?"

"I hope not. I think Tilg does fancy her a bit, despite everything. He only did this to rope me into their crazy conspiracy. Once it's done…I can't see of a single reason they'd keep her. Just make sure you get it all, including Tilg and his goon squad. We may need leverage."

"Okay. What about *him*? Is he good to go?"

"Yes. He's in complete agreement with your plan. Already made da calls. The target is expecting you. Of course, he is expecting him first, so there's that."

"Good. Remind him he needs to be careful," I said. "He's got eyes on him everywh—"

"Um, I'm pretty sure he's aware of that. I wouldn't push it." I heard the crunch of a potato chip in his mouth. It made me laugh. Even in dire times like this, Yancy's appetite could not intimidated. "Let us worry about our end. You just worry you're part 'cause I doubt it's going to be pleasant."

"Trust me, I'm not looking forward to it. Thanks." I hung up the phone, and pretended to glance at my watch. I used my peripheral vision to tag the two agents Tilg had sent to watch me. The first was an Asian, dressed in shorts, black socks, and sandals. A huge Fuji camera hung from his neck. *Sheesh. Talk about offensive stereotypes, Tilg. Come on.*

The second had been a bit more difficult to spot. Probably because he'd taken his cue from the 'Ajax Clean Handbook of Incognito', and had dressed himself up, believe it or not, with rich, yellow robes, a shaved head, and flowers. I nearly lost it when I spotted him up near the entrance, singing the Krishna Consciousness mantra to the chagrin of a couple of baggage checkers. I wasn't sure how long it had been since an airport had actually seen a legitimate Hare Krishna in its midst since the late 70s. Then again, with cultural views straight from the stone ages, why would I have expected anything different from Nathaniel Tilg?

Stretching my arms while faking a yawn, I turned toward the food court where a handful of TSA agents sat eating their breakfast. I approached them with a smile, and leaned forward near their table. "Um, sorry to bothah," I said, faking a broken Chinese accent. I nodded at the Asian man, then at the Hare Krishna. "Not sure how you say. Mans has...have guns. In camera case and in rubes...um, robes. Yes, robes. Both hide guns."

A rather large black man in TSA garb eyed my two government shadows. "You sure?"

I nodded with a naïve smile. "Yes. Seen them talking in...in bath...in toilet room. Not understood what was said, but saw guns being hiding in camera case and robes. Big guns." I held my hands out—big fish tale style—nearly two feet apart to demonstrate just how large the weapons were.

Comprehending my broken pantomime, the five TSA agents shoved their sausage biscuit wrappers aside, unclipped their holster safety straps, and began flanking their two suspects. My stupid grin stretched into a sly one, as I watched three agents approach the Hare Krishna, and two steer toward the Asian tourist. When my two shadows found themselves rapidly explaining their presence to airport security, I ducked around the corner to another hallway, and made my way to a secluded set of employee restrooms. I checked to ensure I wasn't being watched, and entered the restroom. I ripped away my button down shirt to reveal a black Tee with a picture of Master Chiun on it. The caption below him read: *Sinanju is the Sun*. I slipped out of my jeans to reveal a pair of cargo shorts underneath, then walked over to the sink, and turned on the warm water. Satisfied it was the right temperature, I ducked my head into the sink, and wet my hair before pulling out a bottle of dye from my carry-on. I then poured the dye on my wet head, and began kneading it into my scalp. A few more rinses, and I looked up into the mirror to see my old Korean self again.

Satisfied, I dug through my bag, collecting the passport, wallet, and a few odds and ends I might need for this phase of the plan, then tossed the rest into the waste basket before stepping back out into the airport.

This was going to be the tricky part. I'd spent my entire life working my hardest to avoid this very thing. Taking a deep breath, I stepped into the flow of foot traffic, and began making my way to the security queue, and patiently waited for my turn. Twenty-five minutes later, I walked up to a female TSA agent, smiled, and handed her my passport. My hands shook as they held out the documents, and I avoided meeting the woman in the eyes.

"How ya doin' today?" she asked. She had a Hispanic accent and an unusually pleasant demeanor that went far beyond her job description.

My feet fidgeted beneath me, creating a spectacle of nerves for the agent to see. "I, um, I'm doing okay, I guess." My voice was barely a whisper, and I busied myself staring past the X-ray machines, and freedom. From my periphery, I could tell I'd caught her interest, and she scrutinized my passport photo against my own sweating face. She then rifled through a stack of papers, and poorly stifled a gasp a few seconds later.

"Just a second," she said, moving away from her kiosk, and approaching another agent—presumably her supervisor. The two talked in hushed tones, looking back and forth from me to a paper she was holding in her hands. Moments later, they both approached me, hands cautiously gripping the hilts of their guns in their holsters.

"Sir," the male agent said to me, holding up a Wanted poster with a composite sketch of Anton Jax on it. "I'm going to need you to come with me."

CHAPTER 36
AJAX CLEAN

Miami Airport Security Office
Monday, February 12

I sat in the metal chair, its legs bolted to the concrete floor, with my hands cuffed to a ring mounted on top of the interview table in front of me. Another TSA agent sat across from me as he perused the paperwork in front of him.

"Um, are you going to tell me what this is all about?" I figured playing innocent was the best game plan. I wanted to see exactly what my arresting officer knew about my current situation. After all, just because I'd given my two shadows the slip earlier, didn't mean the 'organization' didn't have others within its employ, and if they caught wind of what had happened to me too soon, all bets were off.

The security supervisor flipped through the papers of the file a few moments longer before looking up at me. His firm, squared jaw seemed to pulse with each beat of his heart. He was a brick wall of a man. Muscles on top of muscles, with hardly any fat I could discern. His balding head sheened in the florescent lights overhead. "Well, for starters, you're wanted for questioning in a double homicide that happened last week."

"Wanted? What are you talking about? I was in Chicago last week."

He chuckled. "Tell it to the DEA man coming to have a chat with you."

"D...DEA?"

"Yep. The Drug Enforcement Agency."

"But if I'm wanted for questioning in a homicide..."

"Double homicide."

"Okay. If I'm wanted for questioning in a *double* homicide, what's that got to do with the DEA?"

"Don't know. Don't care." He closed the folder with a sniff. "I've just been told to hold you until he gets here."

"What about a lawyer?"

The TSA agent rose from his chair. "I'm sure you'll get a chance to call one. That's why I haven't asked you any questions myself. Right now, just sit tight." He walked over to the door, opened it, and turned to look at me. "Someone will be by soon with some water if you want." Then, he stepped out into the hall and closed the door.

After he left the room, I took my first good look around. There wasn't much to see. A square, twenty by twenty room with concrete floors, and walls made of painted cinderblock. The door wasn't your standard prison-fare though. The only metal on it were the hinges, and knob. The rest was made of what looked like very sturdy oak. The table in front of me was rectangular, metal, and bolted to the floor like my chair. A single security camera was mounted in the upper corner of the room to my right. A red light blinked on and off, indicating that it was operational.

"Um, excuse me!" I shouted. "Could I have a magazine to read or something?"

But no one answered my pleas, and as time went on, I realized the TSA man had lied about the water as well. No one was coming to my cell any time soon, and since I wasn't sure the next time I'd be able to get any decent amount of sleep, I lolled my head back, closed my eyes, and rested.

It was a gift I'd developed over the years—the ability to fall asleep at the drop of a hat, no matter my surroundings. The nature of my job demanded it, and I took advantage of the talent often. So I was in a very deep sleep when the click of the door handle woke me up with a quick jerk, and a string of drool down one side of my face. I looked up at the door just in time to see a young Asian male—probably in his early thirties—in a silk gray suit enter the room. He was thin, maybe a half a foot taller than myself, with...I couldn't believe what I was seeing...actual honest-to-goodness 90s style shoulder pads underneath his suit jacket, giving the poor impression that he was slightly bulkier than he really was. From the shape of his eyes, and complexion, I pegged him for Korean as well.

Why am I not surprised?

The Asian approached, sat my carry-on and an assortment of evidence bags and folders on the table, and held open a wallet to reveal his badge and ID. "Agent Xian Chang, DEA," he said. Okay, so the name was Chinese, not Korean. Then again, Luna had taken a Chinese name herself before changing it again once she moved to America. "We have much to discuss, Mr. Jax. Much to discuss."

I cocked my head curiously. "Jax? I'm sorry. My name is David Lo-Pan. My passport confirms that. Don't know who this Jax guy is. Like I told the security dude, I was in Chicago when that double murder happened. It couldn't be me."

"David Lo-Pan is the villain from *Big Trouble in Little China*." Chang smiled, pulling out the passport from one of the evidence bags. He opened it, and scrutinized the document. "Rather impressive," he said with a nod. "An excellent forgery. Not sure who made it, but it's almost indistinguishable to the real thing."

"I'll tell my guy you were impressed with his work." There was no need for further pretense. I was exactly where I wanted to be. In the presence of the crooked agent looking out for Jung Ki-yeol. The fact that he thought the passport was a forgery further told me he had no idea who Nathaniel Tilg or his shadow organization was. I gave my captor a shrug. "So what now?" I glanced up at the camera. It was now dark. Someone had turned it off. "Going to put a bullet in my head for your boss now?"

Agent Chang sighed, pulled out his chair, and sat down. "My boss is the director of the DEA. Why on earth would he want me to kill you? Have you done something to him?"

"*Now* who's lying? You know who I'm talking about. He's looking for my father. Wants to draw him out in the open. What better way to do that than by killing his son and daughter?"

He shook his head, his face a stone mask. "I seriously have no idea what you're talking about."

I cocked my head to one side. "Well, you should know, I have a secret about my dad. It's pretty huge too. If you kill me now, Jung'll never find out and I'm pretty sure he'll not forgive you for it."

"I told you. I don't know who this Jung is." He leaned forward across the table to look me in the eye, and for the first time since leaving Tilg's SUV, I was beginning to wonder if I'd made a terrible mistake. "I'm here to take you in for questioning regarding the murders of Dr. Hernandez and Edward Massey. Nothing more than that."

I returned his gaze, trying to sense even the slightest trace of deception. But he was either telling the truth, or one of the best liars I had ever met—outside of Nathaniel Tilg, that is. An all too familiar lump began to form in my throat. "What does the DEA have to do with a murder of dentist and some other guy?"

He smiled. It was a shark-toothed grin. "That's our own business, Mr. Jax. You only need to worry about giving us the answers we're looking for."

He stood from his chair, walked around the table, and unchained me. Pulling me to my feet, he re-cuffed my wrists, and escorted me out of the cell, through a warren of back hallways inside the airport, and out to a waiting black SUV.

CHAPTER 37
AJAX CLEAN

Unknown Location
Miami, Florida
Monday Evening, February 12

The cell that Agent Chang had placed me in was beginning to feel like home. It was pretty much identical to the one Tilg had taken me, which had been near identical in many ways to the security cell at Miami Airport. It was cramped, square, concrete, and had no windows. The major differences in this one, however, were the unnerving lack of a chair, table, or bed. Oh, and the lights that flickered every time the heavy-duty jumper cables attached to the car battery connected with my bare chest.

Chang grinned as he brought the copper connectors to my chest and was rewarded immediately be an arc of electricity that sizzled in the humid air of the cell. His smile widened almost maniacally when he heard me scream. I tried to lift my feet from the metal bucket of water on the floor, but one of his two goons slammed a fist into my gut the moment the electric current was pulled away.

My wrists were chained together, and looped around a series of water pipes bolted to the ceiling. The muscles that did *not* ache from the thirty minutes of electrified torture already, burned with the stress of trying to hold the bulk of my weight from sagging deeper into the bucket.

Needless to say, Agent Chang had not taken me to the DEA's Miami field office. As soon as they'd pushed me into the back of the SUV outside the airport terminal, a bag was pulled over my head, and we drove for nearly an hour, until I was thrown into my current cell. A few minutes later, the torture had begun with a vengeance.

"Now, Mr. Jax," Chang said. "Tell me where your sister is, and the pain can end."

"I already told you, I've no idea." I spat a glob of congealing blood onto his recently polished penny-loafers, aiming as best I could for the shiny copper coin tucked inside the slot. "Knowing her, she's probably already autopsying your boss."

Another jolt shot through me an instant later. The shock would have caused an involuntary release of urine and bile if I had any left. As it happened, another anguished scream would have to suffice for the DEA agent's insatiable lust for torture.

"Okay. Another question then. Where's your old man? You said you had news about him. Tell me and all this pain can end."

I couldn't stand any longer. My knees buckled, and I felt the chains bite into my wrists with iron teeth. I tried to suck in a breath, but my diaphragm rebelled against even that simple act. They say Christ died in a similar way. Death by crucifixion had nothing to do with nails being driven into your wrists or ankles. Had nothing to do with exposure to the elements or the torture one faced prior to being hung upon a tree. Death came from asphyxia and nothing more. The position the body is in while hanging there, places pressure on the lungs. The only way to take a breath was to stretch, tearing muscle and sinew where the nails were imbedded. Eventually, the legs give out altogether—or they're broken—and the condemned man loses his ability to take a single breath. I was beginning to understand just how the word 'excruciating'—a word whose root comes from the word 'crucifix-ion'—came into the English language.

"If your...your boss..." I had to pause for another breath. "...wants to know, he...he can ask me himself."

Chang's shoulders sagged, the jumper cables dropped harm-lessly to the floor, and he let out a resigned chuckle. "You're tougher than I gave you credit for, Mr. Jax. I have to hand it to you. I was willing to bet you'd cave within minutes, but you've hung on much longer than I would have guessed."

I forced a smile through the agony. From the pounding his goons had given my face in between bouts of electric current, it was much easier said than done. I was pretty sure my left *zygomatic* bone—the cheek bone—was shattered. My right eye was swollen nearly shut, probably a fracture in the temporal region, and I thought there was more than a good chance my collar bone buzzed with a hairline fracture as well. But I still managed to show my pearly whites, even though they were probably covered in a thick stream of blood.

"You'll forgive me..." Breath. "...if I don't take the word of a crooked Fed as a compliment."

His eyebrows lifted in surprise. "Seriously? You're a profes-sional criminal. What do you care how I make a little extra spending money?"

"At least I'm an honest criminal," I said, slowly feeling strength return to my rubbery legs. "I don't hide behind the power of a badge to do my dirty work." It was true. As far as I knew, Tilg wasn't planning on giving me one for my new G-man duties. Not that I'd expect him to honor his part of the bargain when this was all done anyway.

Chang's fist slammed against my jaw.

"From what I hear, I'm no different from your own father," he said with a sneer. "I'm Chinese, but even we heard of the exploits of the great police officer from South Korea. Heard how your father arrested one of the biggest crime bosses in your country. Then, we learned the truth. How he'd only arrested Jung Ki-yeol in order to take over his business. We, who had so little hope in our own government…so little respect for our police…witnessed the shame of the once great man, who had been hailed as a shining example of what could be. Imagine how we felt to learn it had all been a lie. A dishonesty. How about that, Anton? How do you feel about that?"

My teeth grinded against the pain—both physical and emotional. I'd heard it all before. Knew the stories all too well. But then, only my sister and I knew the truth, and that was finally about to change. "More lies from Jung. Nothing more. An act of revenge by a desperate man. Your employer has no honor. He's the one who had evidence against my father planted, and you know it. Why on earth would you believe anything from the assholes's lips?"

Okay. Maybe I was putting it on a little heavy, I'll admit. But I was buying time. Had to keep him talking for more reasons than just avoiding another round of torture.

"Honestly, it doesn't matter to me one way or another," Chang said. "As long as his check clears, and he supplies me with enough intel to take down one or two of his competitors, I'm happy. I'm only loyal to him for as long as it serves my purposes."

"I wonder how he'd feel to know that."

Chang laughed. "You think he doesn't? You call him my employer, but in fact, he's my own little lap dog. I hold all the cards. He's free only as long as he stays in my good graces."

Interesting.

"And what stops him from just having one of his loyalists put a bullet in your head?" I asked, probing a mine I hoped would reveal the motherlode. I still ached all over, but the direction of our conversation was beginning to energize me. "Heck, at this point, I might just offer my own services to clean the mess up when it's done."

He eyed me suspiciously, then shrugged. "It's simple," he said. "I have enough evidence to put him away for life. Something happens to me, it ends up in my supervisor's hands. Jung knows this, and because of that, I'm the safest man in the world." He smiled again, then bent down to pick up the jumper cables. "Now. Break's over. Time to get started again."

I was just about to protest when white hot lightening flooded my nerves and I screamed until I blacked out completely.

WHEN I CAME TO, I was laying on my back. It was probably the only part of my body that didn't burn, ache, or throb, and I relished the idea of not moving for an entire month when all this was over. Of course, whether I ever moved at all or not depended entirely on whether the next phase of my plan I'd finalized at the airport worked liked I hoped.

Slowly, I opened my eyes, and found myself in the same cell in which I'd been tortured. The chains still hung from the water pipes above, but the car battery and cables had been removed from the room. I was laying on the floor. A bucket, presumably for urinating, was resting on its side next to my head. I found myself thankful I hadn't used it before losing consciousness.

As I lay there, I strained to listen beyond the walls and door of the cell, trying to hear the slightest trace of movement or conversation on the other side. But if anyone was around, I couldn't tell. It didn't matter anyway. I had no intention of trying to escape. At least, not yet. My only reason for caring whether the building was occupied or not was because I was in no mood for any more of Agent Xian Chang's torture.

Confident I was alone, I sat up and leaned against the wall next to me. As I did so, I nearly screamed as a fresh blast of agony ripped through my broken clavicle. I'd forgotten about that little injury, and once I was able to bite down on my tongue enough to ease my cries, I managed to breathe with only a few intermittent whimpers. As for my face, there were no mirrors to look at the damage, but I could tell by the dull throb all over that I'd be an absolute hit as Quasimodo in a live action remake of Disney's *Hunchback of Notre Dame*.

After assessing my injuries, I sat on the hard floor, my back against the wall, and considered all I'd learned from my interrogation of Chang. It had, surprisingly, been much more fruitful for me, than it had been for the DEA agent. But then, he hadn't been hooked up to a twelve volt battery with his feet submerged in water. I wasn't entirely sure who had gotten the better deal, but as my plan began to evolve, and grow, I was thinking a little more positively. In the end, however, I figured it depended on the next part going without a hitch—which, knowing my luck, was about as likely as hitting a hole-in-one with a watermelon and a sledgehammer for a driver.

I sat there for hours, drifting in and out of consciousness, revising and re-revising my plan as I waited. I had just succumbed to sleep once more when the click of the door unlocking brought me fully alert, and I looked up to see Agent Chang stroll casually into my cell with a wolfish grin. His two goons quickly followed, and were trailed by another tall figure who remained shadowed in the doorway.

"All right, you're about to get your wish," he said, directing his men to lift me from the floor with a nod of his head.

"What do you mean?"

"You told me if Jung wanted to know where your sister or father were, he could ask you himself."

My throat tightened. "Jung? He's here?" My eyes darted to the silhouette in the doorway.

"No. But he's on his way here from Hong Kong. Just for the opportunity to meet you in person. In the meantime, he sent a good friend of yours to keep you company 'til he arrives."

With that, Chang stepped aside, and the shadowy figure stepped clearly into view. I looked up to see a scarecrow of a black man standing over me. A Cheshire grin spread across his face as he fiddled with the bone necklace around his neck.

"Ellis? What the hell...?"

The hitman sneered at me. "Sorry, boss. But the Korean made Mr. Murphy a better offer."

My mouth dropped at the news, which resulted in a hysterical bout of laughter from Xian Chang. "Oh, this is rich. You really thought The Raid would protect you? You thought he would choose principle over a good deal?" He shook his head. "I don't think I've ever met a criminal as naïve as you, Jax. Seriously."

Despite his taunts, I couldn't tear my eyes away from Ellis'. "You Haitian Voodoo bastard," I growled. "I was just starting to trust you. Heck, like you even!"

The hitman only shrugged. "First rule of the biz...I told you this at the hotel...our kind don't have no friends." With that, he strode over to me, waited until the goons had handcuffed me again, then grabbed me by the shoulders, and shoved me out the door. A few minutes later, I was being stuffed, head over feet, into the trunk of Ellis' Chevy, and nearly hurled from pain and nausea when the car accelerated away.

CHAPTER 38
AJAX CLEAN

Fairbanks Condominiums
Miami, Florida
Early Tuesday morning, February 13

sat in total darkness, waiting for the man that held my fate in his hands. If my situation wasn't so dire—and my face wasn't in so much pain—I would have laughed at the absurdity of the course my life had taken in only a week's time. Lured by a ridiculous amount of money to clean a hit that turned out to be a frame job. Hunted by an old enemy of my father's. Cajoled into joining a shadow organization of the United States government who had their eyes set on the same man that wanted me dead. And now, finally I was within reach of everyone's ultimate goals —including my own. The only thing that remained to be seen was: who would come out on top?

That's the big question, isn't it? I squirmed uncomfortably in my seat. *If only he'd arrive so we could get this over with.* Ellis had told me it wouldn't be much longer right before he'd left me in these strange sleeping quarters. Before walking out the door, he had unscrewed the bulb in the ceiling light and pocketed it as he whis-tled an annoyingly cheerful tune. I think he thought it was funny, leaving me in the dark like that. But in truth, I preferred it this way. Alone with nothing but my thoughts and the shadows to keep me company. It was somehow poetic. A metaphor for my entire life.

I heard the clinking of keys in the lock to the apartment beyond my room. The front door opened, then closed. An exhausted sigh from the living room. My heart pounded. It was finally time. A second later, I could hear the sound of liquid pouring into a glass, then silence as the newcomer imbibed the drink and smacked his lips when he was finished.

I nearly groaned at the snailish pace this was taking. My entire body ached from the beating I'd taken earlier that morning, and I couldn't seem to get comfortable for the inevitable confrontation to come. Everything had been going so well until Ellis had shown up to take me away. I was about to get everything I wanted out of the DEA agent. It was only a matter of time—and a few more bruises—and I would have had the evidence I needed to handle all of this with no muss or fuss. Instead, I'd have to settle for my own death instead, I supposed.

The man in the living room yawned, and immediately I heard the soft, graceful tread of his feet brushing against the plush carpet toward the room. It was almost one-thirty in the morning. He had to be exhausted after the day he'd had, which is probably why he was dragging his feet.

I held my breath as the door handle turned, and the shadow of the man stretched across the room's floor, lit only by the moonlight from the living room beyond. He flicked the light switch, but no light came in response. He turned toward the ceiling light, flicking the switch up and down a few times before grunting. Then, his eyes fell on the bed. The beam of moonlight raced past his silhouette to bathe the bed in a silver sheen, revealing the still form of a lifeless Asian female splayed out naked on his expensive sheets.

I cautiously turned on the lamp sitting on the desk next to me, and DEA Agent Xian Chang spun around with a start. Instinctively, he reached for the gun in the holster on his belt, but a blur of motion leapt from the walk-in closet toward him. Two powerful arms wrapped around the agent's torso and heaved him off his feet. The gun slipped from his wrist, dropping harmlessly to the ground. Then, Yancy Fortner hefted Chang and tossed him into the bed on top of the dead assassin. Panicked, he tried to scramble away, but I cleared my throat and caught his attention right away.

I was now standing, his own Glock 17 gripped in my hand. The nerdy, but musclebound Yancy stood at my side. His arms were folded across his steroid-induced chest. "I do believe I don't have to tell you not to try anything stupid, right?" I smiled with the same shark-like teeth he'd shown me earlier that day. "By the way, I'd like you to meet my butler."

"Nice to meet you," he said, with a flurry of a bow.

"Funny thing about him," I said. "He's a horrible butler. Doesn't even know the separate the lights from the darks when doing laundry. But he's one heck of a bodyguard when the need arises." I patted my friend on the shoulder. "I've been trying to learn Kung Fu here and there my entire life. You know, us Asians are expected to know that stuff, right? Well, I never had enough patience. I've taken one or two courses my entire life. Got up to a yellow belt, then decided I'd rather play Mortal Kombat instead. But my Yance? Man! He doesn't need any of that mumbo jumbo. He's like a freakin' Juggernaut or something."

Chang glared at me, still trying to slowly inch away from the dead woman. He was bleeding from his mouth from where Yancy's right hand accidently glanced off his chin. He'd probably bitten his tongue upon impact. It was the least of the pain he'd feel this night.

"By the way, recognize her?" I nodded to the corpse. "I wasn't sure you would. It's been kind of hard to figure out whose side she was on, but thought I'd ask nonetheless. She's an assassin shacking up with the Peyton brothers. Was supposed to kill them, but I got to her first."

"Wh-what do you want?" Chang finally asked.

"Well now, that's an excellent question." I glanced around the room. Like his apartment, the bedroom was luxurious to a fault. Expensive white carpet covered the floor from wall to wall. The sleigh-style bed was covered in exquisite thousand count Egyptian cotton sheets. Next to the black cherry wood desk I'd been sitting at, sat an entertainment unit sporting a 72-inch flat panel television, a slew of Blu-ray discs, and a gorgeous antique Japanese sword. "How about the evidence you have on Jung for starters?"

Chang's eyes darted away, then back to me. "I don't think so," he growled. "It's the only thing keeping me alive."

I shot him an apologetic face. "Um, not really. See, I already found it." I reached into my pocket, and withdrew a USB thumb drive. I turned and nodded to the sword. "Neat little trick, carving out a space in the sword's scabbard like that. Nearly took me ten minutes to find it once I put my mind to it."

"What? How?"

"Forensics, my good man. Forensics. Well, not really. Just observation and inductive inference actually." I moved over to the entertainment center, and rubbed my index finger across the surface near the TV. A thick coat of dust covered my fingertip. "Tsk. Tsk. You really must do something about your cleaning lady. Well, actually, from the immaculate state of the rest of your apartment—and this room—I'd say she's actually very good at her job. But you couldn't very well have her poking around your most prized treasure, could you? The one thing keeping you alive and in the graces of a vicious gangster.

"No, you told her to clean everything but the entertainment center. Then, you couldn't be bothered to clean it yourself." I picked up the sword, and tested its weight in my hands. "But you did take time to clean this one. Or rather, while everything else in the center was covered in a coat of dust, this sword didn't have a speck on it. Either you really treasured it, or you picked it up frequently. Stood to reason, there was something special about it...so, voila!"

He sat up on the edge of the bed, and sneered. "It's encrypted. Just because you have it, doesn't mean you can use it."

"Oh, don't worry about that," I laughed, tossing the thumb drive into the air, catching it, then stuffing it back in my pocket. "Yancy here's not just my butler and bodyguard. He's a world class hacker too."

Chang looked from me to Yancy, then back to me. "So, what now? Now that you've got the evidence, what happens to me?"

I gave him a wink, and nodded to the dead assassin next to him.

"No one will believe I did that," he said. "I'll never be charged."

I turned back to the desk, opened the middle right drawer, and reached inside to withdraw a selection of small booklets of varying colors. I tossed the assortment on the bed next to him to reveal his collection of passports for countries all over the world.

"Interesting little collection you have there." I reached down, grabbed a maroon-colored booklet, and opened it. Inside was a picture of Chang. "Who's Chao Hu, I wonder."

"Having false passports doesn't make me a murderer."

"No, you're absolutely right about that. But it makes you someone shady who doesn't have a problem leaving the country on a moment's notice...like say, if you murdered a prostitute in a fit of rage."

Chang's face turned pale.

"See, here's what's going to happen. A few days from now, your cleaning lady is going to come by, let herself into your apartment as she normally does, and discover this poor girl here. We've been refrigerating her, so she's pretty fresh. But by the time Gladys the Maid, or whatever her name is, finds her." I held my nose and shook my head disgusted. "Ew. I feel kind of bad for Gladys. She, or someone within the apartment complex who hears her screaming, is going to call 911, and a whole mess of cops are going to show up to take a look. Any idea what they're going to be asking?"

The DEA agent didn't answer.

"They're going to be asking where you've wandered off to. Then, they're going to search the apartment, and not only find a ton of physical evidence to suggest you murdered this girl—including your own DNA all over her from where Yancy tossed you—but they're going to discover a ton of fake passports to boot. Then they're going to ask, 'Hm, I wonder what other kind of unscrupulous dealings this incredibly successful drug enforcement agent has been up to?' Of course, besides all your dirty little secrets coming to light, you'll be blamed for her death as well." I tossed the maroon passport back onto the bed. "So, how do you like me so far?"

Chang tried to stand up from the bed, but I lifted the gun, silently threatening him to stay seated. His eyes burned with a fury that might have wilted my resolve just a few days earlier, but at that moment, I was too focused on the plan to let it bother me.

"I've got no intention of going anywhere," he hissed. "I'll fight this."

"No, I don't think so. You've aligned yourself with the man who ruined my father's life. The man who ultimately killed him. And for that, you will repay your debt you've accrued to society." I narrowed my eyes. "Just ask the Peytons what I do to people who threaten or harm those I love."

"Come on. It's not like you're going to kill me or something."

I simply stared back at him.

"Seriously. You may be a lot of things, but cold blooded murderer isn't one of them."

I let him stew on his thoughts for several moments before answering. "Let me explain something to you, Agent Chang. Our father was a good man. An honest man. When our mother died shortly after giving birth to my sister, he did the best he could in raising us. In providing for all our needs. I saw him, on more than a few occasions, go without food so that we had plenty to eat.

"No, he wasn't perfect by any stretch of the imagination. He separated my sister and I at an early age, thinking it would be easier to keep at least one of his beloved children alive if we lived on opposite ends of the earth. But one day, after more than ten years suffering from the humiliation you mentioned earlier tonight...over the shame the false accusations had done to his ancestors, as well as the horrible anguish of how it had torn his family apart, his twelve year old daughter comes home from school to find that he's eaten a bullet from his own gun." I ground my teeth, trying to control the anger building inside me. Understanding, Yancy reached out and placed a hand on my shoulder to calm me. "Lies, Agent Chang. Lies kill. Your employer's lies killed our father. And lies will kill you as well." I craned my head toward the bedroom door. "It's time," I said.

A moment later, Archeo Ellis strode into the room, a suppressed pistol clutched in his right hand. Chang's eyes widened at the sight of the hitman.

"You? But..."

Ellis rolled his eyes. "I work for Wade Murphy, not Jung Kiyeol. As long as I owe a debt to him, I kill whoever The Raid tells me, not your boss and not any president on a piece of green paper either."

"You said I am incapable of murdering you in cold blood," I said, heading toward the bedroom door. "You might be right about that, though I was told only recently that my psych profile suggests sociopathic tendencies. But yeah. I'm not going to kill you." I turned to look at Ellis. "But I know someone who will."

Then leaving Ellis behind, Yancy and I walked out of the bedroom, and closed the door behind us.

CHAPTER 39
LUNA MAO CHING

Rosa Villa Pier
Biscayne Bay, Florida
Tuesday morning, February 13

"Why exactly are we here?" I said to Nathaniel Tilg as we pulled up to the parking lot of what looked to be a port of some kind. It was still dark out. The sun wouldn't rise for another few hours, and the place looked completely abandoned except for the few rocking ships berthed along the docks.

I still felt groggy, having been startled from my sleep with the sudden appearance of Nathaniel in my cell. He'd not explained anything to me. He simply told me to come with him. Then, we'd gotten into a black sports utility vehicle, and had driven thirty minutes to the docks near Biscayne Bay.

"Because your brother doesn't play by the rules," he said with a scowl. "He had to do things his way, and he got himself caught. We lost track of him."

"What?"

He shook his head. "You heard me. Your brother tried to pull a fast one on us. Blew the mission all to hell the moment he stepped foot in the airport. Security caught him and he was handed over to Agent Xian Chang of the DEA." The SUV pulled to a stop near a darkened warehouse, and he stepped out, walked over to my side, and opened the door for me. "Watch your step."

He helped me out, gestured toward the door of the warehouse and we started walking toward it. "That's when we lost track of him," he continued. "My guys, however, caught wind of Jung Ki-yeol's arrival to Florida earlier this evening. Supposedly, he's hired a boat and is heading this way now. We believe it's to rendezvous with Chang and, hopefully, your brother."

He used a key to unlock the warehouse door, opened it, and we stepped inside to be greeted by five men in black military fatigues and assault weapons.

"Sir," said a blonde haired man that I instantly recognized as the 'DEA agent' Nathaniel had shot to 'protect' me. "Everything's set up on the top floor."

"You!" I said. I turned to Nathaniel. "It was a trick?"

My former friend grimaced, then shrugged. "Sorry about that, Ms. Luna. It was the quickest way to get you to go with me. This is Agent Moore. He's one of ours."

I glared at both of them, folding my arms over my chest with a disgusted sniff. If either of them minded my rudeness, they didn't show it though. Instead, they led me up a series of metal stairs until we reached the third floor of the warehouse where a series of audiovisual equipment had been set up and was positioned toward an abandoned slip on the southeast end of the docks.

"Any signs of Chang?" Nathaniel asked Agent Moore, who shook his head. "What about any of Clean's associates?"

"Negative. Looks like the entire place is abandoned, sir."

"That'd be Jung's doing. Probably paid the night workers and security guards off to steer clear of the area until there business is done."

"And what, exactly, is there business?" I asked. "What's about to happen?"

Nathaniel only looked at me with apologetic eyes, then

returned his attention to the surveillance equipment. "Do we have ears as well?" he asked Moore.

The blonde agent nodded. "Yes, sir. Three men on various roofs with parabolic microphones. We should be able to catch everything that's said unless Jung's security has scramblers."

Nathaniel glanced at his watch. "Thirty-fifteen," he said, gesturing to a set of chairs near the warehouse's windows. "Ms. Luna, you might as well take a seat. We may be waiting a while."

Though every instinct in my body told me to resist complying with anything he told me to do, I was just too weary to resist. I lowered myself into the seat, leaned my elbows upon the window seals, and looked out on the black-blue lapping waves of the bay.

The next thing I knew, I was being awakened by a firm hand on my shoulder. I glanced up to see Nathaniel hovering over me, a finger to his lips warning me to keep quiet, then he pointed out at the docks. I followed his gesture, glancing down at the slip on the southeast corner to see a tall black man standing behind a much shorter, blood-covered man bound in duct tape.

I gasped at the sight. Though one eye was swollen hideously, and his mouth gagged with more duct tape, I could see that it was an Asian man with spiked jet-black hair. Blood soaked through his strange t-shirt with the Korean master displayed on the front, and he walked with a limp as he was shoved from behind by his black captor.

"Remy," I whispered, bringing one hand up to my mouth. How long was Nathaniel going to let this go on? Would he let my brother die to see his mission completed?

"Son of bitch," Nathaniel said. "That's Ellis shovin' him around too. Bastard went and turned on him." He let out a soft, insensitive chuckle. "Talk about irony. Clean's been insisting the guy was a nutcase this whole time. Refused to work with him because he didn't trust him. Guess he was right not to all along."

As my brother and his captor moved along the wooden pier, the sound of an outboard motorboat rumbled toward us from the darkness of the bay. Seconds later, the boat came into view, coasted up to the slip, and soon docked. Three men clambered out of the vessel, mooring it to the posts, then assisted a thin, aging man out of the boat and onto the dock. The old man pulled what looked like an oxygen tank behind him. The moment he was properly balanced on the swaying dock, he lifted a clear mask to his face, and drew in a deep breath.

"Someone get the sound up," Nathaniel said. "We need to hear this."

A moment later, there was a series of crackles, then the noise from down below on the dock played quietly next to us as if we were standing right beside them.

I watched in silence, holding my breath lest I miss a single word that was about to be said. The old man—Jung Ki-yeol, I assumed—took a few unsteady steps toward my brother and Ellis, and stopped short.

I wanted to cry out them. Save Remy. Curse the old man by the power of my ancestors, but I struggled to keep my emotions in check. This, after all, was the culmination of over twenty-five years of anger, resentment, and pent up vengeance toward the lean, craggy-faced Asian man that was now threatening my brother. It wouldn't do to allow my anger towards the man to make things worse. All I could at the moment, was wait and see what would happen...and pray to the gods above, that Remy would be protected through the ordeal.

My brother stood at the foot of the pier, the parking lot beyond was devoid of cars save the one Ellis had apparently driven them in. The black man's gun, I could see, was pressed in between Remy's shoulder blades as he shoved him forward. He staggered onto the wooden planks of the pier, nearly falling face first until Ellis grabbed his arms, and helped him to stand.

Is he injured that badly?

Ellis leaned forward, whispering something in Remy's ear, so low that the microphones couldn't pick up what was being said. I strained to understand the words through the lip movement shown on the video monitors, but couldn't.

The video monitors showed all this, but it couldn't show everything. It couldn't show, for instance, the agony my brother was obviously feeling. All the video could really show was the pathetic Asian man slouching in front of his captor. Obscured by bandages, and a duct taped gag wrapped tightly around a head bruised and swollen from fractured bone and clusters of blood congealing in the porous tissue just under the skin, the face that had seen better days.

"Where's Chang?" Nathaniel asked to no one in particular. Agent Moore leaned toward the monitors, using a handheld remote to rotate one of the cameras from side to side as he searched for the DEA agent.

"Not sure," Moore said. "Keeping his distance from this, maybe?"

Nathaniel merely shrugged and continued watching the scenario play out. As did I. I couldn't pull my eyes away from the monitors.

Suddenly, the man named Ellis stopped, grabbing hold of my brother's arms and yanking him to a hard stop.

"We've come far enough, Mr. Johns." The parabolic microphone, being manned by one of Nathaniel's men, caught Ellis' deep Haitian voice with rich, digital quality. "If you want your man, you need to meet me halfway. And leave your men behind."

"I am in no mood for games, Mr. Ellis," Jung shouted back. The brisk bay breeze kept his voice from carrying too far, but even from this distance, its icy familiarity chilled me. Though it shouldn't have surprised me, it indeed matched the voice that had called me on more than one occasion in the last week. "We have a boat here at the end of the pier. We will take our guest, and your job will be finished."

"Those weren't my instructions," Ellis protested. "Mr. Murphy gave very explicit instructions not to let him out of my sight until he was dead. After all, you're not the only one with scores to settle. He wants to see him dead just as much as you, and as powerful as you are, I don't think even you would care to disappoint The Raid."

I watched as Jung Ki-yeol consulted with his two men. It looked as if his bodyguards weren't very happy by this new development, but in the end, it seemed as though the Korean crime lord reminded them who they worked for. Drawing a gun from inside his suit jacket, Jung nodded at Ellis, and began making his way over. The squeak of the oxygen tank's wheels screeched through the speakers as he pulled it behind him.

He approached to within five feet of the Haitian, then stopped to appraise his prize.

"Why is he gagged?" Jung asked.

"Because he never shuts up." Ellis smacked the back of Remy's head. I clenched my hands into fists over the act and silently vowed to return the brutality to him one day. "Nothing but moaning and pitiful attempts at screaming. It's unnerving."

He nodded at this. "I haven't been able to get a hold of Agent Chang. Do you know if he told him where his sister has hidden herself?"

Ellis shook his head. "No. But that's not a problem. I know exactly where she is."

Everyone in the surveillance room seemed to tense with that.

"And?"

"I'll share that with you when the job's done."

The gangster's eyes narrowed as he turned to look at the bruised mess in front of him. "Maybe I don't need his sister. Maybe all I need is him." He took a breath from his oxygen mask. "So? What about it, Ryu Nam-gi? Care to tell me where your father is? Maybe I'll spare that whore of a sister if you do." He took two steps closer, and slammed a fist into Remy's gut, doubling him over and bringing him to his knees. He then grabbed at the bandaged chin, and jerked his swollen face up to look him in the eye. "Tell me. Where is your father?"

"That's not going to be possible," Ellis interjected.

Jung's head snapped up to look at him. "Why is that?"

The hitman reached into his pocket, and pulled out a blood-soaked plastic baggie. Carefully, he smoothed out the exterior of the bag, shifting the crimson liquid from a flat, pinkish object. "Because your stooge...Chang...cut out his tongue. But trust me, it doesn't stop the creep from crying like a child."

I gasped, nearly crying out in alarm if not for Nathaniel's calloused hand clamping down over my mouth. "Shhhh," he whispered in my ear. "I know this is tough, but you got to be strong. For Ajax's sake."

Jung Ki-yeol nearly had a similar reaction as my own. His face turned at this news as a low, almost inaudible growl rumbled up from his throat. He took a series of deep breaths from his oxygen tank to calm himself, and rolled his head around on his shoulders to ease the tension back.

"That idiot! Now we have no choice. We must know where the girl is." Jung looked at the black man. "Tell me. Where is she?"

"Why you want to know so bad?"

"Because, idiot! She's the only one who can tell me what I want to know."

"Yeah, about that." Ellis shifted from one foot to the next, as if dreading the news he was about to reveal. "Clean did share something about his old man. Said he offed himself about some time ago because of what you did to him."

"It's a lie! It has to be."

"Mr. Murphy's put in a few calls to some contacts in China. Seems it is true." Ellis cocked his head. "Why does it matter? It's been years ago since he put you away. And with you setting him up like you did...making everyone think he was your Number Two, it looks like you got your revenge on him anyway. I mean, the man ate his own bullet because of it."

I bit back the tears at the harsh, but very true words, but Jung's rage only blistered into a boil. He raised up both his arms, and screamed, "It isn't enough! Yes, I wanted him to be implicated in my business...set the gears in motion to...to suffer the great shame he deserved. And it would have sufficed, had the self-righteous bastard not taken nearly ten million dollars from a private vault I kept in Seoul. Ten million in gold. And he took it with him when he and his daughter fled to China. I need that gold, Mr. Ellis. And Ryu Nam-seon is the only man who knows where it is!"

"Perhaps the daughter…"

"No! Ryu would have never wished to put her in danger of knowing the gold's location. He would not have confided in her." A sudden stillness passed across Jung's face. "Did Mr. Murphy's inquiries discover where Ryu Nam-seon died? Where he is buried?"

"I'm not sure. I suppose if he didn't, it wouldn't take a great deal of effort to find out."

The gangster smiled at this. "Good. Do it." He then looked down at my brother. "Well, Mr. Ryu, I suppose I no longer have need of you." He pointed his pistol, a rather large barreled weapon, at my brother's head. "Of course, you should know…not only will I find the gold your father stole from me, but I will also track down your sister. I will subdue her. Subjugate her to my will. And when I've had my pleasure from her to the point where she is merely a husk of a person, I will sell her to the worst of my associates in Bangkok. How do you feel about that?"

The eyes behind the bandages and gag widened, pleading behind muffled screams. But before anyone knew what happened, Jung Ki-yeol pulled the trigger, and my brother, Ryu Nam-gi, crumpled over onto the pier, as a pool of dark crimson swelled out from his lifeless head.

CHAPTER 40
LUNA MAO CHING

I screamed. At the top of my lungs, my voice rang out as I leapt to my feet and bolted down the metal stairs.

"Someone stop her!" Nathaniel shouted behind me. "Don't let her out!"

The sound of several footsteps bounded down the steps behind me, but I did not care. The only thing that mattered was my brother. Going to his aid. I was a trained doctor. Surely there was time to save his life. Surely I'd misinterpreted everything and he hadn't really been shot in the head.

"Don't shoot her though, you idiot!"

Instinctively, I ducked my head at the sound of the warning, and leapt down the steps three or four at a time. When I reached the bottom floor, two more agents stood in my way. The closest one took a swing at me with his right arm. Still in motion, I dodged, grabbed hold of the arm with both hands, and brought my knee up into his chest. He crashed to the floor hard, heaving for the breath I'd managed to knock from him. His partner followed right behind, diving toward me in a full body tackle. I spun out of his way, bringing my palm down on the back of his head as he flew past. Then, I continued running toward the warehouse's front door. Toward freedom. Toward my brother.

I ran as fast as my legs would carry me, aware of Nathaniel's angry shouts behind me. I wasn't sure how many men he had at his disposal in this particular operation. There'd been five inside the warehouse when I'd entered. I'd taken care of two. Moore was still behind me, sprinting to catch up, which meant there were still two more unaccounted for.

My eyes focused on door ahead of me, I completely failed to detect something large moving fast to the right of me. It slammed into my side hard, driving me to the floor. I managed to twist my body, whipping the large brute of a man around to where he deflected most of the impact as we struck the concrete floor. But when I came to my feet, and slammed my foot down across the big agent's face, I found myself surrounded by Nathaniel, Moore, and the final soldier I'd seen upon entering. They all had their weapons trained on me.

Shaking his head, Nathaniel smiled and stepped toward me. I brought my arms up in a defensive stance, and glared; a silent warning to him not to come any closer.

"I'm sorry about your loss," he said quietly. "I really am. Heck, I liked that pain in the ass brother of yours. He had style. But I can't let you head out there half-cocked, now can I?"

"I can't believe you let him do it." Tears streamed down my face in both anger and regret. "I cannot believe you stood there and watched that vile man kill Remy!"

He ducked his head slightly, a gesture of shame if there ever was one. "It's a horrible tragedy, yes," he said. "But Ajax Clean's death achieved exactly what we've not been able to do. We've got that bastard on video...shooting your brother. Killing him. No jury in the world would let that man go free. He's going to prison now, Luna. You're going to be safe. And it'll all be thanks to your brother."

I leaned forward, reaching for my shoulder, but I blocked his arm with a swift thrust of my right hand, then spat directly into his face. "Do not ever touch me." My shoulders sagged. I was beaten and I knew it. "I will never forgive you for this, Nathaniel."

He nodded. "I know, Luna. I know." He gestured toward the door. "But the good news is, once we clear the scene—make sure all the bad guys are gone—you'll be free to go home. We're even footin' the bill for the repairs to your house for you."

"Is that supposed to be any kind of consolation?"

He sighed. "Not at all. Your country owes you a great deal of debt, that's all. I aim to be sure they pay up."

"And my brother? How will *he* be rewarded for this?"

The former detective—my once good friend—looked down at his feet as he considered his reply. In the end, when realizing he had nothing good to say, merely shrugged, and gestured toward his team. "Take her back to the base," he said. "Once everything's been handled, I'll notify you to escort her back to her place." He looked at me. "I know this has been rough, Luna. You just discovered your brother after all these years…only to lose him again."

"Permanently," I added.

"But I hope one day, you'll understand. Hope you'll get back to your old life, making a real difference in the world. I hope one day, you'll find the happiness you deserve too."

I sneered, then turned toward the door. "Take me away from this place," I said to the nearest agent. "I'm suddenly finding myself very nauseated."

Without another word, two of the black-clad agents led me from the warehouse and into the back of the SUV.

CHAPTER 41
AJAX CLEAN

Eustis, Florida
Monday, February 19

A nton Jax was dead.

At least, that's what the news reports were saying as I kicked my feet up on the coffee table, and flipped through the TV stations.

"...with the discovery of a body floating along the Biscayne coastline, authorities began an intense manhunt for the man they believed to be responsible for the death." The pretty reporter, Cheryl Dalton, brushed a strand of hair past her ears before continuing her report. "Miami businessman Mark Johns, a Korean national whose real name has been identified as Jung Ki-yeol, was arrested today by agents with the Federal Bureau of Investigations and charged with first degree homicide. The FBI is currently looking into Johns's business affairs, and believe more charges may be filed as their investigation continues."

I smiled, as I flipped the channel to the next news story; this one read by a middle-aged anchor with a store-bought tan and teeth whiter than an Antarctic glacier.

"...medical examiner has identified the body found washed up on the beach near Biscayne Bay as that of thirty-six year old Anton

Jax. Jax, a suspect in a double homicide that occurred in a Miami dental office a week and a half ago..."

"Thanks for the invite," said a voice from behind me. I turned to see Nathaniel Tilg standing at the foot of the stairs, holding the yellow sticky note I'd left on the storm cellar door.

"I figured you'd be by sooner or later. Didn't want to have to get up to let you in." I waved him over to take a seat. "Come on. Take a load off."

The black man complied with a sigh.

"Want a beer?"

He shook his head. "On duty."

"When are you not?"

"Twenty-four, seven in this business, kid."

I nodded at this, then took a pull from my Corona.

"Nice work with that, by the way." Tilg nodded at the television screen. "You certainly had *me* fooled."

"I know."

Tilg looked through the open door to my workshop and stared at the broken freezer on the other side of the room. "Is that thing buzzing?"

I shrugged. The bugs were still hard at work on Mr. Muldoon. They'd continue to work away the flesh for another two or three weeks or so, but because of hermetic sealing, no one in my little batcave would have any clue. Tilg hadn't really heard the beetles working their magic. It was his way of letting me know he believed himself still in charge. Still thought he had leverage over me.

"So?" I asked.

"So, what?"

"I know you have something to say. If you didn't, you wouldn't be here."

He inclined his head slightly. "You went off script. We had a plan. Contracted an entire freakin' team, and sent them to Hong Kong. Then, you pulled that stunt with airport security, and went off grid." I detected the slightest trace of a growl when he took his next breath. "I'm not a big fan of improv."

I shrugged. "I'm not a big fan of being beholden to a black-ops organization with no name either. Especially ones that murder my friends. So, I took care of that little frame job you pulled on me, cleared my name, cleared my father's name, and got the bad guy in the process. Not a bad day's work if I say so myself."

"You haven't cleared anything just yet. The jury's still out. Lots can change."

I laughed. "Oh, you haven't heard?"

"Heard what?"

"Not only did an anonymous source provide Miami-Metro *and* the FBI with that nice little cell phone video of Jung putting a bullet in my head and 'fessing up setting up my dad…" I paused for effect, then added, "Hey, I knew you guys weren't going to share your video, so I had Yancy do his impression of Cecil B. DeMille. Thought the video turned out beautiful, didn't you?"

He merely stared me down.

"But that's not all!" I said with a grin. "They also got a bonus thumb drive containing every piece of information Agent Chang had gathered on Jung."

Tilg shook his head. "I think I'll have that beer now." When I handed him one, he popped it open, and took a swig. "So, I'm still not sure how you pulled it off. I was there. Your sister was there."

"Yeah. I didn't really appreciate you bringing her along to see me get murdered, by the way."

He scowled. "Anyway, we all thought you were dead for sure…until chatting with that little sister of yours a few days ago, that is. Her silence told me most of what I needed to know, but not everything. I figured you were just going to plant evidence on him or something. Had no idea you were going to let him murder you."

"Nah. I did the whole fake evidence thing with Chang. Dead hooker assassin. Buttload of passports. He decided it was in his best interest to leave town."

Tilg's eyes widened, and he downed the rest of the beer in a single gulp. "Oh, jeez. Tell me you didn't."

"I didn't. Jung Ki-yeol did." I pressed my beer bottle against my bruised cheekbone. "I'm Asian. He's Asian. You say we all look the same, so I decided to put it to the test. Ellis played makeup artist with Chang's face. I think he rather enjoyed that a little too much. Then we bandaged up his head, duct taped his mouth—even got a little creative with a cow's tongue Ellis picked up from a butcher shop—and presented the DEA jerk to Jung as if he was me. The tricky part was getting him to talk about my dad, but Ellis is a surprisingly good actor. Bastard started singing like a canary in minutes."

"Did he say why he was so adamant about finding your father after all these years?" I knew Tilg had heard everything up in their little surveillance hideaway. I knew he knew the answer to his own question. And he knew I knew it. But we both knew I was going to lie anyway, so I decided not to disappoint.

I eyed the Fed in silence for a moment, then shook my head. "Nope. Just shot me in the face, met back up with his goons, and they sped off in a go-fast boat they had docked at the pier."

Tilg stared back at me. "That's the way you're gonna play it?"

I answered by taking another swig from the beer.

He shook his head. "Gotta admit. It's pretty clever." He paused. "So when did Ms. Luna find out the truth about you?"

I shrugged. "The day you sent her home. A little note attached to the collar of her cat that mysteriously returned to her the same day she did. We connected a few times after that, filling her in on how it all went down. She wasn't happy with me about it, but she understood it was the best way to handle the situation in the end."

My phone beeped. I glanced down at the text message and smiled.

"I'm guessing she's the M.E. who identified Chang's body as your own?"

I shrugged non-committedly. "No idea what you're talking about."

He smiled as he got up from his seat, and placed the empty beer bottle on the coffee table. "And with Anton Jax dead, law enforcement is no longer looking for you, and you think you're free and clear from our organization."

I stood up to face him. "Pretty much."

"Are you so sure?"

I shrugged. "You know that text I just got?"

He nodded.

"That was Ellis. Just telling me that the eight goons you have up in my yard have been taken care of." I held up my hands. "Don't worry. They're alive. Just tied up." I nodded behind him and he turned around to see Yancy pointing a pump-action shotgun at him. "So, as you can see, I have everything well in hand, don't you think?"

He turned back to me with a scowl. "You don't think this display is going to change my mind about your usefulness, do you?"

"No. It's simply to be a message to you." I walked up to within inches of him and jabbed my index finger into his chest. "I won't forget what you did to Ed Massey. I won't forget my promise to you...you're going to pay. One day. In the meantime, however, I am a working man. I've got bills to pay. So I'll tell you what... anytime you need a good cleaner for a job, you can contact Wade Murphy. He'll know how to contact me since I'm giving up this place after today. And I've got to tell you, I'm not volunteer in your little operation either. My regular rates will apply."

I held out my hand. He glared down it for several moments, the accepted it with a tight-gripped shake. "Fair enough. For now anyway." He waited for Yancy to lower the shotgun, walked over to the cellar stairs, then stopped. "By the way, what do you plan to do now that you're a free man?"

"Ah, I don't know," I said, sitting back down on the couch to watch a bit more news. "I'm on vacation now. Maybe I'll take a trip to China or something. Maybe a little treasure hunting just for fun."

The G-man eyed me suspiciously. "Mmm-hmm," he said before lumbering up the steps, and exiting the cellar door in contemptable silence.